# THE PERFECT WIFE

HANNAH PRICE

*First published in 2025*
*Concept created by Black Swan Digital. Developed by Mark Coleman.*

# PROLOGUE

The morning light poured through the hotel curtains, and for a moment it felt as though it was blessing me. Gold spilling across the bed, and the carpet, and onto my dress hung carefully from the wardrobe door. It felt like a sign, as though the whole world had been holding its breath for me and me alone, waiting for this day.

I smoothed the silk bodice with my hand, marvelling at how soft it felt under my fingers. I had dreamed of this since I was a girl. I had dreamed of the day I would finally belong somewhere. Not just drifting on the outskirts of other people's lives to be tolerated or pitied. I dreamed of being central to someone's life. Essential even. And now here I was.

I listened to the muffled bustle from the corridor outside. Laughter, clinking glasses, the cheerful chatter of relatives who had accepted me so quickly, and so easily. Paul's family would be my family now. Mercer. Such a solid name, with real weight to it. A name people recognise and respect.

Paul had looked at me during the ceremony as though I were the very air in his lungs, and I returned his gaze with all the tenderness I could muster. He really does love me, and I love him too. Or something close enough to it. Love, after all, can be shaped. It can be built brick by brick, if you know what you're doing.

What matters is that I am no longer that girl from a modest town, working too many hours for too little pay, overlooked and underestimated. Today I stepped into a different life. A far grander one, that will hold me securely, wrap me in its traditions, its privileges, and its wealth.

When the vows were spoken, I promised to cherish him. And I will. Because Paul is more than a husband. He is my doorway. Through him, I have been welcomed into a home, a family name, a history, and, soon enough, a sizeable inheritance.

So yes, today I have everything I ever wanted. Love, family, respect. And if those words mean something a little different to me than they do to everyone else, well... that will be my secret.

# 1

The tannoy was blaring something about unattended luggage when Emily and Paul were swept into the arrivals hall, two more faces drawn along by the great human tide of trolleys, baby buggies and duty-free bags. Heathrow always smelled of scorched coffee, aviation fuel and damp overcoats. Inside the terminal, voices ricocheted into one another and dissolved into a generic airport roar. Fluorescent strips flattened everyone's features to the same pallor. It should have been ugly and graceless, but Emily found it oddly thrilling. There was theatre here if you knew how to see it. All those openings and exits, entrances to be made, masks to be adjusted, tearful welcomes home and even more tearful fond farewells. She slid her hand into Paul's and pitched her smile to something soft, private, gently luminous that read as newlywed.

"Still can't believe you let that man charge you that much," Paul said, nodding at the slim paper bag looped over her wrist. His eyes were brighter than the lights, a little glazed with travel, rimmed with sleep he'd promised to catch up on and never would. "He saw you coming."

"He saw good taste coming," Emily said lightly. "It's silk. And it was Florence." She could feel the scarf inside the bag as if it had a pulse, a bright thing against her palm. It would drape just so at the hollow of her throat. She'd watched the shopkeeper's eyes flick to her left hand and to the ring, and she'd watched him count. She had let him.

"And the magnet?" she added, tilting her head at Paul's rucksack. "Your little... masterpiece?"

He grinned, guilty and pleased. "An object of beauty. Kitsch is the new classic. It'll look excellent next to the bottle opener shaped like a sardine."

She laughed and allowed the sound to carry just far enough, as if to say to the passing families and the suited men with their rolling cases: look at us, laughing in an airport, terribly in love, terribly ordinary. A little girl with plaits stared at the glitter of Emily's ring and Emily wiggled her fingers so the stone threw a quick shard of light across the child's face. The mother caught Emily's eye and smiled, and Emily returned it with a warm and non-threatening smile of her own. The trick was to be the kind of woman other women liked. It was amazing what doors that opened.

They were spat out on to a moving walkway and then off again, pulled towards passport control like filings to a magnet. Paul reached automatically for the e-gate, and they were through in seconds, a thousand faces shifting around them into a new configuration as the carousel crowd awaited their baggage. The metal tongue of the conveyor belt lay dark and silent as people arranged themselves in resigned semicircles, stamping their feet, checking their watches. A boy in a football shirt leaned his cheek against his mother's sleeve and slept standing up. A businessman argued in a sotto voce hiss about a conference room on Tuesday. Somewhere behind them a baby howled with the clean fury of the newly wronged.

Emily pressed her shoulder to Paul's and rested her chin

briefly against the wool of his coat. She could feel the steady drum of him, the terrier energy he carried even when standing still. There had been moments in Italy when he'd managed to surrender to the heat and the wine and to her. They'd enjoyed afternoons that tasted of warm sun and lemon rind. Yet, even then, his phone had sat between them on café tables like a second wedding band. She had stroked his wrist and said nothing. You did not discourage a man like Paul from his work. You just curate it, and you make yourself the only still point in his turbulent day.

The belt juddered, shuddered, and came to life. Suitcases emerged like seals from black water. Their bags arrived in good time, straps familiar under their hands. They poured through the last glass doors with everyone else, were breathed on by English air so much colder than Florence, carrying a tang of wet tarmac. They fell in line and followed the small procession to the trains.

On the platform, Paul peered down the track as if that might summon the carriage sooner. He hated waiting. He was always two steps ahead in his mind, pre-empting, preparing. Emily stood very still and let the chill climb the inside of her sleeves. She looked like a woman who could wait for anything. She let her mouth relax slightly, almost a smile, and looked up at him in a way that said I am perfectly content to stand here so long as you stand here, too. It cost nothing and yielded so much.

The train slid in, brakes squealing, doors sucking themselves open. They found two seats together by the window. As they settled, Emily laid the paper bag with the scarf on her lap and tucked her hands on either side of it. London began to unwrap itself outside. Flyovers and car parks, a sequence of back gardens with trampolines and wheelie bins, then terraces with blinkered windows and sudden pockets of allotments like quilt squares stitched between rails and brick. The sky had that grey you could taste.

Paul's phone lit his knee before the train had cleared the airport perimeter. His thumb moved without him looking at the screen, as if it knew the way by heart. She watched the muscles in his jaw flex. The screen reflected briefly in the window, and she glimpsed words client, rate rise, and red flag, before the angle shifted and she saw only their faces in the glass.

"Can't you leave that for one day?" Emily said, lilting the words, running a finger down the grain of them to make sure they came out playful, not peevish. Her head found his shoulder, and her hair found the crease of his collar. She felt him take a breath, a small inward fight she pretended not to notice, and then he put the phone away with a performance of contrition.

"You're right," he said. "You are absolutely right." He kissed the top of her head, and she allowed herself the smallest sigh, as if to say good boy, and shut her eyes. The students across the aisle were spreading crisps across their laps like maps and arguing about which Tube line would get them to Brixton fastest. A woman two rows up was talking to a friend about a hen weekend in Faro that had left her battered by happiness. An elderly man with a face like old leather sat with his hands neatly parked on a folded newspaper, looking nowhere at all. If any of them had looked at Emily and Paul, they would have seen what she intended them to see. A happy couple. The picture of good beginnings.

She cracked one eye and studied their reflection again. The ring did not look too large, but it looked inevitable. She was a Mercer now. She rolled the name along her tongue without moving her lips. It sat differently in her mouth than the one she'd been given at birth. This was heavier, carved from something that didn't chip. She remembered the wedding morning as if it were unspooling in the window. The hotel curtains had billowed like sails, the flowers of her bouquet had been fat-headed with scent, and she'd had the sensation of being inserted into a frame that had already been waiting. His parents had not been unkind, but they'd hardly been effusive about the relationship. His mother, Dorothy, had clearly wanted better for him.

Dorothy's mouth had been a straight line when Emily walked down the aisle. It wasn't unkind, exactly, but it was... contained. That kind of control was a language Emily was still learning. Emily had spent her life learning languages.

She left the thought alone before it went prickly and opened the paper bag instead. The scarf slipped over her fingers like water. The colour made her think of the Duomo at dusk and the way the sky in Florence had gone the colour of the inside of a fig before it went black. She looped it once loosely around her neck. Paul glanced and smiled.

"See?" she said. "Not a mistake."

"On you, nothing's a mistake," he said, and she turned her face slightly so he couldn't see the flicker of satisfaction that wanted to move her mouth.

The train cut across a river, and for a moment there was only the black water with grey smeared along the top of it like thumbed charcoal. The carriage clacked and hummed and steadied back on terra firma. Emily imagined their flat the way they'd left it, with their coffee cups drying on the rack beside the sink, the bed pulled up anyhow in their haste to leave for the airport, the post stacked on the little hallway table. She imagined the walk there from the station, and the way the wheels of the suitcase would snag at that broken bit of pavement on the corner by the chemists. She pictured the small square of the kitchen with its gentle light, the bottle of champagne she'd chilled for their return because it was what you did for the ritual of it, the reassuring nonsense of bubbles in the afternoon. And then, she thought about settling into life after honeymoon. The messages to send, the thank-yous to compose in a voice that said effortless and grateful and ours was understated, just family, just friends. She would write something to Dorothy that was perfectly judged to be warm and respectful, with a touch of self-deprecation that invited correction while also declining it.

"What are you thinking?" Paul asked. He always seemed faintly disconcerted when she fell quiet, as if silence were a room he could never find the light switch for.

"That I'll make us a proper dinner tonight," she said, turning her mouth up. "Something simple. Pasta, maybe. We can look through the photos and choose the ones to send to your mum. She'll want to see every detail." She let the word want carry an implication of willingness to be the one to give her what she wanted.

Paul's face softened.

"She'll love that." Then, a beat later, because he had to add it since duty and affection were braided for him. "She'll love you, too. In time."

Emily touched the scarf as if checking it was there.

"I hope so," she said, so lightly it almost wasn't audible.

A notification lit Paul's thigh. He didn't move, but his attention leaned towards it and then away. Emily slid her hand into his again, and he squeezed as if that were its own form of agreement. He had been born into a house where things matched, and the silver knew its place in a velvet-lined drawer. She had learned very early that hands were what you held when you didn't have anything else. She was grateful for his hand. She was grateful for the curtains and the flowers and the ring and the name. Gratitude, she had discovered, was one of the most persuasive shapes her love could take.

A toddler in the row ahead flung a plastic giraffe and began to wail. The mother looked mortified, and passengers did their British best not to look. Emily bent, hooked the giraffe with two fingers and passed it forward with a smile that said don't be silly, it's nothing and we've all been there. The mother gave her a grateful, exhausted grin. Emily tucked a strand of hair behind her ear and eased back against the seat. There. A tiny thing, but these tiny things stick. If you're the kind of woman who retrieves a child's toy on a train, you're the kind of woman who is kind. People don't interrogate kindness, they lean into it and hand it their version of events.

She felt Paul looking at her and turned her head as if caught unawares. He mouthed you're lovely, practical embarrassment washing pink over his cheekbones, and she widened her eyes a fraction. Am I? Well, imagine that. And she looked out of the window again.

They skimmed past a rank of new-build flats, balconies full of bikes and succulents, then older streets with fox-gnawed bin bags and a mattress propped against a wall like a surrender flag. Emily watched the city change its mind about itself between one road and the next. She loved this part of the transit, the nowhere of it. In transit you could be anyone because you weren't anywhere yet. On the last afternoon in Florence, she had stood at the Ponte Santa Trinita and thought about how bridges were the most beautiful lies, like two places pretending to be one. She had thought, too, about Dorothy's voice on the phone that morning, polite and exact, asking what time their flight landed. We'll be here when you're home, Dorothy had said. It would be lovely to see you.

"We should stop by the shop on the way," Emily said now, casually. "Milk, bread, that nice butter you like. Lemons. It'll save going out again later."

Paul made a contented noise that started low in his throat.

"God, I've missed toast," he said. "Italian bread is a national failing."

"Blasphemy," she said, smiling. "But I'll forgive you." She liked the way the words sat in the air. I will forgive you. It set the terms with a grace that felt like flattery.

The phone quivered again against Paul's leg. He didn't reach for it this time, but his attention snagged on the sensation like a thread on a nail. Emily let her thumb stroke the back of his hand. It soothed him, she knew this, but it also reminded him of the scales, reminded him where he would find rest when he'd finished clambering around inside his head. He exhaled and let his weight fall more fully into the seat. The train's pace eased as the suburbs thickened into themselves and then loosened again, industrial estates clarifying into terraces, terraces dissolving into something wider, then knotting back to roads she half recognised from maps rather than memory.

She thought of the flat. She thought of the people who occupied the flats above and below theirs. The young couple who fought with a performative gusto on Saturday mornings and then played music too loudly in the afternoons. The man downstairs with his quiet, expensive bicycle, always wheeling it up the stairs as if it were an extra limb. She saw all of it as if she were descending in a lift towards it. The corridor with its cheap carpet, the door to their place, the moment where the lock turned and the small, stale sweetness of the air inside kissed her face. It wasn't a grand place. It didn't need to be. It was an address in London. It would do for now.

A row of allotments went by, the late autumn earth turned in fat furrows, sticks marking out the geometry of someone's future. She had always admired people who understood soil. She was learning a different kind of ground now. Plots that thrived best when tended in patience, and stories pruned carefully so they bore the fruit you wanted when you wanted it.

"Do you think we did enough nothing?" Paul asked suddenly. He seemed to be asking the window.

"In Italy?" She let a beat pass. "You are incapable of doing nothing." She softened the verdict with a smile and bumped her shoulder against his. "But you did more nothing than I've ever seen you do."

He looked properly at her then and the expression that crossed his face was one of love, gratitude, and an almost superstitious relief. It warmed her like a drink. She had never been worshipped before. It turned out to be a very useful form of heat.

The train began to slow. People stood too early, clutching bags to their chests as if the doors might decide against them. Someone's suitcase toppled and there was a little flurry of laughter as it was restored. Emily gathered the paper bag and her handbag and slid them over one shoulder. Paul took the suitcase handle with a kind of pride that said husband. She let him.

"Home," he said, and she echoed it in a tone so precise it could mean the square footage they rented, the station platform, the future, his mother's house if you wanted to be poetic about heritage.

"Home."

That was the loveliness of certain words. They were capacious. You could move around inside them without anyone noticing.

As the doors sighed open and the first gust of platform air brushed their faces, Emily tightened her fingers round Paul's. To anyone watching, it would look like the reflex of a woman who didn't want to be parted by the crowd. It was also, of course, what it looked like. That was the thing about holding on. The reasons could be layered so neatly no one could ever say where the truth stopped and the story started. She stepped down with him into the noise with the luggage wheels snapping over the yellow line, and the two of them were taken up again by the city, an easy, polished pair with matching rings, moving forward.

The flat was waiting for them in the same indifferent way it always did, a box of rooms arranged with rental precision. It had a grey carpet, off-white walls, curtains that whispered polyester each time you touched them. They stepped inside with their case dragging behind them, and Emily caught the stale note in the air. The flat had been too long shut, the ghost of old toast and old trainers hadn't had the chance to breath out. There was nothing welcoming about it, but that was fine. She knew how to make aa welcome from nothing.

Paul flicked on the hall light and dumped his jacket on the hook. He looked rumpled but content, blinking around as if reacquainting himself with the place. Emily saw it differently. After the terracotta blaze of Florence, and the glossy boulevards of Rome, the flat seemed starved of colour, as though someone had wrung the life out of it and left only the outline. Half-unpacked bags still cluttered the corner where they'd abandoned them before the wedding. Another scarf of hers trailed like a flag from an open suitcase, a reminder of their rush to catch flights and trains.

"Home sweet home," Paul said, tugging her into the dim sitting room. He tried for enthusiasm, and she rewarded him with a smile.

In the fridge waited the bottle she had left chilling before they left, knowing they'd want it. Champagne, not prosecco. A proper marker. She freed it from its foil and wire cage while Paul fumbled with plug sockets and his phone charger, his attention already snagged by the glowing lure of his inbox.

"Here," she said, tipping the neck of the bottle towards him, the suggestion of ceremony in her tone.

He abandoned his cables and took it, popping the cork with

a celebratory crack that seemed to rattle the windowpanes. Foam spilled eagerly down the dark green glass, and Emily pressed her glass beneath it before it could soak the carpet.

They laughed, clinked, drank. The fizz was sharp and cleansing, a line of bubbles burning pleasantly down her throat. Paul sank into the sofa, tie tugged loose, while she drew her phone from her bag and opened the camera roll.

"Ready?" she asked, and before he could answer the images were tumbling across the small screen. Tiled rooftops glowing orange, narrow streets that looked as though they had grown from the bones of the earth, themselves in sunglasses with their heads pressed together, laughing at something they'd already forgotten.

Paul made a noise of mock despair when the fridge magnet appeared in a shot, his hand proudly holding it aloft in the marketplace.

"Proof of my impeccable taste," he said, trying to sound solemn, and she leaned against him, her laughter feather-light.

The pictures kept sliding past. The restaurant table lit with a single candle, the piazza where they'd sat for hours drinking spritzers, the hotel balcony where he had kissed her neck as no one had ever done before. It was a story, and Emily loved stories. She loved even more the way others believed them.

She tipped the phone screen aside, and he kissed her cheek, then her mouth. Their empty glasses rolled onto the carpet. They folded into each other on the sofa, the dim little room transformed by champagne and photographs into something almost tender. For a while, Emily allowed herself to forget the colourless walls and the sound of traffic groaning outside the window. She let herself think only of the silk scarf still draped around her throat and the weight of Paul's body warm against hers.

The phone broke it. A shrill, insistent ring that sounded less like communication and more like intrusion. Paul jolted upright, fumbling, already pale before he'd even seen the screen. Emily sat back, smoothing her skirt, watching the way his hands shook as he answered.

"Robert?" he said, frowning. "What? Slow down, I can't..."

Emily caught the name. Their parents' neighbour. She leaned forward slightly, brows raised in question.

Paul listened, colour draining. "Collapsed? When? God. Paramedics?" He pressed his palm over his eyes, voice cracking as he repeated the words back, as if rehearsal might change them.

Emily placed her hand firmly on his arm. He looked as though he might bolt, and she could feel the pulse racing beneath his skin, a wild trapped thing. Robert's voice spilled faintly from the phone, flustered, apologetic, drowned in static. Paul stammered reassurance that he was on his way, though he could barely form the sentences. When he hung up, he was already reaching for his coat, his movements jerky and half-formed.

Emily rose more slowly, slipping her shoes back on, collecting her bag with unhurried grace.

"Keys," she reminded him gently, because in his panic he'd have forgotten. She pressed them into his hand, closing his fingers around them like a mother teaching a child.

Paul's mouth opened, a wordless attempt at control. She smoothed his sleeve and met his eyes. "We'll get there in time," she said, softly but with iron beneath.

To him she must have looked like salvation. Inside, she thought only of the champagne still fizzing in the bottle, the photos glowing briefly on the screen before the call came, and how quickly joy could be eclipsed by the intrusion of reality.

This, she knew, was the beginning of something.

# 2

A&E hummed like a hive with a bad temper. The lights were bright, the air a mixture of bleach and anxiety, the soundscape a restless layering of trolley wheels, clipped voices, and the intermittent sting of alarms on monitors. Emily felt the temperature of it on her skin as the specific heat that lives only in hospitals, made of breath and movement and the friction of people trying not to think the worst.

Dorothy was a fixed point in the current. She stood by the sliding doors as if they were gates to a private country, handbag clenched under one arm, hair neatly set, coat immaculate in a shade that wouldn't dare show creases. For a moment, she didn't move at all, only watched them approach with that assessing calm she wore like a second face. Then her mouth thinned.

"Why is it," she said to Paul, each word clipped off at the stalk. "Whenever I need you, you're away."

It wasn't a question. Paul absorbed it like he always did, a flinch you couldn't see if you weren't looking for it. He dropped Emily's hand and reached for his mother, not quite touching.

"Mum. I didn't know. Robert phoned... We came as soon as we could."

Dorothy's gaze slid past him and landed on Emily, travelling slowly, taking stock.

"What are you doing here?" she said, as if Emily had wandered into a room meant for someone else. "There was no need for you to come. This is family business."

Emily let the emotion show on her face in the tiny recoil, the quick recovery.

"I wanted to support Paul," she said gently. "He wanted me here." She used wanted so Dorothy could hear her message. Your son wants me. She didn't push it harder than that. With Dorothy you never pushed, you just showed you could stand your ground.

Paul inhaled as if to say something, but a nurse appeared with a badge that said Sophie and an expression that said come quickly, and ushered them down a corridor that smelled more sharply of disinfectant. As they walked, Emily reached for Paul's hand and felt the tremor in him, small but constant, like a machine running somewhere out of sight.

The cubicle was a box drawn in curtain and light. Harold lay in the middle of it, impossibly diminished, like someone had turned the volume of him right down. White sheets, a greyed-blue hospital gown, hands pale against the blanket. An oxygen mask fogged and cleared, fogged and cleared, in gentle cycles. His eyelids did not flutter. He looked like a man beneath ice.

"Trust him to trip over his own patio," Dorothy said, not moving closer. There was something almost relieved in the crispness of it, as though she was relieved to have said the normal thing.

A doctor in navy scrubs came with a clipboard and a careful voice. He explained that Harold was in a coma. The fall itself had been minor, the head injury not catastrophic, but what concerned them was his heart. Long-standing issues, he said. The shock of the fall likely triggered an arrhythmia. His words were neutral, and not unkind. He added other words like monitoring, observation, best course. All the good furniture of such conversations. Emily watched Paul translate it into 'I wasn't here' and then into 'if I had been here, it would be different'. She could feel the weight of his guilt filling the small room, heavy as a storm.

"We were away," he said to the doctor, as if that were the flaw in the machinery. "We were on our honeymoon."

The doctor's mouth made the shape of sympathy. "I'm sorry it's under these circumstances," he said, which was the sort of sentence that meant everything and changed nothing.

Dorothy stepped forward at last, not to touch Harold but to stand square with him. She studied his face as if hunting for evidence of something she could use later in a conversation. Perhaps proof that he had done this to himself, proof that she was right about the patio, the shoes, the way he never listened when she told him to be careful. Emily moved to the other side of the bed and placed her fingers lightly on the blanket near Harold's wrist. She kept her eyes on Paul, not on Dorothy, because that was the arrangement that made everything proceed without further incident.

"Dad," Paul said, and his voice snagged on the first letter. He reached for Harold's hand and took it between both of his as if he were bracing it, as if he could thread a rope through it to tether his father to the world. "I'm here now."

Emily angled herself so she occupied the space just slightly behind Paul's shoulder, close enough that the warmth of her could reach him, far enough that she didn't overshadow. She murmured nothing words in a soft, low voice that was the right shape to hold back panic.

"He knows you're here," she said. "Keep talking. He'll hear you."

She watched the monitors with the peripheral attention you

give a clock in a room where everyone is late. The green pulse traced itself obediently. The oxygen mask misted, cleared, misted again in such gentle industry for something that was far from gentle. There is a kind of theatre to this, she thought, and then corrected herself. No, not theatre. Ritual. The modern rituals of endings, wrapped in plastic, cotton, beeps, the choreography of hands doing what they have been taught to do.

Dorothy's coat creaked faintly each time she breathed.

"Harold hates hospitals," she said to no one. "He always says they make well people ill."

Emily could have smiled at that. So very Harold. But she didn't smile. She saved it. She saved most things.

"He's comfortable," she said, because that is what you say over white sheets.

Time moved differently here, as though it stretched, then snapped forward. Nurses appeared with syringes and quiet competence, and the doctor murmured instructions in a tone that did not match the urgency in his hands. A porter pushed a trolley past the mouth of the curtain, tyres whispering on linoleum. Somewhere nearby a woman sobbed on a crackle of plastic chair. A pair of policemen, no more than boys really, spoke in undertones at the nurses' station about the price of a season ticket. It all belonged.

The monitors began to misbehave. The neatness of the green line blurred, then broke into uneven bursts, a Morse code Emily did not speak. The oxygen mask fluttered against Harold's moustache as if undecided. A nurse moved briskly to the head of the bed, fingers adjusting something, the action practised and swift. Another nurse appeared with a trolley and then, as if conjured by the sound of the first alarm, the doctor was there again, sleeves pushed up, eyes gone very intent.

"Mr Mercer?" he said, and the weight of the room shifted

towards him. "We're just going to..." He didn't finish the sentence. There is nothing at the end of that sentence that makes a difference.

Paul's grip tightened on his father's hand and his knuckles paled.

"Dad," he said again, as if repetition were a prayer. "I'm right here."

Emily leaned slightly, bringing her mouth close to Paul's ear.

"I'm here too," she said. "Breathe, love." She could feel him trying to obey.

Dorothy's hands were folded so tightly that the knuckles were polished. Her eyes were dry, her nose sharp with a tension that had nothing to do with tears. She looked like she was at the theatre after all, and someone on stage had fluffed a line she'd expected to be delivered correctly.

The alarms rose in a sound designed to puncture the air, and to insist on attention. The doctor's voice cut through: "Okay." The nurses moved in fast, brisk loops, purposeful, precise. And then there was a moment that felt so brief it was almost nothing, when Harold's chest rose and released with a sigh that seemed to belong to another man in another bed, and after that the room slowed.

Stillness is not the absence of sound, it is what happens to sound when it hits a wall and falls down. The doctor's shoulders eased the tiniest degree. He looked at the monitor, then at Harold's face, then at Dorothy and Paul and the young woman standing slightly behind them who was already arranging her features into something that would be remembered as stoic, as kind. He said the sentence all doctors learn to say with a certain shape to it.

"I'm very sorry. We've done all we can."

Paul bent, as if an invisible hand had pressed between his

shoulder blades. He made a sound that had nothing adult in it. The hand around Harold's went slack, and then he put both hands over his eyes and sobbed into the damp cave they made. Emily was already there, sliding an arm across his back, drawing him against her, using the gravity of her body to stop him tipping forward into the bed. She let her cheek touch his temple and didn't make noise. She held him as if she had been built for this exact weight.

Dorothy did not move. She let the doctor's words pass over her and then shook her head once, small, almost irritated.

"It was always going to happen," she said with no tremor in her voice. She sounded like a woman reading out a timetable. "His heart couldn't go on."

Emily turned her head, met Dorothy's eyes for the first time since they had come through the doors. She did not let anything flash across her face, but merely blinked and looked back at Harold, whose mouth had fallen open a little the way dead mouths do. She thought of how many times Dorothy had cooked for him, ironed for him, scolded him for scuffing the carpet, of the decades of their shared language that would never be spoken again. Coldness is one word for what Dorothy was showing, but another is defence.

A nurse reached gently for the monitor and made it quiet. The room changed at the touch of her hand. A curtain of noise drew back and what was left was ordinary. The rasp of fabric, the faint hiss and click of something being turned off, the squeak of a shoe on the tiled floor.

"I'll leave you for a few minutes," the doctor said, and he did, taking the urgency with him. The nurses ghosted away too, their withdrawal practised and kind. The cubicle breathed out.

Paul's sobbing settled into tremors. Emily felt each one in her own muscles, translated them, filed them. She kept her voice low and practical because that was what steadied people.

"We should phone Robert," she said softly. "Let him know."

Dorothy touched it. "He'll want to help with the funeral," she said, brisk again, and tipped her chin at Harold's chest as if he'd left it in the wrong place. "Not a church service. Harold he always thought vicars made everything about themselves. Something simple at the crematorium. A proper notice in the paper, too, none of that internet nonsense." She looked at the bed, then past it. "He wanted his ashes in the garden, near the apple tree. He told me that, you know. Years ago."

Paul made a broken noise that could have been agreement, could have been pain. Emily kept her hand flat between his shoulders, anchoring him as best she could. She nodded once as if Dorothy were a senior colleague detailing next steps.

"Of course," she said. "We can call the undertaker in the morning. I'll help with the calls."

Dorothy's eyes flicked to Emily again, long enough to register that Emily was already allocating tasks and smoothing edges, making a shape around the void. There was a flare of something that looked like resentment, or perhaps recognition of competence in a quarter where she did not wish to see it. Emily lowered her gaze as if acknowledging the rebuke without accepting it.

For a little while they stood in silence. Paul with his head in his hands, Emily holding him, Dorothy upright and untouched. Emily thought of the champagne rolling on their carpet at home, the photographs on her phone of their candlelit faces, their sunglasses, the silly magnet. The world can be two things at once, she thought. A happy day is still a happy day, even if it ends in a hospital cubicle with a mask going still.

A porter's voice outside said someone's name as if he were calling a taxi in a noisy pub. A child cried, hiccupped, and went quiet. A woman at the desk asked someone to spell their surname and repeated it carefully into the air. The world went on, as it always does, without waiting for anyone to catch up.

Eventually Paul stood and wiped his face with the heel of his hand, ashamed of the salt. He kissed his father's forehead in a clumsy, boyish gesture, and then looked at Emily like a man who had misplaced something important and only just realised she was where he'd left it. Gratitude rolled off him like heat from a radiator. It warmed her.

"I need to go home," Dorothy said, not unkindly. "There's nothing more to be done here. I'll speak to Bridges in the morning." Bridges, Emily knew, was the undertaker. Of course there was a name. Of course there had always been a plan.

Emily squeezed Paul's arm.

"I'll drive," she said, though she had no intention of doing anything so dramatic as taking the wheel if he insisted on it. What she meant was I'll get us from here to there. I'll make sure nothing falls apart in the gap.

They stepped out of the cubicle and the curtain sighed closed behind them. The corridor was the same corridor, the hum the same hum. Only they had been altered. Emily reached for Paul's hand as they walked, not demonstrative, merely practical. There were things ahead that required good balance. Dorothy walked at a pace that suggested other people should move faster, and they did.

At the sliding doors, the night leaned in, cool and damp. Emily breathed it in and tasted the city on her tongue, full of exhaust fumes and rain and the faint sweetness of leaves bruised underfoot. She pictured the Mercer house, all its lamps on, all its corners prepared for visitors who would need to sit and be told. She pictured the kettle and the cups and the biscuits Dorothy would say were too good for ordinary days and then press on people anyway. She pictured the phone calls, first to Robert, then others. She pictured Paul in a chair with his head bent and his hands empty, and herself beside him, close enough to lend him her steadiness.

She understood, with a quiet, almost professional click of comprehension, that from this moment forward, the story would have to be told in a way that made sense to people. She would see to that. It was, after all, what she was very good at.

# 3

The Mercer house announced itself before they even stepped through the door. Its brick façade loomed, its windows looked down like they were watching, its roofline was drawn sharp against the February sky. It was the kind of house that carried itself like a person. All upright, dignified, and suspicious of strangers. Even the gravel drive, crunching beneath their shoes, seemed to warn her to remember where she was.

Inside, it smelled faintly of flowers, their sweetness already beginning to curdle. Emily thought it smelled like a waiting room. Paul pushed the door wide, letting the cold spill into the hallway before it swung back with a heavy, self-important thud. He carried himself with an air of reverence, his movements softened by grief. Emily followed, brushing her fingers against the frame as she passed over the threshold. Dorothy entered last, her heels clicking briskly, her handbag like armour against her side.

The silence struck immediately. Not the silence of peace, but the hollow kind that arrives after a presence has gone. Every room seemed to echo with Harold's absence. Emily felt it press against her chest, even as she smoothed her expression into something gentle.

Dust lay along the polished top of the piano, as if time itself had lost the energy to be wiped away. Harold's slippers sat by the hearth in a way that suggested he might come padding back at any moment, complaining about the draught. His reading glasses perched neatly on a side table. The house was holding its breath.

Dorothy, however, was not. She swept forward, shrugging off her coat with a flourish that made her seem taller, stronger.

"Shoes there," she instructed, pointing to a mat tucked beneath a radiator. "Not on the rug. It was handmade in Istanbul. Harold never let anyone trample dirt on it."

Paul bent automatically, untangling his laces with the obedience of a boy who'd heard the command before. Emily unzipped her boots more slowly, her smile polite and composed. Dorothy continued, her voice slicing through the air.

"Tea in the blue pot, not the white one. The white is for Sundays."

Paul gave a strained smile, trying to turn the edge of it into a joke.

"Mum, I'm sure it doesn't matter..."

"It matters," Dorothy said sharply, not looking at him. "It always matters."

Emily set her boots neatly by the skirting board and moved towards the kitchen with the soft-footed efficiency of a guest who wanted very much to appear at home. She filled the kettle, set out cups, found the blue pot. Her hands knew how to be careful in rooms like this. She poured with patience, offering the tray as though the gesture itself might pacify Dorothy.

Dorothy took her cup without thanks.

"Not too strong," she muttered, though she hadn't tasted it yet.

Paul hovered, hands useless in his pockets, his smile brittle. He tried for conversation.

"I should make some arrangements for a notice in the Times. Dad would have..."

Dorothy cut him off.

"Your father hated the Times. It'll have to be the Telegraph."

She sipped her tea, eyes closing briefly, as if she were listening to some echo only she could hear. Emily stayed quiet. She sat with her cup, her smile steady, though Dorothy's dismissals landed like small cuts against her skin. It was easier to bear them in silence. She let her gaze drift, drawn inevitably to the study door at the far end of the hall. Its curtains were drawn, the glass dulled with dust. Papers lay in untidy stacks beyond the threshold, shadows heavy in the corners. The room seemed to hum with the weight of what it had lost, as though Harold's voice, his presence, the thrum of his authority was still trapped in the air. Emily lingered on it, sensing how it would feel to walk inside, to sit in the chair that was still indented with his shape. The silence there was not peace but pressure, like something waiting to be broken. Dorothy's voice drew her back.

"You'll have to see to talk to the undertaker, Paul. Bridges. He rang this morning. He's expecting to hear from you. Don't leave it to the last minute."

Paul nodded, gaze lowered. His mother's words folded him smaller. Emily studied Dorothy more closely. Beneath the immaculate hair and the starched coat, the sharpness of her cheekbones had deepened. Her hands trembled slightly as she lifted the teacup, though she held her back straight, her chin high. Frailty disguised by discipline. The sight stirred something in Emily that was not quite pity, not quite scorn. A recognition, perhaps, of a weakness hidden carefully beneath all the rituals.

The house loomed around them. The furniture seemed too big, the ceilings too high. It was as though Harold had filled the rooms with his presence and now, without him, the walls sagged, the corners gaped, the silence turned oppressive. Emily could feel it in her bones. This was not just a house, it was a stage. And Dorothy, despite her commands and her costume and her clipped words, was only one of the players left standing.

Emily clasped her hands in her lap, keeping her smile intact. She could wait. She had always been good at waiting.

The house had grown quieter with every passing hour, settling into its night-time hush. The clocks ticked more loudly after dark, echoing along the corridors like reminders that nothing could be stopped. Upstairs, Dorothy's footsteps had faded, her door clicked closed in that precise way she had, never a slam. Yet the stillness felt fragile, as though one wrong movement might shatter it and send the whole place into mourning again.

Paul sat in Harold's study with the lamp turned low, his head bent over a half-empty glass of whisky. The amber liquid caught the light in fractured glints, a poor substitute for firelight. His tie had come loose, his shirt sleeves were rolled back, and his hair was untidy from fingers running through it too often. The papers spread across Harold's desk were yellowed at the edges, marked with Harold's neat, uncompromising hand. A ledger lay open, figures standing like sentries in their columns. Dust softened the spines of books lined in rows, their titles faint with time. It was as if Harold himself lingered in the margins, disapproving of Paul for touching his things.

The air was heavy with silence and the faint sting of whisky vapour. Paul stared at the glass as though it might deliver answers if he only looked long enough. He looked smaller here, Emily thought from the doorway. Like a boy caught in his father's clothes, the shoulders too wide, the weight too much.

She entered quietly, careful with each step on the old floorboards.

"Paul," she said softly, her voice a thread against the hush.

He turned, startled, though his eyes softened when they found her.

"You should be in bed," he murmured.

Emily crossed to him, her presence measured. She laid a hand lightly on his shoulder. His shirt was warm under her palm, damp with the day's exhaustion. "I couldn't sleep," she said. "Neither could you, it seems."

He gave a hollow laugh.

"Too many ghosts in here." He gestured vaguely at the shelves, the papers, the chair that still seemed moulded to Harold's shape. "I keep expecting him to walk in and tell me I'm holding the glass wrong."

Emily squeezed his shoulder, lowering herself so she could look him in the eye. Her face was tender and her smile subdued. She let silence bloom for a moment before speaking again, weighing her words carefully.

"I've been thinking," she said, quiet and careful. "We shouldn't leave your mother here alone. She needs us." She paused, watching his face. "This has come as a shock, and I'm not sure she's even begun to process it. Especially on top of her own illness. The cancer will make her frail, and now she doesn't have Harold to support her. She shouldn't have to face this house by herself."

The suggestion landed like balm on a burn. Paul blinked, a film of moisture rising in his eyes. He looked at her as though she had just offered him absolution. His lips parted, but no words came. Instead, he set down his glass, caught her hand and kissed it, holding it to his mouth longer than necessary.

"You're remarkable," he whispered against her skin.

Emily allowed a faint blush to reach her cheeks, lowered her gaze with modesty she knew would please him. She didn't need to say anything. The silence between them brimmed with his gratitude.

In the corridor beyond, a shadow stirred. Dorothy, shawl pulled tight around her shoulders, had stopped at the sound of their voices. She lingered just out of sight, her ear tilted towards the door. The words she caught rang in her head like a bell she had not asked to hear. For a moment she stood in the half-dark, back rigid against the wallpaper patterned with roses delicately faded. She did not step inside, nor announce herself. She simply listened to the hush of their voices, the low intimacy of them, until the sound of Paul's murmur reached her. You're remarkable.

Her lips tightened further. Quiet as a ghost, Dorothy turned away, retreating down the hall. Her cane tapped once against the floorboards before she lifted it, silencing even that sound. She moved back to her room without a word, but her silence carried more weight than any reprimand she could have spoken aloud.

Back in the study, Emily leaned her head lightly against Paul's shoulder. His hand found hers again, gripping as if she were the only solid thing in the room. And in that moment, for him, she was.

# 4

They moved in on a Tuesday, because it felt appropriate to do it on a weekday. Tuesdays were brisk and practical, easy to disguise as an errand if anyone asked why newlyweds were carting boxes into a widow's house not a fortnight after the funeral. The weather had taken that damp, indecisive turn England favours in late winter, and mist clung to the hedges and made the iron railings sweat. Emily stood beneath the porch while Paul wrestled with the front door, the key stiff in a lock that had never like being hurried.

The Mercer house stood in Bray, Berkshire, a village of discreet affluence on the Thames, a short drive from Windsor and still close enough for Paul to commute daily into the City. Among streets lined with fine Georgian homes and old coaching inns, the Mercers' residence was the grandest. It was an imposing, ivy-framed house with manicured lawns sweeping down to the river, its windows tall and symmetrical, its rooms high-ceilinged and echoing with old money. It was the sort of property that spoke not just of wealth, but of generations of careful cultivation of status, the kind of grandeur you didn't buy, but inherited.

"Try lifting it a fraction," she said, even though she'd never opened this door in her life. Men like Paul liked to be told what to do in ways that let them keep charge. He jiggled and lifted, and the door swung open with a little groan, as if roused from sleep against its will.

The hallway yawned at them, a long perspective of polished floorboards and runner rugs, the walls crowded with discreetly expensive art that managed to look both bland and important. Cardboard boxes already cluttered the skirting, stacked two high in places, their black marker pen labels that read KITCHEN, BOOKS, BEDROOM, like temporary tattoos on the house's pale skin. The air was cool and held a faint lily-sweetness that felt almost medicinal now the flowers were gone. Someone had cracked a window a few hours before, and the cold seeped in as if to inspect the newcomers.

Dorothy materialised from the drawing room with the same economy of movement she brought to everything. Her cardigan, a soft grey that matched the light, sat perfectly on her narrow shoulders and her hair was set in its usual helmet of white, every wave obedient. She looked at the boxes as if they were stray dogs that had strayed too far. Her gaze flicked once to Emily's face and then away, the visual equivalent of a sigh.

"You've scuffed the paint," she said to Paul. "By the banister. I'll have to get Robert in to touch it up."

"It was the removal men," Paul said, eagerly apologetic. "I told them to be careful."

"They never are," Dorothy said. "That's why you have to stand over them." She stepped aside with a little wave of her hand that could have been welcome or dismissal. "Shoes on the mat. Not the rug. It was handmade in Istanbul."

"We remember," Paul said, smiling as if he didn't, and unknotted his laces.

Emily bent to unzip her boots, buying herself a moment

with her head lowered and her hair a curtain to peep from behind. She knew how to enter a space that believed itself above her. You didn't stride in as if you belonged, but you behaved exquisitely, as if the house itself might be nervous of you. Then you got to work.

They ferried the boxes through to the kitchen where the light tilted in from the garden and found the dust no one had had time to chase. Harold's slippers were still by the hearth in the morning room next door, one slightly crooked as if he'd half-turned back. Emily tried not to look at them. She lifted the few belongings from paper and set them on the counter, the rhythm quickly soothing. Unwrap, stack, decide, place. Paul carried, fetched, asked where, and she told him, and he placed the boxes where she pointed and then looked over his shoulder towards the hall, half expecting commentary.

It arrived, of course, right on cue. Dorothy appeared in the doorway, regarded the two mugs Emily had just arranged in the cupboard nearest the kettle and said, "We don't keep mugs there."

Emily let her face do that pleasant, obliging thing it had learned years ago.

"Oh?" she said lightly. "Where would you like them?"

"In the cupboard to the left of the Aga," Dorothy said, as if this were a matter of faith. "The one near the kettle is for the good china."

"Of course," Emily said, as if this were a charming household quirk she'd never forget, and moved the mugs without a sound. When she opened the recommended cupboard she was greeted by a jar of desiccated coconut from a decade ago and three unmatched egg cups. She moved those too, carefully, to a shelf where they could live with their kind.

Paul hovered, a man in need of instructions. "Anything else?" he said, smiling, as if to sweeten the air.

Dorothy's glance skimmed the countertops. "Do not put the knives in the drawer near the sink. That drawer is for tea towels. And the small frying pan. Harold liked it on the hook by the clock. Not the larger hook. It will bend."

"Right," Paul said, and he looked at Emily as if to say she'll forget, and Emily smiled as if to say no I won't. She placed the knives where Dorothy decreed. She hung the small pan on its designated hook. She adopted another family's muscle memory as if it had been waiting for her.

By late afternoon, the kitchen had begun to look like somewhere that might, with concentration, yield a meal. Paul flourished a supermarket bag from the village shop like a trophy. He had managed potatoes, rosemary, garlic, the expensive salt in its twee cardboard tube, and a shoulder of lamb wrapped in paper that had bled a little at the corners.

"I thought," he said, almost boyish in his hope. "A proper dinner. Your roast potatoes."

"My roast potatoes," she echoed, touching his wrist. It had the potential to be a small triumph. A table was set, the house warmed by the oven, the aroma of rosemary and fat turning to gold. A gesture that said I'm making a home out of this, for you and for her. Emily knew those kinds of gestures mattered. They lodged in the memory like grit in an oyster, working at becoming a pearl.

Dorothy watched them lay the table with a supervising air, not hostile so much as alert. She corrected the position of a fork by a millimetre. She rotated a tumbler so the tiniest chip faced away from the seat she chose for herself. She placed her own napkin on her lap with a precision that made Emily think of an altar.

The lamb came out blushing and glossy, and the potatoes crunched under the knife. The carrots had caught at their tips and were sweet and singed, and she'd even made proper gravy, from the sticky squares of flavour left on the roasting tray. It coated the spoon like silk. Emily presented the platter like an apology and a promise. She watched Paul's shoulders lower a notch with relief at the sight of something he recognised as care.

Dorothy carved herself a slice with neat brutality and placed it in her mouth with the expression of a woman about to sit for a photograph. She chewed once, twice. Her jaw paused.

"A cheap cut," she said. The words were not cruelly delivered, but they were deliberate. "Harold would never have eaten this. It's too fatty."

Paul laughed in the way men do when a room has turned and they want it to right itself.

"Mum," he said, half-reproach, half-pleading. "Don't be..."

"It's not a criticism," Dorothy said, though of course it was. "Merely a fact. Harold was very particular. He preferred leg to shoulder."

Emily let her smile hold. "I'll remember for next time," she said, and her fingers, already resting on the carving knife, tightened until the knuckles whitened. She felt the pressure as a private contrition and released it before anyone could see.

Paul reached for her hand under the table and gave it a squeeze.

"I think it's delicious," he said, loudly, too brightly. "Honestly, Em, you've outdone yourself." He took a larger bite than he wanted and chewed dutifully, and she wanted to forgive him and pinch him at the same time.

"I'm sure it's perfectly adequate," Dorothy said, cutting her potatoes into exact quarters. "For people who like that kind of thing."

Emily chose a piece of lamb that fell apart when the fork touched it and ate it slowly, her face arranged around appreciation. This was data, not disaster. You could work with data. You learned where people's lines were drawn and you painted your words inside them. The meal made its way to a conclusion. Plates were cleared, and Dorothy grudgingly allowed Emily to stack the dishwasher, though not before pointing out that glasses went on the top rack, not the bottom, and that the silverware should sit handles down, not up, so the business ends could be properly scoured.

By the time the last pan was dried and placed, by the time the tea had been poured into the blue pot (not the white), by the time the lamps had been turned to the correct, dignified level and the curtains shut against the mulch-black garden, the pattern had quietly established itself. Dorothy issued. Paul placated. Emily accommodated. It was almost elegant, the way the three of them moved around the house like pieces figured on a board.

After tea, they migrated to the drawing room. Dorothy chose the chair that allowed her to see both the door and the mantelpiece. She looked smaller in it, though the straightness of her back denied frailty any permission to be witnessed. She asked Paul about the bill for the undertaker and recited, with crisp efficiency, the list of mourners who had written and ought to be written to in return. Emily offered, gently, to draft letters. Dorothy said she would manage with the ones that mattered, and Emily smiled as if she had asked only to be polite.

Paul's phone lit the inside of his pocket like a lighthouse. He tried to ignore it, but failed. When he glanced down, he winced.

"It's just work," he said to no one in particular. "They know I'm..." He didn't finish the sentence because the phone vibrated again, insistent, and he took this as absolution and retrieved it. Emily watched him look down into his little screen-world, his mouth set and thoughtful. She knew that concentration was a refuge for him. She was not threatened by it. Especially as it kept him still while she took the measure of a room.

Dorothy, the teacup at her lips, tipped her head and

considered Emily as if she were a painting she couldn't decide upon.

"You've done well for yourself," she said, the compliment shape perfectly cast, the content flawed at the core. "Coming from such an ordinary family."

Paul didn't look up. His thumb moved across glass.

"Mum," he said absently, a reproach stripped of relevance.

Emily felt the point land, small and precise. She did not reach for it. She left it where it was and turned it into something useful. She placed her cup down gently, took the breath you take before answering an exam question you know you'll score highly on.

"I only hope to do my best for this family."

Dorothy sniffed, a sound both satisfied and sceptical, and took another sip. As statements of intent went, it pleased her to be told exactly what she believed she was owed.

Paul's face lifted from the blue light.

"What's that?" he said, too late to catch it.

"Nothing," Emily said brightly. "Work?"

He looked guilty. "Just an email." He saw his mother watching and put his phone on the sofa arm with performative reluctance. "It can wait."

"I should think so," Dorothy said. "Your father would never have..." She stopped herself, but the ghost of her disapproval was audible anyway.

It grew late in the kind of way time grows late in big houses. Dorothy declared she would go up, but not before she deigned to praise Emily for putting the mugs away properly. Perhaps not the act itself, but the obedience contained within it. She allowed Paul to help her from the room though she didn't truly need it. The stairs accepted her, and up she climbed, measured and exact.

When she was gone, the drawing room seemed to breathe

differently, as if a window had opened. Paul let his shoulders drop and turned towards Emily with an expression that asked for a verdict and for forgiveness at once.

"Are you okay?" he said. He meant: How are you surviving this?

Emily reached over, straightened his tie, a silly little gesture at that hour, and smiled with her mouth closed.

"It's her house," she said. "It's her way of staying in control. It makes people particular."

"You were incredible," he said, earnest, a hand over his heart. "Really. I know it isn't easy."

"It isn't difficult," she said, and made sure the tone implied that if it were, she would happily shoulder it. "She's grieving."

"And you're a saint," he said, and he meant it. He leaned forward, put his forehead against her shoulder, exhaled into the space where the hollow of her collarbone kept secrets. "Thank you."

She let her cheek rest on his hair. "She's also ill," she said, quiet, practical, reminding rather than complaining. "The cancer... we can't underestimate the toll it's taking. And her memory seems rattled, too. She repeated herself three times about the mugs. She might not realise it. We just need to be gentle."

He lifted his head to look at her, guilt running bright behind his eyes.

"You're right," he said. "Of course you are. I'll do better. I'll try to be here more. It's just," he gestured vaguely to the pocket where his phone had returned to roost. "Work is so..."

"Important," she supplied, merciful. "I know." She brushed an imaginary fleck of lint from his sleeve. "And so is your mother. Between us, we can do both."

He kissed her then, brief and grateful, the kind of kiss you give someone you think might save you. She absorbed it like water. They climbed the stairs together, the house creaking in the way old houses do, as if passing judgement on the weight of new people. In the bedroom that had become theirs, which had been one of the guest rooms at the back with a view of the orchard, boxes still leaned against the wall like shy guests. Emily opened the wardrobe and encountered a faint smell of cedar and somebody else's perfume, long evaporated. She hung two dresses and a cardigan, establishing a foothold, and folded underwear into a drawer that slid like a whisper.

Paul, already in a T-shirt and an expression of bone-weariness, checked his phone again and then thought better of it and set it face down on the bedside table. He crawled beneath the duvet as if gravity had sharpened while he stood.

"Come on," he said, voice muffled by pillow. "Before tomorrow starts."

Emily moved through her tiny rituals, applying face cream, fetching a glass of water, a slow brush through her hair as if calming a horse. The mirror yielded a girl-woman whose face could be anything at all depending on who was looking. She smiled at herself briefly as if to practise for morning.

She slipped into bed. Paul turned towards her and wrapped an arm around her waist, anchoring himself.

"Mum will warm to you," he murmured into her shoulder. "She will. She'd be mad not to."

"Mm," Emily said. She could feel the word's shape against her teeth. "I hope so."

"She will. She's just..."

"Grieving," Emily finished, saving him from having to say it again. "Yes. And tired. And frightened."

"And difficult," he said, so quietly it hardly counted as disloyalty. He lifted his head, found her face in the near-dark, and kissed her brow with a reverence that startled her.

"You're a saint. You know that?"

"Don't," she said with a little laugh that softened the admonition into something gentle. "You'll have me canonised before I can make breakfast."

"Eggs," he said, sleep already tugging him under. "Those soft ones. The way you do them."

She listened to his breathing slow. In the silence, the house began its night talk. Downstairs, a pipe settled. Outside, a fox tried the bins. In the hall, the far-off tick of the grandfather clock measuring out the dark. Emily watched the ceiling, barely visible, and let her thoughts move across it like faint light.

She had not lied earlier. Dorothy was tired and frightened. She was also exacting to the point of pettiness and more than a little proud. Both truths could exist. Emily had spent a lifetime learning to hold two truths in the same hand and turn whichever one the room required to the light. What mattered was not which was truer, but which one people believed when they told the story later.

She closed her eyes and pictured the kitchen cupboards, already partly reordered to her satisfaction beneath the cover of Dorothy's rules. She imagined the weekly shop arriving on a Friday morning and the way the delivery man would start saying hello to her by name. She pictured herself in the garden with secateurs, pretending to tame the roses, while the neighbour over the hedge spoke of the weather and the cost of living and how dreadful it all was since Harold passed. She imagined the sound of her own name in the mouths of the village. Lovely girl. So good to Dorothy. So good for Paul. It was not ambition so much as architecture built by laying the bricks of perception with a careful hand.

Beside her, Paul made a small sound, the ghost of a worry surfacing and sinking. Emily placed her palm flat on his chest and felt his heart reckoning with itself in its sleep.

"Shh," she said, the syllable barely born.

In the morning there would be eggs, soft the way he liked them, and a gentle reminder for Dorothy about the visiting nurse and the question of whether she wanted Emily to book the hairdresser for Saturday. There would be a detour into the village for milk where Emily would learn the shopkeeper's name and use it lightly, as if names were compliments. In the evening there would be Dorothy's disapproval served in teaspoons and Paul's gratitude poured out like wine. And through all of it, Emily would keep her smile steady and her step quiet, and the house would get used to the shape she cast in its rooms.

It was not that she liked being belittled. She felt each small sting. But a pattern establishes itself because patterns long to be established, and in their predictability lies a kind of power. You can braid your intentions right through the middle of them and no one sees the plait until it tightens.

Down the corridor, a door creaked, then closed. Dorothy's nocturnal patrols, Emily thought. Keeping an eye on things, patrolling the borders. Fine. It was wise to know the lay of a land before you planted anything that mattered.

She let herself drift then, the house's breath rocking her, the future arranging itself in quiet lines behind her eyes. In the morning, she would move the mugs back, not to the kettle cupboard, since that would be a declaration of war, but to the one above the plates, which was more sensible. Dorothy would notice months from now and be irritated and then forget, and it would become one of those small household facts that no one could remember setting. Harmless and invisible, but entirely consequential.

Emily smiled into the pillow. It was work, yes. But she had never been afraid of work. Not the kind that built something.

~

The cracks, when they came, did not look like cracks. They looked like air passing between two people in a kitchen. They looked like courtesy slightly misapplied. It began with the breakfast after their first night. Emily poached the eggs perfectly, coaxing the whites into domes, the yolks like small suns trembling under their thin film. She buttered toast to its corners. She set the table with the everyday plates and the blue pot for tea, because she wasn't an idiot.

Dorothy joined them dressed for the day, cardigan buttoned, pearls in place as if someone might take a photograph at any moment. She sat, took up her knife, and tapped the side of the egg with its rounded tip. The top opened and the yolk spilled out. She looked down and said nothing at all. The silence was a compliment to her restraint and a rebuke to the egg.

"I can do them firmer," Emily said cheerfully, as if Dorothy had asked. "Tomorrow."

"No need," Dorothy said, which meant there is. "I prefer porridge on weekdays. The old-fashioned kind. Not those sachets. We aren't animals."

"Of course," Emily said. "I'll make some tomorrow."

"And the post," Dorothy said, nodding at the tidy stack Emily had placed by the fruit bowl. "Harold always sorted it by hand before breakfast. Anything that needed attention went on the tray in his study."

"I can do that," Emily said. "If you show me which tray."

Dorothy made a noncommittal sound. Paul, who had eaten his egg in two bites because he was late for a call he had promised not to take, kissed Emily's hair.

"You're the best," he said. Then he bent and kissed Dorothy's cheek, and left a trail of coffee steam behind him like a cartoon.

The morning folded into errands. Emily discovered the vacuum cleaner's obstinate moods and the trick of its cord. She learned where the spare bin bags lived and that Dorothy kept a special cloth for glass that must be washed by hand and dried on the radiator. She moved through the house like someone in a museum who'd been given temporary permission to touch.

Lunch was soup and bread, which seemed simple and safe. Dorothy ate with neat sips, dabbing at the corners of her mouth with a napkin folded into origami. After, she sat in the sunny rectangle in the morning room and read the Telegraph from back to front, because Harold had refused to begin anywhere else. Emily wrote three sympathy replies in her neatest hand and left them by the phone for Dorothy's approval. Dorothy adjusted a comma and corrected "organise" to "organize," a habit she had inherited from a Canadian aunt and refused to relinquish to the British dictionary.

By dinner the weather had pressed its face to the windows and smeared them, as the day tired itself out at last in a dreary grey. Emily made something she thought couldn't fail to satisfy. A cottage pie crowned with potato peaks, green beans with toasted almonds, a fool-proof crumble. Dorothy ate it without comment and then, as she set down her fork, turned to Emily with a mild expression that had a knack of making the words sharper.

"You have some good skills," she said, as if stating the day's weather. "Considering your background."

Paul, in his work bubble, didn't surface. His phone lit the underside of his jaw an unhealthy aquarium blue. "Mm?" he said, noncommittal.

Emily felt that neat little needle again and smiled as if it were a sewing pin in the mouth of a dressmaker about to fit a bride.

"I do my best," she said. The words were gentle and utterly true, though what counted as best would always depend on who was choosing the definition.

Dorothy sniffed, satisfied she'd placed the table ornament precisely where it annoyed her least.

"We'll see," she said, which was more honest than most people manage after two glasses of wine.

Paul looked up belatedly and, discovering he'd missed something, smiled into the gap, hoping charm might paste it over.

"Mum, be nice," he said lightly, and stood to clear plates as a penance he could perform publicly.

Emily wanted to be irritated with him. Instead, she watched the angle of his shoulders and the way his mouth turned down when he thought the women weren't looking, and she forgave him for being himself. He could no more change his responses than Dorothy could change her rituals. That was the point. They were predictable, and predictability, in the right hands, was a tool.

After Dorothy had taken her habitual evening turn through the downstairs rooms, checking the switches, drawing curtains, aligning a cushion to the angle Harold had preferred, she excused herself and went up. The moment her foot lifted from the last stair, the mood altered. Paul sat with his head back against the sofa and exhaled.

"I'm sorry," he said into the ceiling. "She shouldn't have said that."

"She's grieving," Emily said, the line well-rehearsed now, and then, because she refused to be martyred in her own head, she added, "She's also not entirely well."

He sat up. "What do you mean?"

"She repeats herself," Emily said carefully. "And she's... forgetful. Small things. And she's much thinner than at Christmas." Emily had only seen photographs at Christmas, but the point stood; Dorothy was diminished. "Your mum is proud.

Pride can look like rudeness when it's trying to cover fear. The cancer is a lot for anyone. And if there are memory issues..."

"Dementia," Paul said, the word like a cold coin in his mouth.

"Perhaps only the beginnings," Emily said at once, soothing the coin warm in his palm. "But we should be mindful. Gentle."

He reached for her hand, which had made a habit of being where he could find it.

"You're a saint," he said, helpless. "I don't deserve you."

"Don't be silly," she said, smiling as if saints were a ridiculous category and she had no interest in beatification. "You deserve exactly me."

In the days that followed, the pattern of Dorothy's corrections, Paul's half-apologies, and Emily's placid competence settled into a more peaceful existence. The mugs stayed where Dorothy wanted them. The lamb, when it appeared again, was a leg, roasted to Dorothy's exacting definition of done. The tea went in the blue pot. The slippers remained by the hearth, one crooked, and Emily left them there, a relic that consoled Dorothy and cost her nothing.

And if, every now and then, Emily shifted a small thing, or moved the spare keys from the hall table to the little dish by the back door because it made more sense, or tucked Dorothy's letters into a folder arranged by week so nothing went astray, or spoke to the chemist about a pre-payment certificate because prescription charges mount, no one called it encroaching. They called it helpful. They called it remarkable. They called it love. But Dorothy made sure to correct them.

# 5

The Mercer dining room was never meant for three people. It had been built, furnished, and polished for scale. It was a table stretching long enough to seat two dozen with ease, chandeliers hung heavy with crystal to scatter light across silverware that gleamed like little daggers. On the walls, oil portraits of ancestors peered out of dusky frames, faces painted with the same hauteur Dorothy had perfected in life. Tonight, all that grandeur seemed to mock them, because only three places had been set, and the emptiness on either side felt cavernous.

Emily had done her best to soften the atmosphere. She'd chosen Harold's favourite ivory damask cloth with its faint lattice pattern, and laid out polished cutlery, arranging each fork and knife as carefully as a florist positioning stems. She'd placed a small vase of roses in the centre, a gesture of brightness against all the dark wood. She wanted the room to feel alive, to show Dorothy that she honoured tradition, that she could be the caretaker of this house too.

All afternoon she had worked in the kitchen. She'd planned a menu that balanced reverence with flair, a nod to the Mercer standards but with her own touch of elegance. The starter was beetroot carpaccio, the slices paper-thin and glistening with balsamic glaze, arranged like petals across the plate. The main, venison fillet, seared at exactly the right moment, plated with roasted parsnips and shallots caramelised in their skins. For dessert, she'd made a lemon tart, the pastry blind-baked until golden, the filling smooth and sharp, the top kissed with a caramelised sheen.

She had laid each dish on the table with care, hoping that, just for once, Dorothy might nod in approval, however small. But Dorothy had other plans. She lifted her fork with an air of reluctance, as though food itself might fail her. One bite of the beetroot and she dabbed her lips, her face sour.

"Too salty," she pronounced, as though delivering a verdict from the bench.

Paul, seated between them, gave a strained little laugh.

"Mum..."

She moved on to the venison, her knife slicing cleanly through the fillet. She chewed twice, her expression tightening.

"Too bland. A blessing Harold isn't here to taste this. He had very high standards. As do I."

Her tone wasn't sharp in volume, but in delivery, it was the chill of a knife edge drawn slowly across glass. Paul darted a look at Emily, guilt stamped across his features. He attempted a smile, offering it to her like a plaster he hoped might cover the wound.

"It's lovely, Em. Truly. You've worked so hard."

Emily smiled back, but it cost her. Beneath the table, her hands clenched until her knuckles ached. She kept her expression serene and composed as the smile of a wife who understood, who forgave, who would not make a scene. She had learned long ago the value of never letting a critic see you bleed.

Dorothy took another delicate mouthful, chewed, swallowed, and set her cutlery down with the finality of a gavel.

"Paul deserves better."

The words dropped into the silence with a weight that seemed to vibrate along the table. Paul froze, fork halfway to his mouth. His face went slack with shock and then filled with colour. He opened his mouth, breath catching as though words of defence or fury were struggling to form. He even lifted a hand from the table, as though to slam it down, to make his voice heard at last.

But Emily caught his eye. Her lips shaped the words silently. Leave it. The plea was tender but urgent, a warning dressed as patience. Paul faltered. He blinked, exhaled, and slowly lowered his hand. His fork slipped from his grip, clattering against the porcelain with an ignoble clang. Dorothy gave the faintest sniff of satisfaction, a queen certain of her dominion.

Emily held her smile. She swallowed the lump of humiliation that threatened to choke her, pressing it down into her stomach like an indigestible stone. Her face remained pale but poised, the picture of composure under trial. To anyone glancing in from beyond the drawn velvet curtains, it might have looked like a family dining together in solemn grief. But inside the room, the air vibrated with a tension that could not be softened by chandeliers or roses.

Paul shifted in his chair, his hand twitching as though he might reach across to take Emily's. But he didn't. His silence, whether born of cowardice, exhaustion, or misplaced loyalty, settled over the table heavier than Dorothy's words.

Emily carved a piece of venison, placed it carefully on her fork, and raised it to her lips with steady grace. She chewed slowly, savouring nothing, and swallowed with dignity. The humiliation burned, but she held it down where no one could see. She smiled again, serene, patient. The perfect wife. Inside, though, something cracked, so small it barely made a sound.

~

The café was warm and humming with life, the windows fogged with condensation where the early spring chill pressed against the glass. Outside, the streets of Windsor bustled with parents ferrying prams, office workers snatching a quick sandwich, and the faint rumble of traffic heading towards the bridge. Inside, the hiss of the coffee machine and the clink of cups against saucers created a kind of sanctuary. The air smelled of ground beans, butter, and the faint tang of orange zest from a tray of muffins cooling behind the counter.

Emily sat at a corner table, her scarf still knotted neatly around her neck though the room was too warm for it. Steam curled upwards from her cappuccino, blurring her reflection in the window. She watched it drift before she looked back at Isla, one of her oldest friends, who sat opposite, elbows on the table, hands wrapped around her mug as if absorbing its heat.

Isla had travelled out from London that morning, swapping the rush of the city for the quieter rhythms of Windsor. She lived in a narrow townhouse in Islington, where bicycles were chained to railings and neighbours knew one another only by the sound of their footsteps on the stairs. The train ride west was a release for her, a stretch of time where emails could wait and her phone could buzz unanswered in her bag.

She worked as a solicitor for a mid-sized firm in the City, specialising in employment disputes. Her days were a carousel of grievances and negotiations, the air in her office heavy with the smell of photocopied paper and strong coffee. Isla had always thrived in environments that demanded sharpness, her Glasgow upbringing instilling in her a refusal to be intimidated. But the work was draining too. Long hours, endless argument, the constant pressure to be cleverer than the next voice across the table, all took their toll. Coming to Windsor to see Emily felt like stepping into another world altogether. It was slower here, and leafier. It was the kind of place where people still talked about gardens and Sunday roasts rather than contracts and settlements.

"I don't know how you bear it," Isla said, shaking her head. Her voice was low but urgent, carrying the indignation Emily had withheld the night before. "I mean... to say that to you at the table. In front of Paul. It's just cruel."

Emily lowered her gaze, tracing the rim of her cup with one fingertip. Her voice, when it came, was soft, weary. "I just... keep trying. For Paul's sake. He's caught in the middle, and it would be unfair to make him choose."

Isla leaned forward, eyes bright with sympathy, but there was something else there too, that was more cautious. She had always been protective of Emily, but she was no fool. A solicitor by training, she was used to weighing words, measuring the intent beneath them. Her friendship with Emily went back almost a decade, to the days when Emily had worked at a small marketing firm in Reading and Isla had been her colleague, already halfway out the door to a better job. Where Emily had been polished but quiet, Isla had been fearless. She was the sort of woman who would walk into a room and have people remember her voice even if they forgot her name.

Born in Glasgow, she'd grown up in a family of teachers and trade unionists, who didn't have much but who never lacked for conviction. Isla had moved south for university, stayed for work, and eventually built a life that hovered just on the comfortable side of middle-class. A Victorian terrace in Islington, a Labrador called Tess, a partner who lectured in politics. She'd fought for everything she had, and she respected fighters.

That was part of what had drawn her to Emily all those years ago. She had seen the quiet determination beneath the careful manners, the way she never complained but carried herself as if the world could not touch her, even when Isla suspected it already had.

They had bonded properly all those years ago, in the break room of a small marketing firm in Reading where both women had worked, though in very different roles. Emily was the receptionist then, manning the phones with her serene smile, always immaculate in blouses from high street shops that looked more expensive than they were. Isla was a junior solicitor on retainer for the company, called in to handle the dreary churn of employment contracts and minor disputes. Their paths should hardly have crossed, yet fate had a habit of tossing unlikely people together at the water cooler.

Emily had been sitting at the corner table that afternoon, nursing a cup of instant coffee that steamed weakly, her eyes red from the silent tears she thought no one had noticed. Isla, never one to ignore a storm when she saw one brewing, pulled up a chair with a decisive scrape.

"Right," she'd said in her Glaswegian lilt. "Who's upset you, and shall I go and sue them?"

Emily had laughed, caught between surprise and relief, and wiped at her eyes with the heel of her hand. She explained, haltingly, about her mother's latest drama, the messy divorce still rumbling on, and how she'd had to send most of her wages home to keep the heating on in her father's flat. She'd spoken with an apologetic smile, as though ashamed of being ordinary, ashamed of not being from the kind of family who had safety nets and spare bedrooms.

Isla had listened with the unflinching directness she was known for, and then she'd said something that changed everything.

"You're tougher than you realise, Emily. Don't let anyone make you feel small because of where you've come from. You've got more grit in you than half the people in this office."

It was the first time anyone had said such words to Emily without a hint of pity. In that moment, a thread tied itself between them. Isla, the blunt, battle-tested Scot with a sharp sense of justice, and Emily, the quiet observer who absorbed encouragement like sunlight. They began having lunch together, slipping into pubs after work for a glass of wine, confiding more than colleagues usually dared. Isla admired Emily's polish, the way she always seemed composed despite the cracks beneath, and Emily admired Isla's fearlessness, and her refusal to apologise for herself.

From that bond grew a friendship that outlasted the job. Isla left for a bigger firm in London, Emily drifted into Paul's orbit, but they never stopped meeting for coffee dates, exchanging phone calls, little visits. Isla had been the one Emily called first when she got engaged, her excitement tumbling down the line. And now, sitting across from her in this Windsor café, Isla carried not just affection but a kind of responsibility. She knew where Emily had come from, knew how much she wanted to belong to a world that wasn't hers by birth. That knowledge made Isla protective, but it also made her cautious. Because she, perhaps more than anyone, could sense when Emily's version of a story was being tidied, polished, smoothed until the rough edges no longer showed.

Isla's hand reached across the table, covering Emily's for a moment. Her touch was warm, grounding.

"Still," Isla said. "I can't help but wonder... and don't take this the wrong way, but are you sure you're not being... too sensitive?" She softened it with a smile, as if to cushion the doubt. "I mean, she has just lost her husband. And she's ill. People lash out when they're in pain."

Emily lifted her head, her smile faint and rueful. "Yes, you're right. Of course you are. She's grieving, and she's sick, and she's old. I'm sure she doesn't mean it." She sighed, stirring her coffee though she hadn't added sugar. "It's just difficult, sometimes."

"I know. But you're stronger than you think. And Paul. Well, he's lucky. Not every man finds a wife willing to take on all that."

Emily returned the smile, modest, self-effacing. "I just want to do my best for him. For his family. That's all."

But behind her eyes, memories stirred. She thought of her own childhood home, the semi-detached in a Midlands town where the wallpaper peeled in the hallway and her mother's hairdressing appointments paid just enough to cover the leaky boiler. Her father, a delivery driver with restless hands, had been in and out of work, in and out of the house, and then gone altogether. Their divorce had been messy, the shouting spilling into the street. Emily remembered sitting on the stairs, listening to words hurled like crockery, promising herself that one day she would live somewhere quiet, somewhere grand, somewhere no one could walk out of.

That promise had carried her through. Through school, where she kept her head down but her grades up. Through her first job, where she learned quickly that listening and smiling opened more doors than demanding ever did. Through her twenties, when she taught herself how to read what people wanted, what they feared, what would make them believe in her. And now, into Paul's life, and into Dorothy's house.

"I just wish she could see me," Emily murmured, staring into her coffee. "Really see me. Not as an interloper. But as someone who wants to help. To care."

Isla squeezed her hand, her expression full of loyalty. Yet when she drew back, lifting her mug again, there was the faintest flicker of doubt in her eyes. A hesitation, almost imperceptible. What if Dorothy isn't as cruel as she sounds? What if Emily is painting her darker than she is? Isla dismissed it at once, telling herself that grief made everyone say things they didn't mean. But the thought lingered, quiet and unwelcome.

Around them, the café carried on. A waiter with a tired smile delivered plates of avocado toast to a pair of students at the next table. An older couple shared a scone between them, their movements practiced in long marriage. The door chimed each time someone entered, letting in a draught of cold air that smelled faintly of rain.

Emily sipped her coffee, her smile faint, her posture composed. To anyone watching, she looked like a woman confiding in a friend, the very picture of patience and resilience. And Isla, protective but cautious, played her role too, as the sounding board, the one who listened, the one who offered sympathy and doubt in equal measure.

Neither of them said what hung unspoken in the air. That Dorothy's house was no longer just Dorothy's, and that Emily had no intention of leaving it.

# 6

The Mercer house was quiet, though never truly silent, as old houses seldom are. But to Dorothy, seated alone in Harold's study, the quiet sounded vast, like a cathedral that had emptied after a service.

The room was still his. Dust lined the spines of his books, the armchair by the fire sagged where his frame had moulded it, and the faint tobacco ghost of his pipe lingered in the curtains. On the desk stood a walnut frame holding a photograph taken years ago, Harold squinting in the summer sun, his expression caught between irritation and amusement. Dorothy leaned closer, touching the glass with the tips of her fingers, as though pressure might conjure warmth.

"I miss you," she whispered. "And I'm scared."

The words startled her even as she spoke them. She rarely admitted fear, not even to herself. But here, surrounded by his things, she could almost imagine he might answer. Her voice trembled as she went on.

"Everything feels too big without you. The house. Paul. Even her." She paused, swallowing against the tightness in her throat. "She smiles too much. She waits for me to stumble. And Paul doesn't see. He never did. But I..." She pressed her lips together until they thinned. "I can't fight her forever."

Her gaze dropped to Harold's fountain pen lying across a ledger still marked with his tidy hand. She remembered him using it late at night, his mutters about figures and bills, the way she'd scold him for spilling ink on his cuff. Her throat thickened with the memory. Without Harold's gruff reassurance of 'Dorothy, stop fussing, it will be fine'. But it wasn't fine. She wasn't well. She felt the weight of every creak of her bones, every cough that rattled her chest.

She closed her eyes. In the dark behind her lids, she saw the garden where Harold had collapsed, the blur of ambulance lights, the way his hand had felt cold before the end. A tear threatened, but she would not allow it. She straightened in her chair, drawing her shawl tightly around her shoulders. Vulnerability was a luxury, and sharpness was armour.

"I'll manage," she told the photograph, her voice firmer now. "I always do."

She set the frame back in its place and left the study, her spine stiff, her chin raised. If Emily thought she could edge her out, she was mistaken. Harold had trusted her to hold the line, and she would not surrender.

Downstairs, the clatter of keys on a laptop punctured the hush. Paul sat at the kitchen table, his tie still looped round his neck though his jacket lay discarded on the back of a chair. Spreadsheets glowed on his screen, columns and figures eating at his attention. A coffee cup sat cold beside him, ignored for hours.

Emily stood at the doorway, watching him for a moment.

"I'm heading out," she said brightly, reaching for her coat. "I said I'd meet Isla in town for a drink, since I need to collect any post from the flat."

Paul murmured something, his eyes not lifting from the

numbers marching across his screen. His fingers tapped a rhythm on the keys.

"I'll be back before midnight," she added.

"Mm-hm," he said, shifting a cell in his spreadsheet. He hadn't heard.

Emily gave a small smile to herself, collected her bag, and slipped out. The door closed behind her with a sound too gentle to disturb his concentration. On the stairs, Dorothy allowed herself a small smile to acknowledge that Emily had left unheard.

The pub in London was a far cry from the hush of the Mercer house. It was a cosy spot tucked on a side street in Marylebone, its walls lined with battered books and framed black-and-white photographs of city life in another age. Fairy lights were strung across the bar, twinkling against the brass pumps. The low murmur of conversations and the occasional burst of laughter gave the place a warmth Emily could feel in her bones.

Isla was already at a table near the back, her hair pulled into a loose knot, a glass of red wine in hand. She looked up with a grin that softened into concern as Emily slid into the seat opposite.

"You look tired," Isla said, studying her friend's face. "Is it that bad?"

Emily let out a breath, cupping her glass between her palms once the waiter had placed it down. "Nothing I do is right," she said quietly. "I cook, it's wrong. I clean, it's too much noise. If I wash her clothes, she says I'll shrink them. If I don't, I'm neglectful." She smiled ruefully. "I can't win."

Isla's eyes widened, then narrowed with indignation. "That

woman. Honestly. She sounds like something from another century. I don't know how you stand it."

Emily lifted one shoulder, the picture of weary grace. "She's grieving. She's ill. And she's old. I tell myself she doesn't mean it. Paul's worth it, though. That's what matters."

Isla rolled her eyes, but her hand reached across the table and gave Emily's wrist a squeeze. "You're a better person than I am. I'd have packed my bags weeks ago."

Emily laughed softly, shaking her head. "No, you wouldn't. You're tougher than anyone I know, but you're kind too. You'd stay for the man you loved."

The waiter arrived with plates of food, steam curling from bowls of pasta rich with garlic and tomato. Emily ate in small, delicate bites, her voice low as she recounted Dorothy's sharpest remarks from this week. The ones that had cut deepest. Isla listened, shaking her head, sympathy mixing with outrage. Yet somewhere deep inside, a faint doubt stirred. Dorothy sounded dreadful, yes, but Isla knew grief, illness, age could make anyone unkind. She wondered, briefly, if perhaps Emily's patience had simply worn too thin.

But then Emily smiled bravely, her hand lifting her glass. "It's fine, really. I'm just venting."

And Isla, protective to the core, dismissed the doubt and raised her glass too. "Well, Paul had better damn well appreciate you."

The pub's lights glowed golden on the wood tables, and the murmur of strangers' conversations carried around them. For Emily, it was a reprieve. This was a place where she could tell her story and be heard, where she could shape her suffering into something admirable, almost noble. And for Isla, it was a reminder of the girl she had once sat with years ago, a girl with grit in her bones and ambition in her eyes, who had promised herself she would never let the world make her small.

The pub had grown livelier as the evening edged on. The low buzz of conversation had lifted into laughter, clinking glasses, the occasional burst of a song half-sung by the group at the bar. Fairy lights twinkled in their reflections, and the air carried the yeasty tang of spilt beer mixed with garlic from the kitchen.

Isla was leaning back in her chair now, her cheeks flushed with wine, her laughter freer. She had ordered a second glass, then a third, waving away Emily's gentle protests with a grin.

"Oh, don't look at me like that," she teased, swirling the deep red in her glass. "I've had the week from hell. If I have to listen to one more HR manager drone on about constructive dismissal, I'll throttle someone."

Emily smiled, taking a measured sip of her own drink. She hadn't touched more than half. Her hand stayed steady on the glass, her voice even, her expression calm. She was the picture of composure, though she let her smile soften whenever Isla looked at her.

"You're lucky," Isla went on, her words only a fraction slower, looser. "Paul might be busy, but at least you're not wading through other people's battles every day. At least you've got love."

Emily tilted her head, feigning modesty. "Love comes with its own battles."

Isla nodded, serious now, eyes narrowing as she leaned closer across the table. "Tell me something," she said. "Are you and Paul thinking about kids? Or is..." She hesitated and lowered her voice. "Is Dorothy in the way of that for now?"

The question hung there, bold and sharp, slicing through the warmth of the pub. Emily's lashes lowered. She placed her glass carefully on the table and folded her hands around it, as if steadying herself.

"My only purpose right now," she said softly. "Is to look after her. That's all my days are now. I don't have time to think about the future. Or even myself, really." She gave a small, self-deprecating laugh. "Children? I wouldn't know where to begin, not while things are like this. It wouldn't be fair to Paul. Or to them."

Her voice carried just enough tremor to make the words feel raw, but not so much that she seemed self-pitying. She looked down into her glass as though ashamed of the admission.

Isla's face fell. "Oh, Em," she said, her hand darting across the table again to squeeze Emily's wrist. "I'm sorry. I shouldn't have asked. That was clumsy of me."

Emily shook her head quickly, her smile brave.

"No, don't apologise. It's natural to wonder. It's just not the right time. Not when Dorothy needs me so much."

Isla gave a regretful laugh and shook her head, her earrings catching the fairy lights.

"You put the rest of us to shame, you know. We moan about our lives, our jobs, our commutes, and there you are sacrificing your dreams."

Emily smiled, quiet and composed. Inside, she knew the words had landed exactly as she'd wanted them to. Isla looked guilty for asking, sympathetic for hearing, and admiring all at once.

The group at the bar cheered as someone bought a round of shots, the noise spilling across the pub like a wave. Isla lifted her glass again, her eyes a little glassy, while Emily sat perfectly still, her smile unbroken, her hand steady on the stem of her glass. Isla drank, laughed, and leaned against the table with her cheek on her hand. Emily watched the room with calm eyes, her posture serene.

# 7

The City wore its weekday mask. The glass towers like aquariums stacked with anonymous moving figures, screens glowing in blues and greens, the hum of other people's money. Paul swiped into his building and rode the lift up through a vertical garden of offices where plants were kept alive by timers and artificial light. On the trading floor the air vibrated with a constant tension. Phones trilled, keyboards clacked, the air reverberated with the soft thud of a palm against a desk when a price moved the wrong way. Headlines crawled soundlessly along a muted television, showing rates, growth, shocks, stocks. His screen estate bloomed with tabs and charts, liquidity pooling and fleeing at the mercy of decisions he couldn't influence.

He answered calls and spoke in the steady, agreeable voice of a man who made things happen without raising his own temperature. But his attention sloped away in unguarded moments, sliding downriver towards Bray, and towards the house with the gravel drive and the kitchen where the light found dust in the afternoons. He pictured Emily there, with her sleeves pushed to her elbows, hair lifted off her neck with a clip, the quiet industry of her hands. He pictured his mother, too. Small as a pin in a chair that had once looked too small for Harold. The thought needled. He told himself what he always told himself: Emily could handle it. She insisted on it. She wanted to. He was not abandoning them, he was providing for them. That counted for something.

"Mercer," said Rohan, stopping by his desk with two coffees, one for himself, one left on the edge of Paul's keyboard like a peace offering. "How's married life? How was Italy? Have you two come back down to earth?"

Paul's smile came on a fraction too late. "Feels like years ago," he said, turning the coffee cup by its lid as if considering its temperature. "We got back and..." He let his palm open and close, the universal sign for chaos. He didn't say hospital. He didn't say funeral. People here preferred tidied stories.

"Sorry, mate," Rohan said, regret quick in his voice. "I heard about your dad." A beat. "How's your mum holding up?"

Paul glanced at the nearest screen as if the answer might be graphed there. "You know Mum," he said lightly. "Unstoppable. Particular." He kept his tone affectionate. It concealed a multitude of sharp corners. "Emily's... she's been unbelievable."

"Good," Rohan said, relief plain. "You picked a good one there. She must be a saint."

The word landed with a soft thud in Paul's chest. He thought of Emily the previous evening, smooth as water at the door, taking his coat, asking about his day with an interest that made him feel as if there was nothing more important than the answer. The saint thing made him uncomfortable, even though he'd said it himself. It suggested sacrifice and he preferred to believe she was simply good at caring. The way other people were good at languages or the piano.

He made it to lunch without noticing the gap where lunch should be, then chewed a sandwich at his desk while a client spoke in acronyms. His hand found his phone without thinking and he tapped a message with his thumb.

You okay? How's Mum today? x

The reply came a minute later, as if Emily had been waiting with the phone face-up beside her. Quiet day. I'll take her for a little walk later if she's up to it. Don't worry about us. Do your thing. Love you. x

He read the message twice, guilt and relief threading a familiar plait inside him. Do your thing. Permission granted. He closed the chat and tried to translate a yield curve into something that could be explained at five.

Back in Bray, the afternoon folded itself around the house. Emily stood at the kitchen window and watched the orchard huddle under a pewter sky. A blackbird hopped along the lawn where the frost still clung in the places the sun hadn't found. In the glass she could see herself superimposed on the garden as a woman in a calm domestic scene. It was a picture that reassured people. It reassured Paul.

Dorothy came into the kitchen with the slow, stiff walk of someone managing a body that no longer responded to command in quite the way it used to. She wore her cardigan fastened to the top button and a string of pearls that lay too starkly against the papery skin of her throat. Emily turned with a smile she had taught her face to do on autopilot, that lived somewhere between brightness and deference.

"Shall we go out for a little stroll?" she asked gently. "Just round the garden and down to the river gate. Ten minutes, that's all. It would be good to get some fresh air."

Dorothy's hands twitched on the back of the chair she had reached for. Her gaze went past Emily to the rectangle of glass.

The lawn. The patio. The apple tree. Emily watched the way her eyes fixed on a spot beyond the window, as if something invisible were standing there, immovable as weather.

"No," Dorothy said, and the word came out smaller than the ones she usually chose. She cleared her throat and tried again, sharper. "No, thank you. I'm quite comfortable."

"It's very mild," Emily said softly. "We could take it slowly. I thought..."

Dorothy's palm lifted, a tiny pat in the air to tamp down the words. "That is where Harold collapsed," she said, as if Emily might not know. "By the patio door. I do not intend to parade myself around the scene of it like a bit-part in a soap opera." The line should have been barbed. It was, in fact, brittle.

Emily let her hand drift to the kettle and switch it on. The click and hum gave the moment a polite purpose.

"Of course," she said. "We can sit by the window instead. You'll still get the light."

Dorothy studied her face with that cool, narrow look she had, as though she was measuring, assessing, searching for a seam to pull. Emily arranged a little tray with the blue pot, a cup, a plate and a small slice of the ginger cake she had made that morning.

"Just there," she said, setting it by Dorothy's chair in the morning room so the river's silver could make a path through the glass to find her. "Call if you need me."

Dorothy settled with more relief than she intended to show. The blue pot pleased her despite herself. She did not thank Emily, which was its own kind of thank you. Emily returned to the kitchen and resumed her choreography of order, wiping, folding, rinsing, quiet as a tide. She neither sulked nor triumphed. When Paul asked later how the day had been, the truth would be available for him to pick up and hold. I offered to take her out. She preferred to stay in. The shape of the story mattered as much as its content.

Paul took two more calls and sent six more emails and reminded himself that working hard was not guilt, but prudence. By four the winter light had dulled to the colour of old coins. He looked out of the window that faced east and saw the river like a dark belt around the city's waist and thought of the other river that ran past his mother's garden, softer, older, less impressed with men who counted things. He packed his laptop, loosened his tie, and made for the train.

On the platform, commuters gathered with that particular British stoicism that makes standing in the cold look like a hobby. Paul scrolled absent-mindedly through Emily's photos again. She sent them randomly across the day, like small anchors thrown in his direction. A neat pile of folded towels, a saucepan with a glossy stew, a corner of the morning room where the light made a square on the rug, a robin perched on the fence. The last image was of the blue pot beside Dorothy's chair, the river behind her, a slice of cake on the plate. His mother's face was turned away from the lens. He tried to read her posture and decided it was... contained. He pocketed the phone and boarded the train.

Bray always smelled of damp hedges and woodsmoke in the winter. The Mercer house glowed its welcome as Paul came up the drive. Paul carried his bag in and the hallway gave him back his own footsteps.

Emily was there almost at once, as if the house had placed

her within reach on purpose. She took his coat with a small, practised flourish and rose on her toes to kiss his cheek.

"Hi," she said.

The warmth in it was a blanket.

"How was your day?" she asked, already making room for whatever answer he brought. "Did you eat?"

He surprised himself with the confession. "A bit," he said, and felt childlike.

"I'll fix something," she said. "Five minutes. How's the City? Still standing?" She smiled, making the question sound like a joke rather than a demand for proof that his absence had been worthwhile. He reached for her hand and gave it a quick, grateful squeeze.

"You look tired," he said, because he needed to offer care somewhere.

"I'm fine," she said. "We had a quiet day."

From the morning room came Dorothy's voice, not raised but pitched to carry.

"Quiet? She doesn't allow quiet. Never stops bloody cooking and cleaning and badgering me to do things. Hoovering under my feet, clattering pots, nagging about 'fresh air'. Drives me mad."

The words went down the corridor like a draught. Paul kept his face turned towards Emily and let them pass him by.

"I see Mum's in one of her moods," he said, almost apologetic.

Emily's smile didn't alter.

"She's been a little restless," she said. "But we were fine. Truly. I enjoy looking after her." She meant for him to hear I choose this, not I martyr myself. It worked and relief loosened his shoulders.

He stepped into the morning room with the smile he used for clients and mothers. Dorothy sat upright, a book in her lap that she had not turned for twenty minutes. The blue pot, now empty, sat like a small success on its tray.

"How are we?" he said, with a cheeriness he hoped did not sound remedial.

Dorothy tipped her face towards him so he could kiss her cheek, then presented him with an inventory of minor injustices. The postman had rapped too loudly. The neighbour's gardeners had blown leaves on to their drive. A cold draught had crept under the door by the pantry though she had told Harold a thousand times it needed attending to, and now he never would. Paul made the right noises at the right intervals. He did not mention the offer of a walk or the blue pot. He was not collecting wins to set against losses. He was surviving his mother in the only way he knew.

"Dinner in five," Emily called lightly from the kitchen, the words a ribbon that tied one room to the other. "Nothing fancy."

"Never is," Dorothy muttered.

At the table the food was uncomplicated and perfect. She'd made a stew that somehow tasted of patience and loved, bread that yielded with a soft crumb, a green salad slicked with lemon. Dorothy ate without comment, which in her world passed for praise. Paul ate with a real appetite for the first time that day and felt the gratitude surge up in him like heat.

"Thank you," he said to Emily when Dorothy had gone to check the bolt on the back door and to frown at the night. He stood and put his arms around Emily and let his forehead rest against hers. The kitchen smelled of star anise and soap. "For everything. For all of this."

"It's nothing," she said, which only inflated his thankfulness. "We like a routine."

"She says you don't stop," he murmured, with a guilty half-smile, turning the barb into a joke so it wouldn't pierce either of them. "Never stop cooking. Or cleaning. Or badgering."

Emily laughed softly. "She's right about the badgering," she said. "I'll keep at her about fresh air until spring actually arrives. Don't take any notice. She loves it really. We were fine."

He chose to believe her because belief was what he had to offer. He tightened his arms and felt the rightness of her against him, like a human proof that he had made one unambiguous good decision. He was dimly aware of a low thrum under the moment, the unresolved chord that sounded whenever his mother and his wife occupied the same roof. He turned away from it. He had work in the morning. He had done what he could this evening. He had said thank you, sincerely. That felt like enough.

Later, in bed, he checked his emails again and turned the screen face down on the table as penance. Emily slid in beside him, warm and smelling faintly of perfume. He found her hand in the dark.

"Night," he said, not sure what else to say.

"Night," she echoed, making it sound like mercy.

Across the landing, Dorothy sat up in bed with the lamp on, a notebook open on her lap. She had written two lines and crossed both out. The house listened to the three of them not speaking. Down in the garden the apple tree moved its black lace against the sky. The river went on its way, indifferent, carrying everything said and unsaid out towards the sea.

# 8

The wind came up the river and crossed the churchyard with a spite that felt personal, lifting the edges of orders of service and worrying at the hems of black coats. The cemetery sat on a rise beyond Bray, a scatter of tilted headstones and clipped yew, the grass the colour of pewter under the February sky. A handful of mourners stood with collars turned up and hands tucked away like contraband, their breath showing in faint white puffs when they spoke.

Paul stood between his mother and his wife and felt, uselessly, like a hinge. He gripped Emily's hand because she was the only steady thing in a landscape that had learned to make him feel small; she squeezed back with that unshowy pressure that read as strength. Dorothy held herself an inch taller than usual, the line of her spine an accusation. Her face might have been carved in stone. There was no indulgence, no softness, the careful paint at her mouth refused to crack.

The vicar's voice drifted and thinned in the wind. There were words about dust and return and rest. The little bronze, polished urn looked absurdly contained in the vicar's hands. A compromise had been struck without anyone calling it such. A small portion would be interred here in the churchyard's Garden of Remembrance. The rest would go home with them and, when the ground warmed, be buried by the apple tree Harold had planted the year Paul was born. Everyone could live with that. Public sorrow here, private obedience there.

Emily stepped forward when the service paused for gestures. She laid a spray of white flowers on the narrow plinth before his name. Her choice was not lilies, but hellebores and paperwhites, winter-blooming and clean. Her eyes were lowered, the angle of her head composed, her gloved fingers lingering a second on the bow as if the ribbon might need reassuring. There was a murmur among the mourners of approval shaped like sympathy. Such poise. Such care. The young Mrs Mercer is a blessing. The words didn't have to be spoken aloud to exist.

Dorothy glanced down.

"He hated lilies," she said, very clearly, so that the wind could not steal it.

"They aren't lilies, Mum," Paul said softly, a reflex from some earlier version of himself who still believed corrections mattered. "They're..."

"She means well," Robert from next door said into the space, patting Dorothy's elbow in a way that would have earned anyone else a snapped hand. "A lovely thought, Mrs Mercer."

Dorothy's lips thinned. "Lovely thoughts are free," she said, and stared at the urn as if daring it to contradict her.

The vicar resumed his monologue with a few more lines read into the wind, and then it was done. Paul felt the moment he had been bracing for pass like a wave under a boat. He squeezed Emily's hand harder than he meant to. She tilted her face up to him, her eyes bright but steady.

"I'm so sorry," she murmured, pitched just loud enough for those nearest to catch, and then, turning to Dorothy, gentled her voice further. "This must be unbearable for you, Dorothy. To lose him like that, and with everything you're facing yourself. The lung cancer... all that awful treatment. It's a lot at your age." She said it in a way that made the words sound like care rather than a statement of the obvious, but they carried, as she intended them to, and heads tilted. Poor Dorothy. Brave Emily.

Dorothy's chin rose a fraction, offended by accuracy. "We were married for forty-two years," she said. "I do not require your commentary to understand what I have lost, or the challenges I now face alone."

"Of course," Emily said, lowering her eyes at once, the model daughter-in-law conceding ground. "But you aren't ever alone."

After, there were hands to shake and phrases to deploy. He was a fine man. A terrible loss. Do come for a cup of tea. The wind made everyone brisk, and the river, a dark ribbon beyond the yew, hurried away with no patience for human ritual. Paul thanked the vicar, who spoke of Harold's steadiness as if it were a sacrament. Emily listened to Mrs Harcourt from the post office recall the time Harold had insisted on paying for the stamp on a parcel the queue had been arguing over. Emily smiled at the right points and laid a hand on Mrs Harcourt's sleeve at the exact second the story wavered into tears. Dorothy stood apart, receiving condolences with the efficient nod of a woman accepting deliveries.

They walked back to the cars along the gravel path, the little cortège rearranging itself instinctively so that Dorothy led, Paul half a step behind, Emily tucked in at his side. Bray's sky pulled low and heavy. It felt as if the weather itself wanted them off the hill and back among walls. When they reached the road, Paul opened the car door for his mother and watched her fold herself in with slow dignity, the seat belt fastening like a punctuation mark. Emily got in beside him, her hand still in his, the heat of her a quiet, measurable thing.

The house, when they returned, hummed with the kind of

low, continuous conversation that belongs to sombre gatherings, punctuated by small, remembered bursts of laughter that people immediately apologised for. Side lamps glowed gently in every room as if warding off the dark mood, coats bloomed across the hall stand, umbrellas dripped into the tray by the door. The smell of tea and ginger biscuits and beeswax polish made a balm of the air.

Emily moved through it as if it had been built for her. She seemed to carry her own pool of warm light as she went, offering a plate, refilling a cup, taking a hand for a second and holding it between both of hers as if the whole world could be compressed into that gesture and made bearable.

"Do sit," she told Mr and Mrs Latimer from across the lane, steering them towards the sofa and the good cushions.

"Let me warm that for you," she said to the vicar, collecting his cup without asking and returning it with the steam just right.

"You've been so good to Dorothy," she said to Robert.

To the other neighbour's teenage daughter who hovered near the doorway, uncertain whether grief permitted crisps, she offered a conspiratorial smile and a napkin unfolded. She listened more than she spoke. People found themselves telling her things they had not been planning to say.

"She's extraordinary," Mrs Latimer whispered to Paul when Emily was briefly out of earshot, her palm still tingling from Emily's touch. "So composed. Your father would be proud of her."

Paul, who had not stopped watching his wife since they'd come in, felt relief uncurl inside him like something thawing.

"She is great," he said, and the words came out like a benediction.

Dorothy sat in Harold's chair by the fire, slightly away from the main drift of conversation. The blue pot had been retired for the day, and now a big brown one presided, that was more democratic. A plate of biscuits rested untouched on the table beside her. She received visitors with courtly efficiency. She enquired after ailments and grandchildren and boiler men. When people, inevitably, steered praise towards Emily, to comment how she was so thoughtful or such a comfort, Dorothy's mouth arranged itself into an expression of bland agreement while her eyes darkened a shade.

"She's very good with people," said Mrs Harcourt, stopping to pay homage before moving on to the sausage rolls.

"She's playing a part," Dorothy said, not bothering to lower her voice. "It's all for show. She isn't fooling me."

Mrs Harcourt's smile faltered.

"Oh," she said, thinking of Emily's hand on her sleeve at the graveside. "Well, I suppose we all do what we can." She moved on, unconvinced, and poured herself more tea.

Emily was everywhere at once without ever seeming to rush. In the kitchen she made sandwiches appear from nowhere, cut on the diagonal because it just tastes better that way, doesn't it? In the dining room she kept the urn of hot water filled as if it were a living thing. In the hall she deftly whisked an elderly man's damp coat into the airing cupboard and later returned it warm. She never occupied a doorway and never spoke over anyone. When she passed Paul, she touched his wrist or the back of his hand with the lightness of someone checking a pulse. Each time he felt steadier.

At one point, Dorothy's old bridge partner, a neat woman with a voice like the rustle of tissue paper, took the seat beside her.

"How are you really, Dorothy?" she asked, a question that invited honesty the way a trap invites a paw.

Dorothy looked past her to where Emily stood refolding a cloth silently, smile composed, profile restful.

"Tired of all this performance," she said. "Tired of being managed in my own house."

"Managed?" the woman echoed faintly, watching Emily offer her a warmed plate without interrupting the conversation.

"She's an actress," Dorothy said. "Watch her. The way she looks at people. She's memorising her lines."

The bridge partner followed her gaze and saw only a young woman who knew when to step aside so two older men could pass without shuffling, who laughed in soft crescents that made other people relax, who took a tray from a teenager with the assurance of someone who had never broken a plate.

"She seems helpful," she said carefully.

Dorothy breathed out through her nose, a contempt that had grown tired of explaining itself. "Helpful to herself."

Across the room, Emily felt the look on her and turned at once, an instinct for attention honed to a fine wire. She met the older woman's eye and offered a small nod of acknowledgement. The woman coloured, unable to help smiling back. Dorothy's lips pressed thin as thread.

The afternoon wore on. People thinned. The vicar left early for another service, apologising with that peculiar professional sorrow that implies a schedule of griefs. Robert stacked plates and refused to be told he didn't have to. The Latimers took charge of the washing-up with the proprietary air of people who have washed up in this house for twenty years of parish lunches and will not be dissuaded today. Emily let them, which made them love her more.

By four, only the closest neighbours remained, clinging to the comfort of structured kindness. Paul stood by the mantelpiece and endured the long, soft wave of condolences with as much grace as a man can be expected to produce. Each time his gaze snagged on the armchair where his father had sat, the world blurred, and each time it did, Emily appeared between that sight and his eyes, offering him another cup, a plate, a necessary interruption. He did not notice he was being handled. He only noticed that the day went on without making a wreck of him.

At last, the house began to empty properly. The hallway bloomed again with coats and goodbyes. The door sighed open and shut. Silence began to reassert itself.

Emily stood in the centre of the drawing room and looked at what remained. She rearranged the tilt of a cushion, lifted a stray teaspoon from the carpet, she tidied a small plate with a smear of lemon curd on it. She moved through the wreckage of kindness and put it all back the way it had been. Paul came to her and put his arms around her and let the weight of his head rest briefly on her shoulder.

"They think you're wonderful," he said into her hair, which was both a report and a plea that it be true. "They are right."

She laughed lightly and shook her head. "I poured tea," she said. "That's hardly difficult."

"It isn't the tea," he said. "It's the way you make everything easier."

She lowered her gaze, as if embarrassed by credit. Over his shoulder she saw Dorothy watching them from the doorway, her hand white on the jamb, the expression on her face old as the house. Emily softened her mouth into something almost apologetic and let her cheek brush Paul's shoulder as if she might hide there a second. It read, to anyone looking, as humility.

"Go and sit with your mother," she said very gently, releasing him. "I'll finish tidying up."

He kissed her temple and did as he was told. In the morning room he sat on the low stool by Dorothy's chair like the boy he used to be and told her inconsequential things about trains and weather and a client who had mislaid a decimal point and caused a minor storm, just to make noise in the place where quiet had lodged. Dorothy listened with her face turned away and did not mention that the house had been overrun or that the sandwiches had been cut into triangles like a children's party, or that she had heard Emily speaking of lung cancer in the churchyard as if it were a ribbon to be pinned to her dress.

When Paul had finished and gone to fetch her a fresh cup, Dorothy leaned her head back and closed her eyes for a moment. The day arranged itself behind her lids in hard little pictures. The urn, the hellebores, the way the wind made the vicar's words fight for sense, the way Emily had moved through her rooms as if she had the lease on the air. She opened her eyes and found the apple tree in the window, black against the last of the light. In a few weeks, she told herself, they would take the rest of Harold out there, dig the small, neat hole with the trowel that fit her hand, and put him where he had asked to be laid. That would be the real thing. This today had been for show, because it's what the village expected.

In the kitchen, Emily soaked the last of the teaspoons and watched the water make small galaxies of the suds. The house hummed to itself, pleased, but a little drowsy. From the hall, the last pair of neighbours murmured that they mustn't linger and then lingered a little longer anyway. One of them said, not lowering her voice quite enough, "She's an angel, that girl."

Emily smiled at the sink, not because she believed in angels, but because people did such useful work on your behalf when they had decided that you were one.

# 9

The kitchen was bright with late-morning sun, spilling across the tiled floor in rectangles that only emphasised the silence. Emily stood at the sink, her sleeves rolled up, the faint scent of lemon washing up liquid rising from the bowl where she had washed the breakfast china. She moved quietly, placing each piece into the rack as though the act itself might keep the house steady.

Behind her, the door creaked open. Dorothy entered with her slow, deliberate tread, her cardigan buttoned all the way up, pearls resting just so against her collarbone. Her eyes went at once to the draining board.

"That set," she said sharply, tapping the counter with one finger. "Is for Sundays only."

Emily turned at once, her expression apologetic. "I'm sorry, Dorothy. I didn't realise. I thought..."

"You thought wrong." Dorothy's tone was clipped, unforgiving. She reached for a cup, tilting it towards the light as though expecting to find a crack. "We don't use the rose-patterned china on a weekday. Harold insisted. He said standards must be maintained."

Emily swallowed, inclining her head.

"Of course. I'll remember."

Her voice was even, but her shoulders sagged, as if the weight of invisible reprimands had begun to accumulate there. Dorothy lingered, her gaze cool.

"Your lack of breeding," she muttered, not quite under her breath. "Makes me wonder what Paul sees in you. Harold thought the same."

The words cut deep, though Emily only blinked. For a moment, her face flickered as something raw, almost furious coursed through her, but she pressed it down, smoothed it over with the calmness she wore like armour.

Footsteps sounded in the hall. A moment later Paul appeared, loosening his tie, his phone still in his hand.

"Everything alright in here," he asked, dropping a kiss on Emily's cheek without glancing at her eyes. He had not caught the silence, or if he had, he chose to ignore it.

Emily's smile was instant, a mask slipping seamlessly into place.

"We were just talking about what to do for dinner," she said brightly.

Paul grinned, distracted, already half elsewhere. "Perfect. You always think of everything." He looked at his phone again, scrolling as he left the room.

Dorothy's lips thinned into something between triumph and contempt. Emily turned back to the sink, her hands steady, her face serene, though inside she burned. The mask held.

London was noisy in a way Bray never was. Buses hissed along Oxford Street, shop windows gleamed with mannequins dressed for spring, and the pavement pulsed with shoppers, couples, tourists. Emily walked beside Isla, her steps measured, her hair pinned neatly, a shopping bag looped over one wrist.

They ducked into a boutique filled with the scent of expensive candles and leather handbags. Isla, ever decisive, plucked up a silk blouse, holding it against herself in the mirror.

"Too much?" she asked, and then laughed before Emily could answer. "Everything's too much in here. Come on, try something."

Emily shook her head gently. "I don't need anything."

"You never do," Isla said, narrowing her eyes. "Except patience, apparently. So? What's she done now?"

Emily let out a breath, quiet, and recounted Dorothy's morning tirade.

"She told me the china I used was only for Sundays. I apologised, but she said..." Her voice faltered, then steadied. "She said she wonders what Paul sees in me. That Harold thought the same."

Isla's eyes widened. Then she laughed, sharp and incredulous.

"Good grief. She sounds like a caricature! Honestly, Em, it's like living with a character from a bad play."

Emily gave a wan smile, folding the handle of her bag more tightly around her wrist. "I know. But I want to make it work. For Paul's sake. He's caught between us, and it wouldn't be fair to make him choose."

Isla set the blouse back on the rack, shaking her head. "You've got the patience of a saint. I don't know how you do it."

Emily's smile held, serene and self-effacing. "I just keep reminding myself she's grieving. And she's unwell. That makes people... sharper. I can't take it personally."

Isla studied her friend for a moment. Emily's words were steady, her face smooth, her tone modest. But Isla noticed, not for the first time, that Emily never spoke about her own feelings.

Never said she was angry, or hurt, or exhausted. Only that Dorothy was cruel. That Dorothy was impossible. That Dorothy was ill and grieving. Emily herself remained a blank surface, however pitying, patient, and endlessly good.

Isla looped her arm through Emily's as they left the shop, smiling because she wanted to believe the story. But unease pricked at her. There was something too polished about the way Emily recounted it, as though the hurt were rehearsed. As though Emily's mask was so firmly in place it had become her face.

On the street, the crowds surged around them, the lights changed from red to green, and Emily walked on, calm and composed, her voice soft with stoicism. Isla laughed at her own expense, saying she'd lose her mind if she had to live in Bray. But Emily only smiled, the model wife, the patient daughter-in-law, never complaining, never cracking.

They stopped at a café tucked behind the high street, a quieter place away from the swirl of shoppers. The tables were small and the crockery mismatched, but the smell of ground coffee and warm pastries lent the room an intimacy that made people talk more freely. Isla ordered two cappuccinos and a plate of almond croissants, insisting Emily share even when she protested she wasn't hungry.

For a while, they chatted about lighter things, like Isla's impossible client who had sent a twelve-page email at three in the morning, or the dog walker who had apparently lost Tess for an entire hour in Regent's Park, or the new partner at her firm who wore waistcoats as if auditioning for a period drama. Emily laughed at all the right places, her smile gentle, her voice low. But Isla's eyes kept searching her face, not satisfied with the polite brightness.

At last, Isla leaned forward, elbows on the table, her expression softening.

"Tell me the truth, Em. Isn't all of this putting a strain on your marriage?"

The question landed between them with a kind of hush, muting the background chatter. Emily's smile faltered, then returned, slower this time, touched with sadness. She lowered her gaze to the swirl of chocolate powder dissolving into her coffee.

"Paul's grieving too," she said quietly. "He's lost his father. And he's worried about his mother. I can't add to that. He needs me to be steady, for both of them. If I started falling apart…" She shook her head, letting the sentence trail away, and gave a small, almost embarrassed laugh. "It wouldn't be fair."

Isla frowned, her heart tugged between admiration and concern. "But what about you? Who's steady for you?"

Emily's smile deepened, modest and brave. "I don't need that. I just need to keep going. For Paul. That's all that matters right now. It will get easier, with time."

Isla reached across the table and squeezed her hand, her eyes bright with sympathy. But inside, unease stirred again. Emily spoke as if her life were entirely sacrifice, entirely for others. Isla wanted to shake her, and demand to know what she felt, what she wanted. Yet Emily's calm expression, her quiet dignity, made protest feel almost cruel.

So, Isla let it go, withdrawing her hand and lifting her cup.

"He's lucky to have you," she said instead, her voice warm.

Emily smiled at that, a small, sad curve of her lips, and sipped her coffee. Outside, people hurried past with shopping bags and umbrellas, their lives brisk and ordinary. Emily was a portrait of grace under pressure, while Isla wondered if beneath it there was anything Emily allowed herself to keep.

# 10

Dorothy kept her bedroom like a museum of proof. Harold's cufflinks remained lined up in the little leather tray, the onyx pair and the engine-turned silver. His pipe stand waited on the chest of drawers though the bowls had long since cooled. His three favourite ties hung from the back of the wardrobe door. The navy with the discreet dots, the club stripe, and the one she'd always said made him look too jolly. She had dusted them yesterday, and yet the fine pale film had settled again, as if the house preferred its old things soft around the edges.

She sat at the dressing table with its triple mirrors and regarded herself as if she were a witness called to give evidence. Her face had thinned. The good pearls lay heavy against the ladder of her collarbones. Beside the central mirror Harold watched her from the silver frame propped against the perfume tray. A summer photo, mid-squint, the ghost of a smile pulling one corner of his mouth. The look that said don't fuss, Dorothy. He had said it so often she could hear the cadence even now.

"I am not fussing," she told him, although she knew she was. "I am making a record."

She lifted the photograph, thumb resting on the cool glass.

"Paul is still working, even on a Sunday," she said. "'Deadlines', 'markets'." She let the words out with a small curl of contempt. "The City always wants more than it gives back. You said that. You were right."

Her gaze shifted, the angle catching her own face doubled and trebled in the side mirrors. Three Dorothys, each more tired than the next. She turned the frame so Harold was looking out at the room instead. "And now she is here," she went on, the pronoun landing like a pin. "Smiling at everyone. Pouring tea as if she were born to it. Moving my things and then putting them back badly as though I won't notice."

She placed the frame down carefully and adjusted a hairpin. The effort made her hand tremble. She watched the tremor with irritated curiosity, as if it belonged to someone else.

"They all think she's an angel," she said, keeping her voice low as though the walls might repeat her if she raised it. "Robert said so on the path after the service. 'Your Emily's a marvel, Mrs Mercer.' He said it twice, as if repeating a thing made it truer. The Latimers called her 'a blessing'. The vicar, well, he's paid to bless people, isn't he."

The room pressed in on her. The curtains were drawn against the brightness over the river, the bed made exactly as Harold had liked it, hospital corners and the quilt smoothed twice with the flat of her palm. She remembered the last winter he had grumbled about the apple tree losing its leaves, how he'd gone out with the long-handled loppers and come back in flushed with triumph and a small cut on his forehead where a branch had caught him. She had scolded him then, fiercely, because fear often chose the language of anger. If she closed her eyes ,she could see the exact place on the patio where he had fallen. Sometimes she thought if she stood very still, she would hear the soft, wrong thud of a body meeting stone again.

"She's waiting to take my place," she said to the photograph, almost conversationally. "You can't see it because you never looked for those things. You never had to. Men are allowed to find the surface adequate." She paused, hearing herself, the prim sharpness of it, and felt the unsteady heat behind her eyes.

"I am afraid," she admitted, the words surprising her mouth with their shape. "That is what it is. Not just of the illness." She refused to say the word cancer today. Even saying it tired her. "But of becoming irrelevant. Of being tidied away. They'll start with small things. The mugs. The drawer for the knives. Then one day the piano will have been 'moved to a better spot' and no one will remember where the original spot used to be. And in no time I will be the thing no one remembers."

She sat very straight. The habit would not leave her even when she wanted it to. "I am not unkind," she said, more to herself than to the photograph. "I never have been. But I am precise, and that's not a sin. It kept this house standing."

In the frame, Harold did not argue. He wouldn't have, even if he'd been in the room. The years had taught him when silence was the safer choice.

Dorothy moved the frame, aligning it with the edge of the tray the way it usually was.

"You trusted me to hold the line," she said. "I am holding it." Then, much more quietly, as if promising a child something she might not be able to give, "I will not be erased."

She stood, feeling the ache uncurl in her ankle and the small catch in her breath. The room swam for a second. She placed a hand on the wardrobe door until it steadied. Below, the house gave nothing but silence. Dorothy smoothed the bed once more, for the look of the thing, and prepared herself to go down to lunch.

Sunday lunch had always been a ceremony here, even when it was only the three of them. Today the table was set simply, almost austerely. There was a linen runner down the middle, three places set with the good silverware but not the candlesticks. Emily had laid it all with the same deftness she applied to everything. The knives were all aligned, the napkins folded in soft triangles, a water jug was sweating faintly in the heat of the room. From the kitchen came the gentle clatter of plates and the smell of roasted chicken and thyme, a comfort for people who could still be comforted.

Dorothy took her chair and noted, without comment, that the seat cushion had been flipped to the right way after two days of sitting the wrong way up. Paul poured water for them all and sat, his movements economical, the politeness of a man who is late for something even when he isn't.

They began with the soup. Carrot and coriander, bright and smooth. Dorothy lifted her spoon and found the taste serviceable, which she translated into a barbed comment.

"It's very savoury."

She dabbed the corner of her mouth with her napkin. Her stomach felt unsettled. She'd started feeling ill from all the sweet tea after the cemetery and her body had not quite righted itself since then. Indigestion shaped itself as complaint. She knew this but still could not help the tone.

"I shouldn't have the chicken," she said. "It will lie on me like lead."

Paul put his spoon down at once. "You don't have to have the chicken," he said quickly, as if the plates might reverse course back to the kitchen of their own accord. "We could..." He looked to Emily for an alternative, and the glance carried its usual freight, asking her to make it easy.

Emily's smile remained calm, a temperature under which sauces never split. "There's fish as well," she said. "I poached a little salmon with lemon. Or I can make you tea and toast instead, Dorothy. Whatever would sit best."

"Tea," Dorothy said, irritated by their hovering yet soothed by the options. "But not too strong." She glanced at Paul. "And don't let her drown it."

"Of course," Emily said, and rose at once.

Paul followed her into the kitchen, fuss blooming in him like algae.

"Mum's off colour again," he murmured, guilty and baffled and tired of his own guilt. "I think... look, maybe after lunch I'll take her for a drive. She likes the long road by the river."

Emily lifted the lid on a small pan, checked the heat, turned it down without drama.

"Or she could nap," she said gently. "She was up in the night."

"How do you know?"

"I heard her door." She kept her tone neutral. Information, not accusation. "She's exhausted, Paul."

He looked at her with a flicker of shame, and a rush of gratitude, the way he always did when she voiced something he had failed to notice.

"You're so good to her," he said under his breath, as if praise were a hand to be smuggled into hers.

Back at the table Emily set the tea tray down with that neat ballet of hers. She'd laid out a cup, saucer, the teapot, with the milk to the left because Dorothy preferred it there. Dorothy's face had pinched as if in anticipation of something being done wrong.

"Stop hovering, both of you," she said suddenly, as Emily adjusted the angle of the milk jug and Paul, unhelpful, asked if she wanted a cushion at her back. The words shot out sharper than she intended. "If I wanted help, I'd ask for it."

A little silence pooled in the middle of the table. Paul retreated into it, his gaze dropping to his plate, the old boy's posture returning to him like a lesson learned. When the air crackles, be smaller. He broke a piece of bread with fussy concentration.

Emily, who did not retreat, kept her voice level.

"Let's keep it simple, then," she said, as if the whole exchange had been about crockery. "Eat what you can. We'll all get some rest after."

Dorothy eyed her with a suspicion that had hardened into habit. The problem with Emily, she thought, was that even her appeasements felt like manoeuvres. Every sentence smoothed the surface of the water and hid the current.

Lunch faltered forward. Dorothy picked, then pushed her plate away. Paul did not press. Emily stacked plates quietly and did not, for once, offer pudding. The house felt charged with tension.

After, Dorothy stood, the thought of her room a relief and an admission.

"I'll go up," she said. "And I won't be disturbed." She caught Emily's tiny nod and resented it for how reasonable it looked.

The staircase rose before her, with its pale runner pinned with brass rods, the banister polished to a gloss that remembered every hand. Halfway up, where the light from the landing made a shallow pool on the steps, her ankle turned. It happened so quickly she did not even prepare the little cry as the world tilting took her by surprise. Her foot slid, her knee buckled, and the pain ran up her leg bright as a blade.

The sound she made was sharp, and undignified, and summoned them both at once. Paul reached her first, taking two steps at a time, hands under her elbows, both strong and clumsy with alarm. Emily was there a second later, already sliding a palm to the small of Dorothy's back, steady and warm.

"I'm all right," Dorothy said through her teeth, and the lie felt like a necessary armour. Her face had gone grey. Even the pearls seemed too white against it.

"Let's sit," Emily said, not a suggestion. She guided Dorothy back to the broader step where the curve of the banister made a little pause in the climb. "Breathe. We'll have a look at that ankle."

Paul hovered, appalled at himself for hovering. "Does it hurt? Of course it hurts. Sorry. But can you move it?"

"Don't ask her to," Emily said, gentle but firm, and set her own body as a brace against Dorothy's shoulder so she couldn't overbalance. "Let me feel."

It was the work of a minute, practised and careful. Emily's fingers probed at the ankle, the assessment done with a nurse's quiet competence though she'd never trained as one.

"A twist, not a break," she declared. "Cold cloth first, then elevation."

Dorothy watched her from very close, the details of Emily's face enlarged by proximity. The faint line between her brows became more pronounced when she concentrated, as did the steadiness of her mouth. Her lashes cast small shadows on her cheek. Dorothy wanted, wildly, to bite her hand. Instead, she let her head rest against the wall and saw, to her own shock, the inside of her own fear. It shocked her how light she suddenly felt in their hands, and how small. The truth of it pulled at her. The body she had commanded all her life had begun to negotiate behind her back.

They got her to her room between them in a quiet, awkward, efficient procession. Emily's arm took more of Dorothy's weight than her size suggested it could. On the bed, Emily lifted the ankle onto a pillow and fashioned a cold compress with a tea towel and a bag of frozen peas before Dorothy could protest about peas being for eating. Paul brought paracetamol and water, but he held the glass too close, as if either thirst or pain were things you could fix with proximity.

"Thank you," Dorothy said at last, because the forms

mattered even now. "That'll do now." She made it sound like a reprimand.

Emily nodded once. "I'll check on you in half an hour," she said. "Call if you need me sooner."

"I won't," Dorothy said, then heard the childishness in it and added. "I'll be fine."

Paul lingered a heartbeat, torn between the old loyalty and the new.

"Try to get some rest, Mum," he managed, and touched the quilt as if contact with fabric could stand in for what he could not say.

In the hallway, with the door half-closed, Emily's face softened in that private way of hers.

"She's more frail than she lets on," she said quietly, a diagnosis spoken to the air as much as to Paul. "We need to be careful of the stairs."

Paul nodded, chastened and grateful and full of a guilt that had nowhere to go. He looked at his wife as if she were the only adult in a room where he had been a child too long.

"What would I do without you?" he said, and meant it without seeing how it sounded.

Emily smiled the smallest smile.

"You won't have to find out," she said, and went down to the kitchen to put the kettle on, because in this house tea remained the one ritual everyone understood.

Behind the door, Dorothy lay very still and stared at the ceiling. The pain in her ankle throbbed in time with her pulse. She listened to their movements below and the low murmur of their voices, and let the fear rise and settle, rise and settle, like the river ticking along beyond the garden. She would not be erased, she told herself again, and found the promise harder to hold than it had been an hour before.

# 11

Paul's office was the same as it had been the day before and the week before that. The glass towers still reflected one another's ambitions, the faint hum of the trading floor remained constant, colleagues paced with headsets pressed to their ears. Yet the ordinary rhythm seemed fragile today, as though the day was just waiting to change shape.

The call came just after eleven. His mobile lit with an unfamiliar number. He excused himself from the desk and ducked into one of the glass-walled conference rooms, shutting the door with more force than he meant to.

"Mr Mercer?" The voice was careful, professional, the weight of officialdom carried in the syllables. "Detective Inspector Rawlings here. I wonder if you might have a moment."

Paul sat heavily in the nearest chair. "Yes. Of course." His throat was dry. He reached for his water bottle and found it empty.

"It's regarding your father's death," the detective continued, each word placed with deliberate precision. "We've reviewed CCTV from a neighbouring property. A week before your father's collapse, the footage shows a hooded figure loitering near the garden boundary. It's unusual enough that we'd like to speak further with you and your family."

Paul's stomach dropped as though the floor beneath him had given way.

"Loitering?" His voice sounded thinner than he intended. "What? What are you saying?"

"I'm not saying anything," Rawlings replied, calm, neutral. "We'd just like to clarify a few details. Could be nothing, call it routine, but we need to follow up. Are you available to come in later this week?"

Paul closed his eyes briefly.

"Yes," he said, his voice hollow. "Yes, of course. Just let me speak to my mother first."

"Thank you," Rawlings said. "We'll be in touch to arrange a time."

When the line clicked dead, Paul sat in the silence of the conference room. His reflection in the glass opposite looked pale, his tie skewed. He ran a hand down his face. A hooded figure? At the house? The words sounded foreign, like something from a bad thriller, and yet his chest ached with the weight of implication. Guilt gnawed at him. Not because he had done anything, but because he hadn't been there. Because he hadn't seen. Because his father had been injured while he had been drinking wine in Florence and Emily had been buying scarves in a square that smelled of lemons.

He forced himself to return to his desk. The numbers on his screen blurred. When a colleague asked him a simple question about a trade, he gave the wrong answer and had to correct it a moment later. His smile, when Rohan cracked a joke, felt brittle, plastered over unease. The whole day stretched long and thin, a thread straining toward the evening, when he would finally tell them.

The house was quiet when Paul came in. Emily greeted him at the door with her usual warmth, slipping his coat from his shoulders, pressing her lips briefly to his cheek. Dorothy was in the morning room, lamp on already though dusk had barely settled, her knitting untouched on her lap.

Paul waited until they were all gathered at the table before speaking. His food remained largely untouched. He twisted the stem of his wineglass, watching the red liquid catch the light.

"I had a call today," he began. "From the police."

Dorothy stiffened at once, her fork poised in mid-air. "What could they possibly want now? They were nothing but a nuisance when Harold died, with their silly questions, like they're looking to blame someone for a silly accident."

Paul drew a breath. "Apparently, they've got CCTV from a neighbour's camera that shows someone hanging around the garden. A week before he fell. A hooded figure, they said."

Dorothy's face tightened, her spine locking upright.

"So what are they saying? That it wasn't an accident? What are they insinuating?" Her voice rose, sharp as cut glass. "We don't have hooded intruders around here, do we? This is a respectable area. We don't have low-lifes snooping about."

Emily laid her hand lightly on Paul's arm, her voice calm and low, the very picture of reassurance. "It must be something they just need to follow up on," she said. "They'll have to tick every box. I'm sure it doesn't mean anything."

Dorothy turned on her, her mouth twisting. "Routine? This family doesn't need more meddling. I'm still grieving my husband, and the police should respect that. How insensitive of them, stirring things up."

The room fell silent. Paul stared at the table, guilt pressing down on him, though he could not have said why. He only knew he should have been here, should have protected them both. Emily's hand remained steady on his arm, the only anchor in the room.

When at last Dorothy pushed back her chair and declared she was retiring early, she moved stiffly, her face still set with fury. They listened to her slow steps up the staircase, the creak of the banister under her hand, the final shut of her bedroom door.

Paul exhaled, pressing his fingers into his eyes.

"I shouldn't have told her," he said. "I've upset her for nothing."

Emily shook her head gently. "Better she hears it from you than from someone else. She'll calm down. It's just shock."

They sat for a while in the softened quiet, the sound of the clock marking the moments. Then Emily reached across the table, her expression thoughtful.

"Paul, I've been thinking. Perhaps it's time we set up a room for her downstairs. The library would work. It has the downstairs bathroom, which could act as a kind of ensuite, and she wouldn't need to manage the stairs. She's still so frail after her fall. It would be safer."

Paul looked at her, a flicker of relief crossing his face.

"That's an excellent idea. She'll fight it, of course, but I think it makes sense. She'd be independent, and we wouldn't have to worry every time she goes up and down." He smiled then, brief but genuine. "You always think of everything."

Emily returned the smile modestly, lowering her eyes. "I just want what's best for her. For all of us."

Paul leaned across and kissed her hand, grateful beyond words. He did not see the faint tension in her shoulders relax.

Upstairs, Dorothy shifted in her bed. She stared at the ceiling, anger knotting with unease. The police, Emily's calm voice, Paul's silence, all whirled in her mind. She closed her eyes but found no rest.

Downstairs, Emily cleared the plates in silence, the picture of composure, while Paul watched her, his unease buried under gratitude, never noticing how much more at ease she looked than he did.

# 12

They called it an interview room, but it felt like a waiting room that had given up pretending. The walls were a neutral not-quite-white, the kind of colour that made you second-guess your eyes. The table was laminated wood with a puckered edge where the finish had bubbled, and the chairs were the sort that suggested temporary penitence. A little black dome in the corner watched without blinking, and a red light glowed on the recorder box as if the machine had a pulse. The air smelled faintly of bleach and stale coffee, threaded with a tired artificial pine scent from a cleaner's cloth.

Paul and Emily sat side by side. He had chosen the chair that faced the door, as if he could manage the room better that way. His jacket was unbuttoned, and his tie sat a fraction off-centre, as though he had tugged at it in the lift. Emily's coat lay folded on her lap, her hands resting on top, fingers laced as if in prayer. They looked, to anyone glancing through the glass pane in the door, like a couple waiting for a verdict on a mortgage.

The detective, Rawlings, was formal without being unfriendly, a man whose shirt collars had learned the shape of his neck. He had a pen that made a quiet, confident scratching noise on the pad and a second, younger officer, DC Patel, sat beside him with her laptop screen casting a soft light on her face. Rawlings offered coffee in paper cups that were too hot at first and never quite warm enough after that. He apologised for the cups as though cheap containers might break a case.

"Thank you for coming in," he began, and the formula buffered them from whatever would follow. "We appreciate you making the time."

"Of course," Paul said, with that polite briskness he used for clients, that made his assent sound like part of the detective's plan. He cleared his throat. "We want to help. If there's anything we can help you clarify."

Rawlings nodded, ticked something invisible in his head. "We're speaking to a number of people," he said, a phrase designed to spread the weight. "Neighbours, the vicar, the gentleman from next door... Robert?"

"Yates," Emily supplied gently, her voice pitched low. "Robert Yates. He was the one who phoned Paul. On the... on the day." Her eyes flicked to the table at that word and then back up again as if she'd apologised to the wood for making it a witness.

Rawlings's gaze moved to her, not unkindly. "Yes. Mr Yates mentioned that. The call was to you, Mr Mercer?"

"To me," Paul said. He could feel the little place under his jaw where the muscle liked to knot. "We'd just got back from our honeymoon." He forced a small smile that didn't quite reach his eyes. "It feels like a long time ago now."

"How long had you been back?" Patel asked, checking something on her screen and then looking up. Her voice was lighter than Rawlings's, conversational, a tone that suggested friendlier rooms.

"Only a few hours," Paul said. "We landed around four, wasn't it, love? It was later by the time we got to the house, of course. The train was slow." He pressed his palm to the table for a moment, grounding the sentence. It wobbled anyway. "Robert called shortly after. Half an hour. Maybe." He hated that he didn't know exactly. If he had kept the times carved into him like numbers on a stone, perhaps his father would not be dead. No, that was ridiculous.

Emily's fingers tightened, just enough for him to feel.

"It was all a bit of a rush," she said, her voice careful with sympathy for the detectives too, as if she understood how poor a tool memory can be and didn't hold it against anyone. "We went straight to the hospital from our flat. They were wonderful. They did everything they could."

Rawlings nodded. "Could we go back a little," he said, the pen waiting, patient. "We're trying to establish the days around the incident. Who saw Mr Mercer, who spoke to him, that sort of thing. When did you last see your father alive, Mr Mercer?"

Paul swallowed. A particular image surfaced unbidden of his father's hand on his shoulder the afternoon before the wedding, a grip that had been more cautious than firm. He pushed that away and reached for the correct memory.

"The morning we flew to Italy," he said. "We came by to say goodbye. He was fine." He searched for a word that wouldn't sound like a verdict. "Tired. He said he'd been out in the garden early. Pruning. He said the apple tree was getting away from him."

"Was anyone else there?" Patel asked.

"Dorothy," Emily said. "His wife." She caught herself. "Paul's mother. She made tea. She always makes tea."

"I understand Mrs Mercer has been unwell," Rawlings said, the sentence shaped like a question but left open.

Emily inclined her head. "She's being very brave," she said, and the praise felt like a small, solid thing she could place in the middle of the table where it would do no harm. "She tires quickly. But she never complains." Her mouth softened on the last word, as if the compliment hurt.

Rawlings wrote something, then lifted his eyes.

"As we mentioned on the phone," he said, turning to Paul. "We've been reviewing CCTV from a neighbouring property, after a series of complaints about a suspicious character hanging around the area. The footage shows a hooded individual spending some time near the rear boundary fence in the week prior to Mr Mercer's fall."

The word hooded snagged in the air again, flimsy and theatrical until you thought about it at your own window. Paul felt sweat prickle at the back of his neck despite the room's bland chill.

"Spending time," he said, as though he could argue the phrase smaller. "How long?"

"Several minutes," Patel said. "Perhaps longer. The footage is motion-activated, so it records in bursts. We're attempting to obtain more from another angle."

"Was there a break-in?" Emily asked, calm, earnest. "Anything taken?"

"No," Rawlings said. "No reports of theft, no signs of forced entry. It could be nothing. A passerby lingering. A fox caught in a hood that fooled the lens," he added dryly, and his mouth twitched, an attempt to offer them a less sinister image. "But we prefer to rule things out properly."

Emily nodded once. "Of course," she said. "It's sensible."

Paul was aware of his own breathing. He wanted to ask if the figure had looked in through the kitchen window, or if the head had turned towards the morning room, or if the camera had seen hands held low or raised.

"If this was a week before my father slipped, I don't understand. Do you think this has anything to do with his heart?" He nearly said death and did not.

Rawlings arranged his pen next to the notepad, parallel. "At present, we're not treating Mr Mercer's death as suspicious," he said. "But an unexplained presence in the week before is interesting. We're simply following the thread."

"Threads can be knotted to look like ropes," Emily said softly, then immediately apologised for speaking in metaphor, as if a literary turn might impede justice. "I only mean, it's not so easy to see patterns when we're grieving."

Rawlings's eyes moved between them, weighing. "You'd be surprised how often grief clarifies," he said, and then, with a nod, let the subject pass as if it had been a kite tugging at its string and he had decided not to let it go.

They walked, between the four of them, back over the day of the fall. The phone call from Robert, the drive to the hospital, the colour of the light in A&E, the blink and hush of machines. Patel asked the questions that tidied the edges about times of arrivals and departures, without poking hard at the middle. Emily let her voice tremble once, and the tremor looked like truth as the syllables escaped her control for a second before she reined them back. It was only a small deviation from how she felt when she allowed herself to remember Dorothy saying Paul deserves better. She borrowed that heat and used it to colour her words just enough.

"Had your father expressed any concerns in the weeks before?" Rawlings asked at last. "About anyone in the area? Tradesmen? Delivery drivers? Anyone new?"

Paul shook his head, perhaps too fast. "Not to me," he said. "But we were busy with the wedding. He seemed... himself." The phrase rang hollow, and he hated that it did.

Emily tilted her chin in thought. "He did mention the teenagers who cut through the lane sometimes," she said, then frowned at herself for tattling. "But that was more a lament about manners than a warning. He said they dropped crisp packets."

She smiled, apologetic, as if litter were too small a thing to mention in a police station. Patel wrote it down anyway. Small things win cases, her pen seemed to believe.

Rawlings flipped a page. "We'll be speaking to the neighbours who back onto your garden," he said. "And we'd like to arrange a time to view the exterior of your property from their angle, if that's acceptable."

"Of course," Paul said at once. The words came easily. He wanted to be the man who cooperated. He wanted to be the man who had nothing to hide. A thought skated across his mind and was gone before he could see its face. There had been deliveries for the wedding to the house in the week before. What if they'd left the side gate unlatched. What if one of them had spotted something they fancied, and come back for a closer look. The question felt like a bruise he kept pressing.

There were other items on Rawlings' list, like who held spare keys, whether any contractors had been in the week before, whether Dorothy had mentioned anything unusual. Emily answered at once where she could and deferred to Paul where it seemed right. When Rawlings asked how Dorothy was coping, Emily's throat worked and her eyes looked liquid for a second, as if a trick of the light had turned them to water.

"She's very proud," Emily said. "She doesn't like to appear weak. But she's tired. The treatment is difficult. And she's frightened of the stairs since her fall." She stopped, as if suddenly conscious she might be telling tales outside school. "She wouldn't want me to say that. Please don't write that down."

Rawlings's mouth did that small twitch again.

"Noted," he said, and his pen moved anyway, but the letters were smaller.

At the end, if there was an end to this sort of formal conversation, they stood, awkward as guests who don't know whether to shake hands. Rawlings rounded the table and the momentary nearness of him made Emily realise he was taller than he looked in his chair. He held out his hand, and she placed her own in it without fuss, and her grip was cool, brief, and exact. Paul's handshake was firmer than he felt. He maintained steady eye contact, as he had been taught to do, and sensed, somewhere animal-deep, that the detective registered the effort.

Patel gave them a card with a number and the instruction to call if they remembered anything, even if it felt too small to matter.

"It's always the small things," she said, almost cheerfully, and looked precisely like a person who believed that. Emily tucked the card into her wallet as if it were something that needed safekeeping.

In the corridor, the carpet had that council-quality give that makes footsteps sound thoughtful. A constable passed them with a clipboard and nodded as if grief were a uniform he recognised. Through a glass panel Emily could see a woman crying into a tissue with her whole body. The weeping looked extravagant in a place dedicated to restraint.

Outside, the February light sat low and grey. Paul breathed as if someone had told him he'd been holding his breath; he put a hand on the small of Emily's back and a little pressure there steered them towards the street. For two steps she allowed herself to feel the irony of it—how that light touch looked like protection to anyone watching and felt, to her, like a mild attempt at control.

"Thank you," he said, when they reached the pavement, the words tumbling out as if he had to unload them before the red light at the crossing changed. "For coming. For saying the right things. I should have..." He didn't finish. Guilt was a tide, it didn't require grammar.

"You did fine," Emily said. "You were honest. That's all anyone can be." She didn't add that honesty is sometimes an arrangement rather than a state. He kissed her temple hard, like a man paying a tax, and when he pulled back, he kept his eyes somewhere else, as if something in her face might accuse him of ill doing.

"I'm sure it's nothing," Emily said. "They have to follow up complaints, don't they? But it was a whole week before he fell."

He nodded an agreement he didn't quite feel, and she linked his arms as they walked to the station. On the train back, he stared at the river and saw the garden. He told himself his father was the sort of man who noticed gates and latches. He told himself he had always been careful. The stories we tell ourselves, he thought, are like receipts we fold into wallets and never look at again. He closed his eyes and let the rhythm of the carriage give him a lie he could rest on for ten minutes.

Dorothy heard the front door and the murmur of voices in the hall. She heard Emily's low, even tone, and heard Paul's reply, pitched a little too high. She sat very straight in Harold's chair in the morning room and waited to be told what had been said. The river glinted through the window like metal, and the afternoon had flattened into a tired grey. When they came in, she kept her eyes on the view as if they were an interruption.

"How did it go?" she asked, and the question was a challenge rather than an enquiry.

Paul, taking the armchair opposite his mother, smiled too quickly.

"Routine," he said. "They asked about the week before. The CCTV. That sort of thing."

"Routine," Dorothy repeated, tasting the word and finding it sour. "At a police station. With recording equipment." Her gaze shifted to Emily. "And you went along, did you?"

Emily lowered her head, a modest nod. "Only to support Paul," she said. "It's a difficult place to sit alone."

Dorothy turned her mouth down, the gesture delicate, precise, as if pressing out a fold in paper.

"And why did she have to go with you?" she demanded of Paul, as if Emily were a parcel he had signed for without checking the return address. "It's nothing to do with her. I am sick of her poking her nose into family business."

Paul blinked. He looked absurdly like a boy who has been accused of smuggling biscuits.

"Mum," he said, slipping into the thin voice that had never worked on her. "She went to support me. That's all."

Emily kept her eyes on her hands.

"I only wanted to help," she murmured, and the humility in it made Dorothy bristle, because she could hear what sympathy would make of those words.

Dorothy set her palms on the arms of her chair and pushed herself up. The cane stood beside her, and she took it the way a general might take a sword, reluctantly, with impatience for its necessity.

"I don't want to hear any more about it," she said. "If the police have questions about this house, they can put them to me. Not to you." She tipped her head at Emily without looking directly at her. "And certainly not to outsiders."

"I'm not..." Paul began, and then realised where the sentence would take him if he followed it. He let it fall, helpless, and glanced at Emily, who gave him a small shake of the head without lifting her gaze.

Dorothy moved towards the door. The cane's tip clicked on the floorboards, a sound that managed to be both fragile and defiant.

"I am going to my room," she announced. "And I will not be disturbed."

Her steps were slower than she remembered them being, the ankle tender in ways that annoyed her. On the first stair she felt the eyes of both of them on her back. Only one set felt anxious. She refused to turn. The cane tapped and tapped, an angry punctuation climbing towards the landing.

In the quiet that followed, Paul rubbed his jaw as if he had been hit there. "I should have been firmer with her," he said. "I should have kept her from saying that."

"You can't control what she says," Emily replied, gentle but firm. "You can only make things easier where you can." She set a hand on his forearm and he stilled under it.

"Which reminds me. What about the room downstairs. The library."

He looked at her and, briefly, his face lit with something like gratitude.

"We'll do it," he said. "I'll speak to her tonight. If I catch her in the right mood." He hesitated to finish the sentence because he realised, with a small wince, that moods were not to be charted. "It makes sense," he said instead. "For her safety."

"And her independence," Emily added, because the word would appeal to Dorothy's pride. "Her own bathroom. No stairs. We can make it hers. It's not a compromise, but a choice."

Paul nodded, and the movement had something eager in it, like a man grabbing at a sensible idea because sensible ideas protected him from the other kind.

"You're right," he said, and smiled with relief at the shape of himself saying it. "I'll raise it after supper."

"Not after supper," Emily said, and the correction had no sharpness in it. "After tea. She's steadier then."

He looked at her with a mixture of gratitude and dependence that he would have disliked if he had been able to see it.

"All right," he said. "After tea. You know best."

She lowered her eyes, taking the praise as if it embarrassed her. "I only know what I see," she said. "And I see she's tired."

They ate quietly that evening. Dorothy did not descend. Paul took a tray up and returned with it not quite empty and an expression that made Emily think, not yet. After, in the kitchen, she rinsed plates and he dried, and the soft domesticity of it was a drug he welcomed. His phone buzzed on the counter. It was Rohan, a question about the earliest train in the morning. He left it unanswered. Emily noticed and said nothing. Later she would praise him for his priorities, and he would feel good and that goodness would mask the other feeling.

When they went up, the landing light made a shallow pool outside Dorothy's door. From within, a faint cough sounded, but more a clearing of the throat before speech. No speech came. Paul paused and Emily's hand touched his back and urged him on. In their room he sat on the edge of the bed and unlaced his shoes with more care than their knots warranted.

"What if the police think that figure had something to do with my father's..." he began, and stopped.

Emily sat beside him, close enough for warmth, not close enough to trap. "They only ever think what the evidence tells them," she said. "At the moment, the evidence tells them your father fell and his heart failed, which is what happened. The figure on the footage is a curiosity, and they're probably looking at it for robberies or something."

He nodded, pretended to believe it completely. He pushed

his hands through his hair and gave a short laugh that wanted to be a breath.

"You always make things sound manageable," he said. "You make me sound like I'm not failing."

"You're not," she said, because that is what he needed to be told. It sounded like truth, which was as good as any truth in the dark.

Much later, when the house had settled, Dorothy stood in her doorway and looked down the stairs as if they were a slope she might ski. Her ankle twinged, reminding her of her own body's suddenly shabby workmanship. She thought of the police and of Emily's hands on her just above the step, and how they'd felt warm, competent, and inevitable. The fear she had named in her room earlier returned in a new shape. Irrelevance, she thought, is a kind of loosening. You feel yourself unthreading from your own life. She set her hand on the banister, sturdy as a faithful dog.

"Not yet," she said aloud, and the words surprised her with their steadiness.

# 13

Morning wore its best disguise. A pale sun spilled across the tiled floor as Emily moved through the kitchen in the quiet rhythm she had taught herself, preparing breakfast for them all.

Paul was already at the table with his laptop open, phone facedown and vibrating as if it had something urgent to confess. He wore his work shirt with the sleeves rolled to the elbow, the knot of his tie left in from yesterday, ready to be dragged back up the silk at a moment's notice. He peered at an email thread as though it were a landscape he could cross if he just kept walking.

"Morning," he said without looking up. His hand went out automatically when Emily set the coffee down and found it, grateful. The gratitude made her want to forgive him for being emotionally elsewhere.

Dorothy entered as if she were arriving for a hearing. Cardigan buttoned to the top, pearls looped with military precision, cane in hand more as a punctuation mark than a necessity. She paused by the door and surveyed the room with the practised eye of a woman who could locate an error with half her attention.

"It's too bright in here," she said, nodding at the slats of light. "One of you draw the blind." She moved to her chair and sat with care, flinching as her ankle reminded her it had not forgiven her for the stairs.

Emily turned the blind a fraction, letting the sun resolve into stripes, and then she brought the blue pot and poured.

"Weak," Dorothy said, after one sip, like a judge issuing a verdict. "It tastes like hotel tea."

"I'll let it brew longer," Emily said mildly, as if this were information rather than correction. She set the timer in her head to two minutes and added twenty seconds because the morning demanded generosity.

The eggs were ready. She lifted them from the water and dried their shells with the little square of linen Dorothy kept for that purpose. She popped each into their egg cups and delivered them with toast. When she cracked hers, the yolk sat like a small sun, not quite set, the tremor of perfection.

Dorothy prodded her own yolk with the tip of her spoon and watched the gold run.

"Too runny," she said. "You'll never master the art of running a house like this if you can't even cook an egg properly."

"Mum," Paul murmured, eyes still on his screen, the plea almost reflexive. "Please."

Emily, who could have produced half a dozen eggs at different stages of doneness while blindfolded and standing on one leg, lifted the plate away at once.

"I'll do you another," she said, as if her failure were an ordinary accident, like rain. "A minute more."

Dorothy's gaze followed the plate as though it were being removed from evidence too soon.

"And the tea will be stew by the time you remember to pour it," she said. "Honestly. Standards. Your father..."

"...had high ones," Paul finished, too quickly. He rubbed his forehead, the universal sign for 'I am here but I am also in six other places'. His phone trembled across the table, angling itself towards the edge. He caught it without looking and pushed it back to the middle, penning it in with his coffee mug as if it were a living thing.

"Mum," he said again, this time lifting his eyes and forcing a smile that cracked at one corner. "Can we not do this today?"

Dorothy sniffed. "Do what? Eat? Drink tea? Live in my own house according to my own wishes?" She took another sip and grimaced as if Emily had personally soured the milk by thinking herself above her station.

Emily returned the second egg, firmer, the yolk dignified, the white obedient.

"Better," Dorothy conceded, then added, almost kindly, "It's not a failure to write things down, you know. I could make you a chart. Monday to Sunday. Eggs and tea and how to fold towels so they don't develop lines."

When they'd finished, Emily collected plates that had barely been disturbed and set them gently in the sink, running the tap only halfway so the noise wouldn't give Dorothy something else to mind. She wiped a ring of tea from the table and polished it away with the heel of her hand, the movement small and self-erasing. She had learned that the less space she took up while she worked, the calmer Dorothy's breathing became.

"Actually," Paul said, the word lifting like a gate that might slam. "We should talk about something else, too. Something practical." He straightened his shoulders, preparing himself to sound reasonable. "Mum, about the stairs."

Dorothy put her spoon down. "What about them."

"The fall rattled us," he said. "All of us. You were lucky. I've been thinking, and Emily agrees, that it might be better if we moved your bedroom downstairs. Just temporarily." He let the word dangle as if to suggest it might change its mind later. "The library has the bathroom that can be an ensuite. We can set it up properly. It'll mean fewer trips up and down. It'll be safer and easier for you."

Dorothy stared at him as if he had suggested opening the house to tourists.

"I am not moving out of the bedroom I shared with my husband," she said. Her voice was very soft, which was when it was most dangerous. "This is my house. My bedroom is my bedroom. I won't be shifted about like a guest."

Emily kept her eyes on the dishcloth.

"It wouldn't be about shifting you," she said gently, without looking up. "It would be adapting to suit your needs. For now. The library is lovely in the afternoon. You'd have the light, and your own bathroom. No stairs to climb." She made the advantages sound like comforts rather than contingencies. "We could bring your things down. The photographs. The quilt. Make it yours."

Dorothy's hand, where it rested on the table, trembled once, almost imperceptibly, then stilled.

"No," she said. "I won't be banished."

"You wouldn't be," Paul said, and now the softness in his tone went brittle, as if he were trying to handle glass with gloves on. "We've thought about this. I've spoken to someone already. Decorators and the plumber, to put a proper shower in. It'll be sorted in a week."

Silence sat down at the table with them. It was the wrong move. Emily felt it the moment he said it, the way you feel a glass slip before it hits the floor. Dorothy's face altered as something colder moved behind it, a curtain pulled across.

"You've arranged work in my house," she said. "In my rooms. Without asking me."

"It's not..." Paul began.

Emily stepped forward, very slightly, not so much intervening as shading the light.

"We wanted to have a plan," she said. "So you wouldn't be inconvenienced. It's easily un-arranged if you'd prefer to keep things as they are." She lied as gently as she knew how. The plumber had already texted to confirm measurements that afternoon. "It was only a thought, Dorothy. Because we care."

Dorothy's glare settled on her then, as if Emily had spoken too much in the first person. The cane knocked once against the leg of the chair.

"You only care about ordering my life to suit yourself," she said. "You and your charts and your schedules and your lists. You think if you bring enough cups of tea into my rooms I'll forget they used to be mine alone."

Paul pushed back his chair and stood up too quickly. The laptop lid flapped, the phone skittered, his coffee slopped into the saucer.

"This is about your safety," he said, voice too loud for the kitchen. "It's not an argument. It's decided."

Dorothy's mouth opened and closed. For a terrible second, she looked not furious but lost.

"Decided by whom," she said, and the last word was so old-fashioned that Emily felt an ache for the woman she had been when grammar mattered more than stairs.

"By me," Paul said, bravado carrying him the rest of the way because he had already stepped off the edge. He ran a hand through his hair and tried for a smile that wasn't apology. "I'm your son. It's my job to look after you now."

"Your job," Dorothy echoed, as if the sounds had to be tested to destruction. "How nice it must be to have a job that lets you change other people's lives."

"This is why," Emily said quietly, to no one, to the air, and busied herself with plates again so the words could be mistaken for a murmur about the washing up. She knew what would happen next. Resistance would splinter and all that would remain would be resentment, which was easier to contain because it lived in one place.

Dorothy stood, the cane thumping the floor in a rhythm that tried to sound like command and failed.

"I am going upstairs," she said. "To *my* room."

"Wait," Emily said, as if asking a favour she did not expect to be granted. "Before you go, I should tell you. I've invited my friend, Isla, to lunch today. She's arriving shortly." She kept her tone light, apologetic around the edges. "I was going to see if I could encourage her to stay a night or two. She'll be no trouble. And she... well... She's been worried about me. I told her not to be."

Dorothy stared at her as if the space between them had filled with smoke. "This is not a hotel," she said.

"No," Emily agreed. "It's a home. Which is why it's nice to have friends in it sometimes."

Paul, who had been bracing for a blow from one direction, blinked at the one from the other.

"That's fine," he said slowly. "Isla's good people." He glanced at his mother, already calculating what concession would balance this new invasion. "You like Isla," he added lamely, and then wished he hadn't, because the last time Dorothy had "liked" anything had been before he introduced her to Emily.

Dorothy gathered the tatters of her control around her like a shawl.

"Invite whomever you wish," she said, and there was so much scorn in the permission it might have singed the air. "Since my wishes are now apparently not even advisory." She turned for the door, the cane marking her retreat. "And tell your plumbers that if they chip a single tile I shall have their heads on spikes."

The line should have been comic. No one laughed. When she had gone, Paul let himself collapse back into the chair and pinched the bridge of his nose.

"That went well," he said, attempting irony and landing somewhere near despair. "I shouldn't have told her I'd already booked them."

"It was honest," Emily said. She dried the last plate and set it in the rack like a small white moon. "And practical. She'll be angrier if we make and unmake and make plans again. Better to hold one line."

He nodded, grateful for the steadying narrative. "You're right. As usual."

Emily smiled as if the compliment embarrassed her. "I'll go and put fresh towels in the library. Just to see how it looks." She did not say for Isla, though the thought of a friend's voice in the house felt suddenly like oxygen. "She'll be here by four."

Paul reached for his phone, then pushed it away. "I'll try to be back before then," he said, already failing. "There's a call with New York at five."

"Of course," Emily said. "We'll manage."

She glanced up at the ceiling as she left the kitchen, seeing not plaster but the map of rooms above, and Dorothy moving stiffly along the corridor, touching the wardrobe door to steady herself because she would not use the railings, stopping by the photograph of Harold to tell him that treachery had arrived stamped and postmarked under his roof.

The evening sun laid itself along the Thames like burnished gold. The river moved with its usual, indifferent determination, carrying twigs, weeds, and a single plastic ball past the bottom of the Mercer garden and on towards Maidenhead as if there were somewhere it had to be by nightfall. Emily took the path along the bank, her hands deep in her coat pockets, breath making short ghosts in the cooling air. The lights had come on in the houses on the opposite bank—gold rectangles suspended above the water, each a small theatre where other families were getting things wrong and right.

She dialled Isla and held the phone to her ear. The line clicked and filled with her friend's voice, warm and brisk, the sound of a person who believed in the usefulness of words.

"Tell me everything," Isla said. "I'm on the tube, but I can hear you. If I lose you in a tunnel, I'll ring back."

Emily closed her eyes briefly at the relief of it, then opened them again to watch a pair of dog walkers negotiate the etiquette of leads and greetings.

"Breakfast," she said, and put all the weight of her morning into the word. "Tea too weak tea. Egg too runny. And the line of the day, 'You'll never master the art of running a house like this if you can't even cook an egg properly.'" She managed to make it sound almost funny. Almost. "It's like she wants to break me and cause a rift between me and Paul."

Isla's exhale hissed through the speaker. "She's a piece of work. I'm sorry, Em. I know I say that too often, but God. The audacity."

Emily smiled with half her mouth. "And then Paul chose the worst moment in living memory to tell her that he wants to move her to the room downstairs. He even told her he's already booked the plumber and decorators. And the temperature in the room dropped ten degrees."

"Oh no."

"Oh yes. She looked at him like he'd put it up on Airbnb without mentioning it. And she looked at me like I'd posted the listing."

"Do I need to bring boxing gloves?" Isla asked. Emily could

hear the rattle of the doors open and close at a station stop. "Because I will back you up, so help me."

Emily laughed, and the sound made a couple walking past glance over and smile reflexively. "No boxing gloves. Just you. She hates the very idea of guests, so perhaps your existence will distract her from wanting to die on the hill of the upstairs bedroom."

"Em." Isla's voice softened, the way it did in court when she knew she had to nudge a witness into saying the thing they didn't want to say. "Do you think she's just frightened of change? Lots of elderly people are. And it must be hard, seeing a younger woman take control of her home. Not to mention..." She hesitated, then pressed on. "What if she feels like all her power is being stripped away. Sometimes people fight the wrong things because they don't know where to put the fear."

Emily's steps slowed. A cyclist chimed a bell behind her and she moved aside without thinking, watching him weave through the dusk like a moving star.

"I know," she said softly. "I tell myself that every day. She is frightened. And proud. And sometimes so tired I think if I touched her too hard, she'd bruise." She swallowed. "But it's hard not to take it personally when the target is always me, or the things I do."

"Of course," Isla said quickly. "Of course. I didn't mean..." The tube swallowed her words and spat them back. "I didn't mean it to sound like you should excuse everything. I hate thinking of you becoming the punching bag for someone else's terror."

"It's not that," Emily said, and she let the wound show, just for Isla, because Isla had known her before the Mercer house learned her footsteps. "It's the way she does it. The smallnesses. The egg. The tea. The way she says 'my house' like I'm a stain on the skirting board. I can stand being disliked, but I can't stand being made to feel invisible and unwelcome."

The phone went quiet for a beat. Emily listened to the river talk to itself and to a child asking for one more minute on the swings.

"You are not invisible to me," Isla said at last. "Not while I'm around to make a nuisance of myself."

Emily smiled for real then, and the smile reached her eyes. "You'll be here in an hour?"

"Forty minutes if the trains behave. I've got a small suitcase and a bottle of something indecently expensive, because if I'm going to Trespass in Bray I might as well do it properly."

"Dorothy will call it vulgar."

"I'll call it medicinal." Isla paused. "Besides, it's not for her. Now, about the room downstairs, are you sure it's wise to push that now?"

"It's not pushing," Emily said. "It's planning. She nearly went tumbling again on Thursday. The carpet is slippery, the runner has a mean little fold near the top, and her ankle is still tender. It's not safe for her to be upstairs." She exhaled. "And the ensuite down there is nicer. She'd never admit it, but she'd like it. Once we make it hers."

"Maybe," Isla said slowly. Emily could hear her conceding ground and staking a flag at the same time. "But it might feel like being moved off the battlefield. You know? Like you and Paul have drawn a line around a smaller patch of earth and said, 'this bit is yours' because the rest now belongs to you."

Emily stopped at the rail where the path dipped towards the water and looked at her reflection wavering in the dusk. The woman in the river wore her hair pinned and her mouth quiet. She looked like someone who could be trusted with fragile things.

"I don't want the rest to belong to me," she said, and she

wanted it to be true the moment she heard herself say it. "I want the house to stop being a battleground. For her. For Paul. For all of us."

"Then maybe frame it like a gift," Isla said. "Autonomy. Privacy. The library as a sovereign nation. Do that lawyer thing you hate me doing. Put a spin on it."

"I can spin," Emily said, and the honesty of it made her laugh again, low. "Thank you."

"Always." Isla cleared her throat. "And Em, one more thing."

"Go on."

"You've been telling me the ways she wounds you, and I don't doubt them. But you don't tell me how you feel except as an equation. You say, Dorothy does x, therefore I must do y. You're allowed to say, 'I'm furious' or 'I'm lonely' or 'I want to run.'"

Emily thought of the egg, of the tea, of the look on Dorothy's face when Paul said he'd already booked the plumber, of the way the cane had sounded on the floorboards like an old soldier's drum calling a retreat and pretending it was a march.

"I am lonely," she said, surprising herself with the confession. "And I'm tired in a way that sleep doesn't fix. And sometimes I think if I stop moving, I'll cry so hard it will frighten him."

"Then don't stop moving until I get there," Isla said. "And when I arrive, I'll hand you a glass and you can cry at me. I can take it."

"Deal," Emily said. "I'll meet you at the gate."

She hung up and stood for a moment longer, watching the river carry off the daylight. A child trotted past with a stick, a father ambling behind, looking like all fathers look at the end of a Sunday, half content, half planning. Emily turned back towards the house. Its windows were lit already, squares of gold set into the blueing evening. From here, from this distance, it looked like every storybook drawing of a home a child might point at and say: that one.

Inside, she knew, the kitchen would be in order because she had left it that way and Dorothy's footfalls would patter across the upstairs carpet because the need to watch had outstripped the need to rest. Paul would arrive later than he said and kiss her hair and say thank you for something that felt too small to accept gratitude for. And Isla would come with her suitcase and her armoury of words, and the house would rearrange itself around another woman's laugh. Dorothy would hate it and pretend not to. Emily would smile and carry plates and smooth the surface of the water where she could, watching underneath for the snags.

She set her pace and kept to it, returning along the path, feeling the river at her shoulder like a witness that wouldn't speak. The weekend would be a test of them all, but perhaps it would also be a reprieve. She adjusted the collar of her coat and thought of the downstairs library, still smelling faintly of leather and dust, and pictured fresh sheets turned down and a quilt folded just so, a lamp set at the correct height for reading, the ensuite gleaming. A room made safe. A kindness that would look, to the right eyes, like love.

# 14

Isla arrived just before noon with a bag of pastries from a bakery near the station and the suspicion that she was bringing sugar to a wound.

"Paul's still out," Emily said, kissing Isla's cheek and taking the paper bag. "Some corporate golf thing. It's work, but the word 'work' does an awful lot of heavy lifting in Paul's sentences at the moment."

"Corporate events are like hell on earth," Isla said cheerfully, shedding her coat. "Don't quote me." She clocked the neatness of a salad already made with watercress, fennel, pomegranate seeds like rubies, and the bowls warming in the oven for what smelled like parsnip soup, and the cutlery set out without fuss. Emily even made tidiness look tender.

"Will Dorothy be joining us?" Isla asked, casual, looking towards the doorway that led to the morning room.

Emily's smile thinned. "No. She's not hungry apparently. I made her a sandwich, and she took it up. She prefers to eat in her room. She says she's already 'had enough of chatter'." The phrase arrived in Dorothy's voice, a crispness Emily could imitate perfectly without meaning to.

"Right," Isla said, and let it rest. She had learned not to interrogate absences as if they were crimes.

They ate at the little table by the window, knees almost touching. The river showed in the distance, silver where the light found it. Isla listened as Emily told her about the chart Dorothy had proposed drawing for duties Emily had already memorised so completely she could have taught a course. They talked about the move downstairs that was being contested not because it was wrong but because it had been suggested. The words had the texture of small stories, they were precise, and the sharpness was softened with rueful smiles. Isla heard her friend's voice and then, beneath it, the engine of something else, steady as a metronome.

"She'll come round," Isla said, because it was a sentence that didn't make anything worse.

"Paul says she always does, eventually." Emily's smile was dutiful and sad. "But I don't know. I try. I keep trying. Every day I wake up and decide to try again." She said it without self-congratulation, and yet Isla felt the sentence arrive with a curated weight, as if it had been polished by repetition.

"So," Isla said, risking the lawyer's question wrapped in a friend's tone. "Does she ever say anything kind? A thank you? A moment of, I don't know, anything normal?"

Emily's spoon paused, a fraction.

"Not to me," she said lightly, and then, quickly, to soften it. "On good days, she tolerates me. And when she's tired, she says less rather than more. That is almost kindness in this house."

The answer sat between them like a placemat laid for an absent guest. Isla nodded and sipped her soup. She remembered how her own gran was a terror as she shrank. She hoarded sugar in her dresser and told the vicar to take off his hat in her sitting room and once rang the police because the cat looked suspicious, but she also stroked Isla's hair when she had tonsillitis and smuggled her biscuits under the duvet. What she thought was that Dorothy's meanness, as Emily reported it, never contained an accidental kindness. No stray softness, no misfired tenderness. In Emily's telling, Dorothy's cruelty was seamless, like something manufactured.

"Does she like the library?" Isla asked instead, as neutrally as she could. "The move?"

"It's not a move," Emily said. "It's an option." She smiled with professional patience. "And no. She thinks I'm banishing her. Paul's speaking to her again tonight."

"And how does Paul really cope with all this?" Isla kept her voice even. "How does he deal with her."

Emily considered. "He is good," she said at last. "And grateful for my support." She laid her spoon down precisely on the little notch of the saucer. "He tries. He is grieving, too." The last line was offered like an explanation for a debt.

Upstairs, a floorboard made a small complaint. The sound had the same effect on both of them. Their eyes flicked up, their shoulders twitched an apology to the ceiling. Isla glanced at Emily and saw how attuned she was to this house, and the way she had learned its pulse, its throat-clearings, the language of its walls. There was skill in that. There could also be danger.

Isla broke the bread they made you pay too much for in London and dipped it in the soup.

"Look," she said, deciding to commit to kindness even if it turned out to be wrong, "I'm in your corner. You know that. But..." She swallowed. She could feel the edge of something important. "Sometimes when you describe her, it's like watching a storm through a window. All wind and noise and no weather breaks. Maybe you just tell me the worst bits. Maybe you need to. But if there are better bits, small ones, I want to hear those too."

Emily's eyes were steady on Isla's face. For a moment,

something like indignation sparked, brief and unguarded, before being extinguished by that smooth composure.

"I do tell you," she said gently. "When she sleeps well. When she eats. When the pain is less. Those are her good times." She held Isla's gaze. "I know it's hard to hear only complaint. I hear myself and wonder who I have become? I didn't mean to become someone who keeps an account of small unkindnesses. It's just that small things are what the day is made of now."

Isla reached across and squeezed her wrist. The bones felt thin beneath her fingers.

"I'm sorry," she said at once. "I'm clumsy. I just want you to be happy." She pictured her gran, the sugar drawer, the cat. "Sometimes people who are frightened are also impossible to reason with. Both can be true."

Emily smiled as if Isla had just solved a puzzle no one else had been clever enough to see.

"I tell myself that a hundred times before breakfast," she said. "And a hundred times after."

They cleared plates together, the choreography of old friends who had shared smaller kitchens and cheaper crockery. Isla carried dishes to the sink and Emily took them from her, already soaped, already rinsed, already placed.

"You'll stay the whole weekend?" Emily asked. "I've made up the spare room by the orchard."

"Twist my arm," Isla said. "I like the orchard room. It makes me feel as if I'm about to be cast as the sensible aunt in a BBC drama."

"Typecasting," Emily said, and her smile this time had mischief in it. Isla treasured that flash of the old Emily.

"But I can't stay today, I've got to get back for work. How about I come for the weekend?"

"That would be perfect," Emily said, and meant it.

When they had finished, they sat again with coffee. Emily

poured from a French press and the air grew comfortable with the smell. Isla watched her friend wrap her hands around the mug, then set it down untouched, then lift it again in a small loop, calming herself with a prop. She wondered if Emily realised she was performing even for the person who had known her before all this. It was not a deceit exactly. More like a costume that had begun to forget there was a different skin beneath it.

"What would you do," Isla asked suddenly, the question arriving without preface. "If it goes on like this forever?"

Emily looked genuinely startled. "Forever?"

"Yes. The friction. The nitpicking, the charts. What if it never changes. If Paul never notices any more than he notices now."

Emily's mouth parted, then closed, then curved into something like surrender. "Then I would have to go on," she said. "And keep trying. Because Paul is worth it." She added, softer, almost to herself. "And because I don't like losing."

Isla laughed, delighted by the honesty. "There she is," she said. "The girl who negotiated a pay rise for me in the break room because she said I sat like a queen and it was my own fault people forgot to pay tribute."

Emily's eyes widened. "I did not."

"You did," Isla said, mock solemn. "And you were right." She stood and pulled Emily into an embrace that lasted a beat longer than either of them expected. Isla rested her chin on her friend's shoulder and thought, loyalty is easy in public, and suspicion is treachery even in private. She decided to choose loyalty, for now.

From overhead, they heard a faint noise that sounded like the scrape of a chair. Then the slow, deliberate sound of footsteps heading towards the landing and away again. Dorothy, moving her pieces on the board of her day. Isla released Emily and smiled in the direction of the ceiling.

"Your dragon's stirring," she whispered.

Emily's laugh this time was small and real.

"Come on," she said. "Let's go and walk by the river before it rains. She naps after lunch, anyway."

They took their coats and left the kitchen tidy enough to pass any inspection. In the hall, Isla paused by the photographs on the wall showing Paul aged eight in a cricket sweater, a child version of smugness. Beside it was an image of Harold at a regatta, squinting into the sun, and beside that Dorothy as a young woman, looking almost amused by the camera. Isla thought, not for the first time, that time didn't kill people so much as erode them. She followed Emily out. The door made a polite, expensive thud as it closed.

Isla and Emily walked beside the river. The path was slick with yesterday's rain and scattered with small twigs, as if the trees had shed arguments in the night. Isla listened as Emily returned to her litany of the week's upcoming events and told herself it was okay to hold both advocate and witness roles at once.

For now, she looped her arm through Emily's and pointed out a heron standing like a piece of folded paper by the reeds.

"Look at him," she said. "He thinks stillness is dignity."

Emily squinted and smiled. "Maybe he's just thinking."

"Maybe," Isla said, and the word felt like a compromise with the world.

When they returned, Emily put the kettle on by reflex, and Isla took it upon herself to set out biscuits beside the pot. She placed one aside on a separate plate for Dorothy. Emily saw and said nothing. The house resumed the shape it liked best, its rooms linked by quiet industry and the knowledge that every sound had an audience.

Isla left at three with promises to come back on Friday. Emily walked her to the door and they hugged on the step where a thin sun found their faces.

"You're doing brilliantly," Isla said, and meant it. She climbed into the taxi and, as it pulled away, watched Emily turn back into the house that kept asking her to prove herself. Loyalty won the day. Suspicion went home with Isla in the back seat, mild and not yet certain of its own name.

That night, Dorothy drew the curtains in the morning room so precisely that the two sides met as neatly as two lips pressed together. She carried the record from the shelf to the player with both hands, not because it was heavy but because that is how respect sometimes looks. It was Harold's favourite. Sinatra, the late voice, worn round the edges like sea glass. She lifted the arm and set it down with concentration. The tiny surrender of needle to groove still pleased her. A hush, and then strings, and then that voice, conspiratorial and tired. It was a very good year...

She closed her eyes and put her hand on Harold's chair. The leather had grown shiny from decades of his nape, his elbows, the fidget of his fingers on the arms when the answer to a crossword wouldn't come. She could conjure him there. She could almost hear the small throat-clearing before he read aloud from the Telegraph, the way he'd look over at her after a joke as if checking she'd heard and filed it. How quiet the room had become since that look no longer crossed the air.

"They're waiting for me to go next," she said, because the music loosened something in her throat and because Harold had never punished honesty. The words startled her in the room as much as they had in her chest.

"I know what she's up to. Slowly taking over my home.

Twisting things. Making Paul annoyed with me." The last line broke a little, though she had not meant it to.

"He was never annoyed with me before," she added, and knew it wasn't strictly true. Boys grow into men by angling themselves away from their mothers' edges. But his annoyance had changed into something sharper.

She opened her eyes. The lamp made a circle of humility on the rug. Just enough light for one person. On the mantelpiece, the photograph from the regatta held Harold in that crisp beige the camera never quite captured right.

"I wish you were here," she told the picture. "Because I'm tired." She pressed fingers into the tender place at her ankle as if to show him proof. "And I can't fight her forever." The confession arrived without armour, and the room did not punish her for it.

Sinatra went on, patient, generous, making a case for memory as a kind of mercy. Dorothy listened and felt in her chest, not quite pain, but more like a door opening very slowly in a house where it had long been stuck. Fear stepped through first, ungainly and unashamed, and stood where she could see it. She studied it with the curiosity she had once reserved for recipes. A pinch of pride, a handful of habit, a ladle of grief, season with illness, simmer without hope. It wasn't monstrous, she realised, not really. Just too strong for her palette. Outside, an owl tested the night with its question. Dorothy smiled, and stroked the leather of Harold's chair in small, regular movements.

"I won't let her win," she said. "Though I don't know what winning looks like anymore." She wished, suddenly and extravagantly, for something banal and old fashioned. Like a tin of peaches in the larder they could split over the sink after midnight, Harold with a fork, she with a spoon, their shared greed an intimacy. She almost went to look for one, but didn't. It wouldn't be the same without him.

When the record ended, she did not lift the arm right away. The needle worried the end groove in tiny, dutiful circles, sounding like a distant tap dripping. Eventually she rose, slower than she intended, and returned the disc to its sleeve. She switched off the lamp and the room reshaped itself around the dark. On her way out she paused by the door and listened to the house listening to her. She stood there a moment longer, assessing the staircase, the way the banister's polish gleamed, the new fear the carpeted treads inspired. She was so tired. Still, she put her hand against the wall to steady herself and made her way downstairs.

# 15

The dining room had the faint hush of a church where the service has ended but the candles are still burning. The chandelier hummed with soft light, laying it over the polished wood, over the gleam of knives and forks, over three people who had long since run out of things to say.

Emily served quietly, setting plates down with the practiced ease of someone who had learned to move without clatter. Hunter's chicken, crisp potatoes, carrots glazed until they shone. The kind of food that asked only to be eaten and enjoyed.

Dorothy picked with the precision of a surgeon. Fork into potato, lift, inspect, return. A small grimace at the carrots. She pressed the edge of her knife against the chicken, as if testing for structural integrity, then gave a sniff.

"It's dry," she pronounced, though she had not tasted it. "Overcooked, and somehow still lacking flavour. Honestly, Emily, you'd think after all these weeks you'd know how to keep meat from turning into sawdust."

Paul dropped his fork onto his plate with a noise that startled even him. "Enough, Mum."

The words landed harder than he'd intended, the sharpness

hanging in the air like smoke. For a heartbeat Dorothy froze, hand poised midair, eyes narrowing. Emily's gaze flicked between them, and her eyes glistened though her smile came steady, brave, almost apologetic.

"It's fine, Paul," she said quickly, soothing the air. "It's just taking me a while to learn Dorothy's tastes. I'll try harder."

Dorothy slammed her cutlery down, the sound like a gavel. "Oh, for heaven's sake. Must we all pretend?" She rolled her eyes towards the ceiling.

Paul exhaled heavily, burying his face in his hands, elbows on the table like a boy who had been scolded for the last time.

Emily leaned forward slightly, her voice honey-soft, a peace offering shaped like a question. "Have you thought any more about the idea of moving downstairs?"

Dorothy's head snapped round. "I hate it," she said flatly. "Even the idea makes me feel like an invalid, exiled from my own home. Don't think I don't see what's happening." Her eyes drilled into Emily's face. "You'd like me tucked away downstairs, wouldn't you? Out of sight. But I am not falling for it."

The cutlery on Emily's plate gleamed untouched. She smoothed her napkin across her lap, her composure holding like porcelain under pressure.

Paul groaned, dragging a hand down his face, his voice weary.

"Mum, please. It's safer for you. That's all. No one's trying to..." He faltered, the words deserting him. He looked between the two women, knowing he had already lost both arguments.

Dinner went on in silence, the scrape of Dorothy's fork against china the only sound. Emily chewed delicately, the corners of her mouth turned into a brave little crescent, while Paul stared at his plate as if the potatoes might offer a way out.

Later that night, when Dorothy had gone to bed and Paul claimed he had emails to finish, Emily retreated to the orchard room where the phone signal was strongest. She curled into the armchair and dialled Isla.

"It was awful," she whispered, though no one was near enough to hear. "She tore into everything again. She slammed her cutlery down, Isla. She said I'm trying to make her feel like an invalid. Paul snapped at her, finally, but then he just buried his head in his hands and left me to patch it all back together." Her voice quivered as though on the edge of tears but never tipped over. "I don't know how much more of this I can take."

On the other end of the line, Isla's voice sharpened with outrage.

"Emily. That's appalling. She treats you like a servant. And Paul? What? He just sits there? Puts his head in his hands like a child? You're his wife."

Emily sniffed softly, the sound carrying the texture of quiet endurance. "He's grieving too. And she's his mother. I can't ask him to fight every battle for me. I just wish he'd see how hard I'm trying."

Isla was silent a moment, and when she spoke again her tone was thoughtful, tinged with doubt.

"Em... maybe the problem isn't only Dorothy. Maybe it's Paul, too. If he can't stand up for you, if he can't stand up to his mother, then isn't he failing you just as much?"

Emily's breath caught. "Please don't say that," she whispered, and Isla could hear the wound in it. "He's all I have here. I can't... I can't think of him as part of the problem."

Isla closed her eyes, guilt pricking. "I'm sorry. You're right. He loves you. I know he does."

Emily smiled into the receiver, small and sad. "Thank you. I just needed someone to hear me."

She ended the call and sat very still in the darkened room.

~

From the landing, Paul lowered his phone, which he had used as a pretext to hover. He had caught enough of their conversation to hear the report of Dorothy's cruelty, Isla's outrage, Emily's muffled distress. His jaw tightened. For once, he felt something colder than guilt move through him. For one, he had some clarity.

He went to his mother's room without knocking. Dorothy was propped up in bed with a book she hadn't turned a page of in twenty minutes. She looked up, startled by the force in his step.

"Mother. Listen. If you don't like Emily caring for you," Paul said, his voice low and hard. "Then the other option is a care home."

Dorothy's mouth fell open. For a second she looked less like a matriarch than like a woman winded. "Paul..."

He held her gaze, unflinching. "Those are the choices. Think about them."

He shut the door gently but firmly, the kind of close that feels final.

In the hall, he passed Emily as she came out of the orchard room, and squeezed her hand.

"I've had a word with her," he said. "Given her something to think about if she's not happy with the way things are now."

He turned slowly and descended the stairs.

# 16

The kitchen smelled faintly of lemon polish and the ghost of yesterday's chicken. Afternoon light pressed against the glass, cold and unforgiving, painting long stripes across the tiled floor. Emily stood at the sink, her hands braced on the counter, shoulders rigid. Her breath came shallow and fast, each inhale catching high in her chest.

The most recent exchange had been nothing new. Another sharp word, another dismissal, another reminder from Dorothy that Emily's place here was provisional, tolerated, never quite welcome. For some reason, today, the words had lodged deeper, like a barb beneath the skin. She gripped the edge of the counter so hard her knuckles paled, the faint tremor in her fingers betraying the storm she refused to let surface.

The clock on the wall ticked steadily, each second a small cruelty. The sound filled the silence, marking the moment like an interrogation. Emily stared down at the sink, its porcelain gleaming, the water tap dripping once, twice. The room was so orderly, which was her doing, and yet still she felt chaos pressing against her ribs, threatening to spill if she loosened her grip.

For one dangerous instant, she let her face twist, raw and unguarded. Frustration, weariness, and anger lived there all at once, all the colours she never allowed the world to see. Her lips pressed thin, her eyes flashed with unshed tears. It was a private fury, silent and feral, contained only by force of will.

Paul's footsteps sounded in the hall and Emily closed her eyes once, deeply, as though submerging herself in cool water. When she opened them again, the expression was gone. She smoothed her hair back, wiped her palms on the tea towel, and turned, the gentle smile already in place.

Paul entered, loosening his tie, his face marked by the faint strain of another day spent splitting himself between obligations.

"Everything all right?" he asked, a distracted kindness, his gaze already drifting toward his phone.

Emily's smile softened, serene.

"Of course. Just tidying." She lifted the towel as proof, the picture of calm industry. "How was your day?"

He exhaled, relieved by her steadiness.

"Long," he admitted. He leaned over to kiss her cheek, his lips brushing the faint scent of soap and citrus. "But it's better now I'm home."

Emily's eyes glistened, but with warmth this time. "Good," she said softly. "That's all that matters."

He smiled back, weary but grateful, and left the room, humming under his breath as if the weight on his shoulders had been lightened by her gentleness.

When the door closed behind him, Emily turned back to the sink. Her hands lingered on the counter again, just for a heartbeat. But the fury had been folded away, locked beneath layers of composure. The clock ticked on.

~

Upstairs the air in Dorothy's old bedroom felt heavy, thickened by grief and age. Curtains drawn against the afternoon sun cast the room in dim shadow, and the faint smell of lavender sachets lingered from drawers that had not been opened in years.

Dorothy sat in her chair, Harold's photograph propped on the bedside table. His eyes, captured mid-squint in the summer light, stared back at her with the unfailing patience of the dead. She leaned closer, whispering to the glass as though he might hear through it.

"What shall I do, Harold?" Her voice wavered, brittle as paper. "She wants me gone. I know it."

Her fingers traced the frame, lingering on the edge as if gripping it might tether her to him. "She smiles at everyone, but I see the real her. Smiling isn't kindness, it's camouflage. She waits until Paul's not here to keep me safe, and then..." Dorothy's breath hitched. "Then I feel how the air changes. The house doesn't feel mine anymore."

She turned her head slowly, surveying the room. The wardrobe where Harold's suits still hung, faintly musty. The bed, too wide now, one side perfectly smooth each morning as if untouched by sleep. The walls themselves seemed to press closer, listening to her every mutter, waiting to betray her.

"I want my house back," she whispered, her voice breaking. "I don't feel safe here anymore, especially when Paul is at work. I hate being alone with her."

Her eyes darted to the door, half-expecting Emily to be standing there, calm and silent, ready with a tray of tea she hadn't asked for. She saw only the shadow of the landing, but her heart still beat too fast.

She turned back to Harold's photograph, clutching it in both hands.

"I'm so tired," she said, her head bowing. "I can't fight her forever. But I won't let her win. Not in our house. Not while I have breath left."

Dorothy t closed her eyes, the picture held against her chest. The house shifted around her in familiar creaks. To her, the sound was no longer comforting. It was the whisper of an enemy, waiting in the walls.

Dorothy let the photograph rest on her chest, her hands trembling slightly with the effort of holding it. For a long while she sat like that, eyes closed, listening to the house breathe its old, patient noises around her. She felt so brittle these days, so bound up in suspicion, that she almost startled herself when a gentler memory surfaced, unbidden, like a bird returning to a forgotten perch.

She saw Harold as he had been when Paul was small, with his sleeves rolled to the elbow, crouched in the garden teaching their boy how to kick a football without stumbling over his own feet. Harold's laugh, uncharacteristically loose, had carried all the way through the open kitchen window. Dorothy had been at the sink, washing lettuce for supper, pausing now and then just to watch them. She'd seen Paul come charging up to her afterwards, cheeks flushed, demanding lemonade and telling her that Daddy said he'd be a striker one day. She'd given him the biggest glass she could find, filled to the brim, and smoothed his hair back with a tenderness that made her throat ache even now.

Another memory came, of Christmas morning, the year Paul was seven. Harold had insisted on lighting the fire before stockings could be opened, and Dorothy had padded downstairs in her slippers, her dressing gown wrapped tight, laughing at his stubbornness. Paul had appeared halfway down the stairs, face alight with wonder, clutching his stocking as if it were treasure. Dorothy remembered kneeling on the rug beside him, feeling her own excitement mirrored in his eyes. She had kissed the crown of his head, inhaling the scent of sleep and boyish mischief, and Harold had caught her gaze with one of those quiet, knowing smiles that said, See? This is what matters.

Dorothy let out a shuddering breath. She had been softer then, and kinder, her sharp edges dulled by youth and hope. She had loved her husband, her boy, the life they were building together openly. The house had felt alive, full of warmth, of laughter that didn't echo back against silence. She remembered chasing Paul through the hall with a wooden spoon when he'd stolen biscuit dough, Harold chuckling from the doorway, arms folded.

She pressed her lips to Harold's photograph now, the glass cold against her skin.

"We were happy, weren't we?" she whispered. "Before the world got small, before I got old. Before everything turned into rules and battles."

Her throat tightened. She wondered when exactly she had become the woman her daughter-in-law described to her friend. When had she become so cantankerous, unyielding, and impossible. She wondered if she had traded kindness for control without noticing. Tears pricked her eyes, startling her with their heat.

"I miss that version of us," she confessed to Harold's frozen smile. "The one where I wasn't afraid of disappearing."

The words trembled into the dim room, fragile as cobwebs, and for a moment Dorothy felt the faintest flicker of her old self, of the woman who had been loved, who had laughed easily, who had held her child close and believed she was enough. But the moment passed. The shadows closed back in, and suspicion resumed its seat beside her, loyal and heavy. Dorothy set the photograph back on the table, aligning it with the lamp.

"I'll hold the line, Harold," she whispered. "I'll keep what's ours safe."

The softer woman faded, leaving only the one who feared she would soon be erased.

# 17

The city outside Paul's office window was a glittering circuit board, towers lit like circuitry, headlights streaming along roads that curved and bent like wires. From the twenty-second floor, it all looked almost orderly, as though chaos might be managed if you stood far enough above it. Inside, though, the office hummed with the restlessness of men and women who had long ago sold their evenings, and their souls, to the market.

Paul sat at his desk, the glow of spreadsheets flattening his face. Figures blurred into one another, columns rising and falling with a rhythm that made his eyes ache. Around him, colleagues moved quietly, in muffled footsteps across carpet, the clink of coffee cups, the rustle of jackets shrugged back on after midnight. Someone laughed low at a joke only fatigue could produce, but Paul didn't turn his head.

His phone buzzed once on the desk. He let it vibrate, then flipped it over without opening the screen. Later, when the spreadsheet cells danced too much to be trusted, he unlocked it. A row of messages waited, all from Emily.

18:10 – Just started dinner. Something warming tonight.

19:00 – Miss you. Don't be too late.

19:05 – Dinner will be ready at 8. I'll keep it hot if you're not back in time.

The clock on his monitor read 19:50. He wouldn't be back in time. Guilt pinched at his chest, brief and sharp, but he swallowed it. There was work still unfinished, and he told himself Emily knew that. She always knew. She managed, somehow, to keep the world running without complaint.

He set the phone face down again and told himself it was better not to answer than to offer false hope. He rubbed at his eyes, leaned back in his chair, and stared out at the grid of windows across the street, each one a square of someone else's exhaustion.

"She'll be fine," he muttered under his breath, though no one had asked. "She's always fine."

He bent back over the numbers until they blurred.

It was past midnight when Paul finally pulled into the gravel drive, tyres crunching, headlights glancing briefly across the apple tree before dying. The house loomed ahead, its windows mostly dark, but one lamp glowed in the hall, left on like a vigil. He carried his laptop bag inside and shut the door with exaggerated care, as if the house itself might scold him.

The silence was thick, broken only by the hum of the refrigerator. On the kitchen table a plate waited beneath a dome of foil, neatly labelled in Emily's hand with a sticky note. Enjoy. X. He peeled it back and the scent of casserole rose, comforting and accusing at once. He was too tired to eat, but the gesture pierced him. She had cooked, plated, covered, all without complaint, then gone to bed alone.

"Midnight feast?"

The voice came from the shadows. Paul started, turning. Dorothy sat in the armchair by the hall doorway, her cane propped against her knee. The lamp behind her threw her face into sharp relief, every line carved deep.

"So, you finally came home," she said, her tone dry as dust. "Looks like you hate being here as much as I do."

Paul sighed, dragging a hand over his face. "Mum, please. Not now."

"Not now," she echoed. "Always not now. You leave me with her all day, come home when the house is asleep, and expect me not to notice. Do you think I don't see how you can't bear it here?"

Her words hit their mark, but he refused to let them land. He picked up his bag and brushed past, muttering.

"I'm going to bed, Mum. You should, too."

Dorothy watched him mount the stairs, her lips pressed thin, her eyes sharp with something between victory and despair. When his door closed upstairs, she sat back, her hands trembling faintly on the arms of the chair.

Upstairs, Emily lay still in bed, her eyes open, listening to the faint murmur of voices below until the silence returned.

She had left the lamp in the hall burning deliberately, as she always did. Paul's lateness no longer surprised her. She had measured the silence in the house, counted each minute past eight o'clock, and known exactly how the evening would unfold.

She heard his voice downstairs, low and weary, Dorothy's sharper reply, the muted scrape of his footsteps on the stairs. She closed her eyes briefly, arranging her expression into one of drowsy half-sleep. When he entered, she wanted him to see not reproach but serenity.

The door opened. His weight shifted onto the carpet, his sigh filling the room. Emily remained still, her breathing slow, even. She felt the dip of the mattress as he sat, the faint rustle of his tie being tugged loose. He sat there for a long moment, elbows on his knees, his head in his hands.

Emily opened her eyes just enough to let the lamplight shape her profile into the soft, peaceful, expression of a devoted wife. She did not speak. She did not need to. Her silence, patient and uncomplaining, would be answer enough.

Paul lay down at last, the mattress dipping, his arm brushing hers.

"Sorry," he whispered into the dark, though he wasn't sure if he meant for being late, for leaving her to Dorothy, or for something larger he could not name.

Emily's lips curved faintly, her eyes still closed. She let the word hang in the quiet between them like a fragile offering. She would accept it in the morning, when he needed her to. For now, she simply lay still, the picture of grace under pressure, while inside her chest a private calculation ticked on.

The clock downstairs struck once, and she finally let herself drift into sleep.

# 18

It happened on a quiet Thursday, the sort of afternoon that pretends nothing can go wrong. Dorothy stood at the counter with the blue pot beside her like a talisman, as the kettle murmured towards the boil. She had come down without calling. She liked to do for herself, to prove she still could. The teaspoon trembled faintly in her fingers as she set it on the saucer. She told the tremor to mind its manners.

The kettle clicked off. Dorothy reached for it and felt, first, the surge of its weight and then a bloom of breathlessness that seemed to open inside her chest like an umbrella. The room tilted by a degree. A small black moth of dizziness fluttered at the edge of her sight.

She placed the kettle back down too quickly and its base kissed the hotplate with an indelicate clatter. Her hand went to the counter, then slid a little. There was dampness under her palm she didn't remember leaving. The blue pot blurred in front of her. Not now, she thought, both furious and frightened at once. Then her knees folded as if commanded by an old order, and she sat hard on the cold tile, breath trapped high in her throat.

Emily heard the sound from the pantry and was in the doorway at once. The sight made her heart lurch. Dorothy sat small on the floor, braced against the cupboard, the colour leached from her face to match the white of her knuckles.

"Dorothy," Emily said, kneeling, voice low as water. "It's all right. I've got you. Just stay where you are a second."

"Don't fuss," Dorothy snapped, the words coming out in a brittle whisper that tried to sound like command.

"I won't," Emily promised, already slipping one arm steady at Dorothy's back, the other braced under her forearm. "We'll do this your way. Slowly, okay?"

Together they made a careful geometry of movement, with Emily anchoring and pivoting and Dorothy pushing with what strength she could find, breath hissing through her teeth. In small stages, they reached the chair by the kitchen door. Dorothy lowered herself into it like a woman trying to win a bet with gravity. Her chest ticked with shallow breaths and a tiny muscle jumped repeatedly in her jaw.

Emily fetched water, the glass held with an outward calm that belied the prickle of fear in her scalp. She'd learned to move without spooking the moment.

"Have a sip, if you can." She offered the glass and Dorothy swatted the air, as if batting away a wasp.

"I said, don't fuss."

"I'm not fussing," Emily said, setting the glass within reach anyway. "Just parking it there."

Dorothy looked smaller than she had yesterday. The pallor wasn't the chalk of anger, it was the grey that comes when the body is busy elsewhere. Emily wanted to press the back of her hand to Dorothy's forehead like the mothers do in films. Instead, she kept her hands in her lap and watched the rise and fall of Dorothy's chest and counted to sixty twice.

"I'm going to get Paul," she said, as gently as she could. "I'll be two minutes."

Dorothy closed her eyes, the concession disguised as disdain. "If you must."

Emily crossed the hall at speed without sounding like she was rushing, climbed the back stairs two at a time, and found Paul in the little room they called a study, bent over his laptop with the expression of a man trying to balance an equation that refused to equalise.

"She's had a moment in the kitchen," Emily said, pitched calm. "She's sitting now, but I'd like you to come."

He was on his feet before the sentence finished. "What do you mean 'a moment'?" He brushed past her with his heart in his mouth, nearly tripping on the runner at the top of the stairs. In the kitchen he went pale at the sight of Dorothy in the chair.

"Mum." The word broke in the middle like a twig.

"I don't need mollycoddling," Dorothy said at once, hauling herself upright in the chair as if posture could banish biology. "You can both leave me alone. I merely sat down. People do."

"You were on the floor," Paul said, panic trying to muscle itself into decision. "We should call someone."

"I'll ring the surgery," Emily cut in, gentling the urgency before it could escalate into ambulance lights. "Ask for a visit. You don't need hospital, Dorothy. You need to rest and to let us help you."

Dorothy's eyes flashed. "Do not speak to me as if I were a child in a pushchair."

"I wouldn't dare," Emily said, with a small almost-smile that asked the moment to unclench. "But I am going to call the doctor. And then I'm going to walk you back to your room."

They made the journey from kitchen to the newly established library-bedroom like a procession. Slow and deliberate, two steps and pause. Emily kept one hand at the small of Dorothy's back and one at her elbow. Paul hovered, ineffectual, wanting to carry her and not knowing how to ask. In the library, Emily settled Dorothy into the high-backed chair by the window that caught the river's light when it had any to give, and tucked a pillow behind her without comment.

"Phone the GP," Emily said, to Paul, without looking away from Dorothy. "Tell them we need to come in today."

"I am not an emergency," Dorothy said, chin lifted, but the skin at her mouth had the pinched look of someone trying not to flinch.

"You are my mother," Paul said, and Emily saw him working to make the sentence sound like permission rather than possession. He stepped into the hall with his mobile already ringing.

Emily poured the water from the glass into a small china cup, knowing that Dorothy tolerated cups better than glasses, and offered it again. This time Dorothy took it, the fine tremor in her fingers making the surface dimple.

"I simply stood up too fast," she said, wanting a story that did not use the word weakness.

"Of course," Emily said.

By the time Paul returned, Dorothy's breathing had eased into a more even tide.

"They'll send someone out this afternoon," he said. "Dr Ahmed. Or the locum. They're short-staffed."

"They always are," Dorothy said, and Emily could not tell whether it was compassion or condemnation.

Emily stood, smoothing the blanket across Dorothy's knees. "Shall I make tea?" she asked lightly.

Dorothy's mouth shaped a no and then paused, as if the energy for refusal cost more than the tea would.

"If you must," she said. "Strong. In the blue pot." The words were a creed. Emily nodded and left, her footsteps measured, leaving Paul in the chair opposite his mother, holding his hands palm-up as if waiting to receive an instruction.

"I don't want mollycoddling," Dorothy said again, more tired now. "I want to be left alone to do things my way."

"I know," Paul said. He didn't. He wanted to, but he didn't.

He stared at the door through which Emily had vanished and felt the shape of his guilt the way a tongue finds a sore tooth. He looked back at his mother. She had closed her eyes and for a moment she looked like the woman in the old photos on the stairs, only with the colour drained out. The thought frightened him more than the fall.

Dr Ahmed arrived just before four with rain still jewelling his coat. He carried the small case that looks like every GP's case and has, across decades, contained different miracles. He had the manners of a man who had been in enough drawing rooms to know where people kept the good lamps. Emily met him in the hall and took his coat with a smile that reached for steadiness rather than charm.

"Thank you for coming," she said. "She's in the library."

Dorothy had composed herself, as much out of pride as discomfort. She would not be found dishevelled. The blanket was folded so its edge ran straight, the cup centred on the saucer, the line of her mouth set for visitors.

"Mrs Mercer," Dr Ahmed said, warm but not familiar. He washed his hands with the gel he produced from his pocket in an act that remained faintly theatrical even after years of habit and sat on the chair Emily pushed into place without being asked. The stethoscope was warm from his pocket when he looped it to his ears.

"Let's have a listen."

Dorothy opened the buttons of her cardigan with slow dignity and breathed as instructed. Deeply, then again. The bell of the stethoscope made small cold circles on her back and front. He watched her face as much as his watch, counting not just breaths but effort.

"Any pain?" he asked, palping her ankles, checking for the indentations a thumb leaves in waterlogged tissue. "In the chest? In the ribs? Back?"

"Only from being interrogated," Dorothy said. A faint tremor had crept into her wit.

"Mm," he said, the sound neither assent nor rebuke. He checked her pulse, its rhythm a quiet argument. He asked about appetite and sleep and the steps between rooms. He asked about pills, which and when, how many, with food, without.

Emily sat slightly behind him and to the side, present but not presiding. When Dorothy fell silent, either from fatigue or defiance, Emily supplied a word or two.

"The breathlessness is worse in the mornings," she said. "She's more unsteady later in the day." She kept her voice gentle, as if speaking too loudly might bruise.

"We were wondering," Paul added, perched awkwardly on the edge of the bed as if he didn't trust himself to sit properly. "Whether the medication is... still right."

Dr Ahmed nodded. He removed the stethoscope and let it hang, doctor-like, about his neck.

"Mrs Mercer," he said, addressing Dorothy as the sovereign she required him to recognise, "I think what you felt in the kitchen was a combination of things. Your lungs are working harder than they once did. Your body is telling you it needs to go slower."

"My body is disobedient," Dorothy said. "It should be told to behave."

He smiled, quickly, and then sobered. "We can adjust some

medicines to help with the breathlessness. You've had dexamethasone before..." He glanced at Emily, who nodded once. "...to reduce the inflammation around the tumour and make breathing easier. I'd like to increase the dose a little for a short while and see if that buys you some comfort."

Dorothy sniffed. "Steroids make me hungry. I don't want to grow fat and lazy."

"It's about easing the work your chest is doing," he said. "Not about appetite. And only for a time." He hesitated, the next part weighed before he offered it. "You mentioned aches in your hip last week."

"That was walking on bad paving," Dorothy said at once.

"It may be that the cancer treatment has become more troublesome in the bones," he said carefully. "We often use a medicine called a bisphosphonate, a zoledronic acid, to strengthen the bones and reduce pain. It can help. We can organise it without you needing to go into hospital. A community nurse can offer infusion at home, or we can consider an oral alternative if that's easier to tolerate. Given how frail you've been feeling, I'm inclined to treat presumptively rather than drag you in for scans you don't want."

Dorothy's eyes flashed with offence at the word frail and with relief at no hospital.

"I'll not be poked and prodded," she said. "If the thing helps, fine. But I won't sit in corridors."

"We'll keep it simple," he said. "We'll also add something to protect your stomach while you're on the steroid. And, this is as important as any prescription, you must rest. No overexertion. Short walks in the house. Sit to do things you'd normally stand for. Let people bring you tea."

"Everyone talks to me as if I were ninety-six," Dorothy muttered. "I am not a china doll. Do not pat me."

"No patting," Dr Ahmed said mildly. "Only the occasional

telling-off." He looked to Emily and Paul. "I'll leave a plan. We'll review in a week by phone, sooner if there's any change."

"Thank you," Paul said, too quickly, gratitude the first thing he knew how to offer when he felt useless. He stood as if to shepherd the GP out and then hovered, uncertain, realising the consultation had not finished watching him.

Emily rose. "Tea?" she said. "Or will you let me send you away with a coffee to keep you from falling asleep at the wheel?"

"Tea would make my afternoon respectable," he said, and if there was a flicker of relief in his eyes at the promise of being cared for, it was the relief of a man who has sat in too many rooms where the kettle was an enemy. Emily went to the kitchen, and the GP watched her go, then turned back to Dorothy with a few last practicalities about doses, timing, when to call. Dorothy answered in clipped syllables, the edge in her voice disguising fatigue.

In the hall, when he'd shrugged back on his coat, the GP paused beside Paul. He kept his voice low.

"She's very weak," he said, not unkindly. "The lung disease is advancing, I'm afraid. We'll aim for comfort and stability. The steroid should ease the breathlessness. The zoledronic acid may help the ache, if that's what it is. No sense in chasing proof if treatment will be the same."

Paul swallowed, the words rearranging his insides. "Right."

Dr Ahmed's gaze flicked to the kitchen, where Emily was clearing away the tea things, then back.

"She's a rock, your wife," he said simply. "Steady hands. If you've got someone like that in the house, you're fortunate." He didn't see the way the compliment dug under Paul's ribs and stayed there, or the way praise for Emily sometimes felt like a verdict on him.

The moment was pushed aside as Emily came back through to the hall.

"We'll make sure she takes it easy," she said, reassuring and calm.

Dorothy watched the three of them as if they were actors who had learned their lines too well.

"If anyone says 'rest' to me again," she murmured, "I shall scream."

Emily smiled, the corners of her mouth steady.

"We won't say it then," she said. "We'll simply engineer that you get it."

Dorothy gave her a long, narrow look.

"You do enough engineering anyway," she said. The bite in it was real, but the voice carried less force than it had that morning.

"Doctor," Emily said, turning the attention neatly. "Before you go. Her memory's been... slippery." She kept the word kind. "Keys misplaced, that sort of thing. Repeating a story and being surprised she's told it. More sundowning, if that's the term."

Dorothy's chin came up. "My memory is excellent," she said, then faltered. "I think."

"It would be surprising if it weren't worse when she's tired," Dr Ahmed said. "Illness makes the brain economical. We can look at a small adjustment to her medication to take the edge off the agitation in the evenings. Nothing heavy. And routine will be your friend." He looked at Emily as he said it, and it came out as praise.

When he had gone, the house absorbed the absence like a sponge. Rain began again, tapping at the window with the delicacy of a visitor not sure of their welcome. Emily went back to the kitchen and dried the last of the cups quietly. Paul stood for a moment in the hall with the GP's words in his ears. She's very weak, he'd said. Advanced. Comfort. Your wife is a rock. The words bounced into all the parts of himself that wanted to argue and wanted to cry and wanted to be told precisely what to do. He went to the library doorway and watched his mother watching the river.

"Do you want anything?" he asked, hating the stupidity of the question as it left his mouth.

"For everyone to stop asking me what I want, and not bothering to listen to the reply," Dorothy said, but without heat.

He crossed to her, bent, and kissed her hair. It smelled of lavender and shampoo.

"I'll be in the next room," he said, as if proximity were competence.

When he'd gone, Emily returned with another cup, just hot water this time, lemon slice floating on the surface like a small sun.

"No tea," she said. "The doctor will tell me off for the caffeine."

Dorothy took it, fingers warmer now.

"You like being told you do things well," she said, a scalpel of a sentence slid under the skin of a fact.

Emily's smile didn't slip. "Everyone does."

Dorothy let the steam touch her face. She felt older than she had an hour ago. The chair had deepened around her shape. She looked at the door where Dr Ahmed had stood and at the garden where Harold had pruned and fallen, and then at the woman who moved through her rooms as if they were her own.

"I don't want to be fussed over," she said, voice threadbare.

"Then let's call it something else," Emily said. "We'll call it company."

Dorothy closed her eyes. She was too tired to argue and too proud to agree. Back in the kitchen, Emily set the steroid blister pack by the fruit bowl where Dorothy could resent it daily in full view. She wrote the new times on a notepad in a hand like tidy scaffolding and fixed it to the fridge with the apple-shaped magnet. She moved calmly, leaving no trace of hurry, no shadow of triumph. If you watched closely enough, you might have seen her fingertips tremble once before she pressed them flat against the cool door and smoothed the paper into certainty.

In the library, Dorothy opened her eyes and found the river again, darker now, the surface corrugated by rain. She pictured the blue pot in the kitchen, the cup on her table, the record player silent in the corner. She admitted nothing aloud. But the thought came anyway, treacherous and soft. It would be easier if I were kinder. It brushed her like a wing and was gone.

## 19

The café off the Outer Circle had always felt like a secret, the kind of place you stumbled upon one winter and then pretended you'd known forever. Regent's Park lay just beyond the steamed windows, trees black-laced against a pewter sky, the boating lake a dull mirror. Inside, the room was small, warm, and mostly quiet. Two students were bent over laptops, a woman with a pram was bouncing her foot to keep time with a sleeping child, and a pair of baristas conducting their work in murmurs, as if noise were a currency to be frugal with.

Isla was there first, thawing her hands around a flat white and watching London rearrange itself in the glass. She recognised Emily the instant the door pushed open with her tidy silhouette, composed mouth, and the gentle way she stepped over the threshold as though she'd promised the room not to disturb it. A gust of outside followed her in, all cold air, car fumes, and a distant bark, and then the door sighed shut and the café received her with a low hum of welcome.

"Sorry I'm late," Emily said, unwinding a scarf, the apology automatic and unruffled. "Dorothy decided she didn't want breakfast after all, only to change her mind at the last minute."

Isla laughed, because that was what you did when Emily made her domestic comments.

"You look lovely," she said, hugging her, registering at once the thinness under the coat, the fretwork of tiredness at the eyes that didn't quite break the surface. "And cold."

"I'm always cold now," Emily said lightly, rubbing her hands together. "I think the house has winter in the walls."

They found a corner table beneath a dusty fern. Isla ordered for them, the way she always did, coffees, one slice of almond cake "for us to pretend we'll share". For a few minutes they did the lighter dance of conversation. Isla had an impossible client who had mistaken a grievance for a crusade, and a new associate at her firm who wore brogues like armour. Emily smiled in the right places, supplied little glances and hums that made Isla feel, despite herself, like the fascinating one.

And then, as if the air changed pressure around them, Emily lowered her voice and folded her hands around her cup.

"I haven't told you the latest," she said. "The GP's been. He's adjusted some medicines, more steroids. And he's given her something else he says strengthens bones. Zoledronic acid." She handled the words like cutlery, careful not to stab. "He thinks the cancer might have spread."

Isla's throat completed a small, private swallow.

"I'm so sorry," she said. The phrase felt tinny and necessary, the way all the right phrases do. "How is she?"

"Fierce," Emily said with a smile that almost convinced. "And afraid. Not that she'd call it that." She paused, and the pause was a cliff-edge. "Sometimes I wish it would just... end," she said, scarcely louder than the hiss from the milk wand. "Her cancer has spread and she's in so much pain... it's hard to see her like that, it's cruel really."

The words landed on the table with no clatter, but Isla felt them vibrate through her bones all the same. She blinked. In the shock of the sentence she had the absurd thought that the fern above them was listening.

Emily's face changed almost at once, as if she'd heard herself from the outside. She laughed quickly, not unkindly, a small apology stamped with charm.

"Listen to me. That sounds awful, doesn't it? I'm not wishing her dead. God... I only mean... I wish the suffering would end. For her. For Paul. For all of us. The house feels like a sickroom sometimes..." She exhaled, shook her head. "But that's the stress talking."

Isla forced her own smile to behave. "It's understandable," she said. The word tasted uncertain. "Watching someone you love suffer. It scrapes at you."

Emily nodded, gaze lowered, fingers fussing at a sugar packet she would not use. "It's ugly, seeing someone so diminished. She hates being helped. She hates *me* helping. It turns every small kindness into a contest I have to lose just to keep the peace." She looked up then, eyes bright with unshed tears. "And I keep thinking how relieved everyone would be if...." She stopped herself with a soft click of her tongue. "Ignore me. I sound like a monster."

"You don't," Isla said at once. "You sound like someone at the end of tether." Even as she said it, something in her chest tightened, as if a hand had closed around a thread and tugged. The particular phrasing of 'I wish it would just end' clung. She could file it under mercy or she could file it under weariness, but somehow it refused to file neatly.

Isla moved the conversation into the lanes she knew better, like logistics, options, and plans.

"Have you thought about bringing more support into the house?" she asked. "A Macmillan nurse. Respite care. Anything that gives you, and her, boundaries."

"She'd call it invasion," Emily said. "She already calls the GP's visits a parade. And she complains about the district nurse as if she were a kid who'd kicked her cat. If I suggested another nurse, she'd barricade the library with the wingback chair."

"So, you let her be queen of the hill," Isla said gently. "And you run supplies up to the castle."

"Exactly," Emily said, and the agreement sounded both proud and exhausted. "I've become excellent at siege warfare."

"Emily." Isla heard her own voice soften into something like plea. "You need looking after, too."

"I've got you," Emily said, a quick flare of warmth. "And Paul. In his way." She tilted her head at herself. "And the house has its built-in routines that tell me what to do, if I listen. Keep the linens hot. Write the times and doses of medicines. Put the water within reach. Remove the rugs that slide and leave the ones that stick. Tidiness is a language Dorothy understands, and it keeps us from speaking the other one."

A child at the neighbouring table squeaked in sleep and then sighed. The barista set the almond cake down and the sound of the plate summoned them both back to the room. Emily used the fork like a pen, tracing a line in the crumbs.

"What would you do," she asked suddenly, her voice gone small. "If you were me? If nothing changed."

Isla took a breath that felt like a decision.

"I'd insist on help," she said. "Not for you, for her. So that refusing it feels less like punishing you. I'd start making the doctor's words louder than yours, and Paul's louder than anybody's. And I'd be honest with Paul about how late nights and silence make all this worse. He can't outsource her care to you."

Emily's mouth tipped. "He has a talent for assuming I'm all right."

"Because you're excellent at acting all right," Isla said, and heard the crispness she used in court intrude. She softened it at once. "I know why you do it. But if you don't give him your edges, he'll keep admiring your polish."

Emily laughed, properly, this time, and the relief of it moved through both of them like heat.

"You should put that on a mug," she said. She took a bite of cake and then another. "I just miss us, sometimes," she added, the words floating to the surface of their talk like something honest that didn't know how to hide. "The way me and Paul were before the house, before the hospital, before every conversation was a programme we had to stick to."

"Then book a change in the programme that's only yours," Isla said. "A night in London. A hotel room. No phones. I'll sit on your house like a dragon."

"Dorothy would call you vulgar," Emily said, and the joke landed where it should. They smiled at each other, a quick, clean flash of the friendship that had outlasted jobs and flats and lovers with bad ideas.

Still, when Emily went to the counter to pay, Isla watched her in profile and felt that small tightening again. *Sometimes I wish it would just end.* The phrase returned like a song you hadn't realised you'd learned, and no amount of rationalising scrubbed it out.

Outside, they walked a circuit of the park, collars turned up, the wind flicking hair into eyes. Emily tucked her hand into Isla's elbow, and they looked, to anyone passing, like women whose problems were manageable and whose coats were warm enough. They parted at the tube entrance with a long hug that both of them extended by a second and neither mentioned.

On the escalator down, Isla stared at the chequerboard of adverts and felt loyalty and suspicion do their familiar tug-of-war. She chose loyalty in public, but suspicion rode home with her, quiet as a thought you promise you will not say aloud. She would visit at the weekend, she decided, and she would watch. If there was anything to see beyond exhaustion and fear, she would be the one to see it. She owed Emily that, and she owed the truth whatever shape it chose.

Evening drew itself over Bray with the practised grace of a curtain that has always known its cue. The river ran black and low, and somewhere along the bank someone burned damp wood that sent up a reluctant smoke. In the kitchen the lights were warm, and the oven slow and obedient. Emily moved with her tidy choreography, filling a saucepan, chopping onion and fennel. She made a fish pie because it was gentle, because Dorothy had once almost hinted she liked it, and because it sat kindly on a tired stomach and tasted of patience. Parsley, a little lemon, a breadcrumb top that would go to gold and stop there. She made a salad for Paul, who had already texted to say he'd be late, in case his appetite remembered him, and filled a jug of water.

The house had learned to keep its volume low in the evenings. Even the clock in the hall seemed to tick with manners. Emily set three places at the smaller table because the dining room made everything sound like a performance, and because she still hoped Paul would come home in time to join them. She carried the plates through and placed them just so. She could feel, without turning, when Dorothy had entered. The air altered, static gathered, the faint contact of cane to floorboards felt like a military percussion.

Dorothy sat with a care she disguised as disdain. Her face wore the colour of winter. Emily set the plate before her.

"If you'd prefer something else," she said. "Please just say. I can do an omelette."

Dorothy looked at the pie, at the steam, at the little island of parsley where the crust dipped. She lifted her fork, pressed it into the surface, then withdrew as if she'd tested the strength of a bridge and found it suspect.

"I'm not hungry," she said, but did not push the plate away. Not yet.

Paul was late enough that his absence felt like an excuse. He arrived at last with apologies in his pockets, shrugging off the cold, his hair damp with drizzle, face closed in its apologies. He kissed his mother, then kissed Emily's temple, and both touches felt like something to be corrected later.

"Smells amazing," he said, as he sat, and tried for normal. "Did you see the swans?" he asked. "Two of them by the gate as I came in. Looking as if they own the river."

"They do own it," Dorothy said. "Nature ignores deeds and contracts."

Emily passed him the bowl of salad and he took it as if accepting a verdict. For a minute they ate in a quiet that might have passed for peace if you didn't know how to listen. The pie yielded generously. Emily watched for the small signs, like Dorothy's mouth softening when the taste was right, the second spoonful taken without fuss. They did not appear.

"Not eating?" Paul asked gently when Dorothy's fork hovered and then fell. "Do you want something else? Toast? Yogurt?"

Dorothy pushed the plate three inches from her and spoke as if confiding to the table, voice pitched perfectly to reach the one person it needed to.

"I'm not eating her food anymore," she said. "Lord knows what she's put in it."

The words were so quiet and so corrosive that even the clock in the hall seemed to stall. Emily's hand paused, mid-reach for the water jug. It was the smallest of pauses, a blink of a gesture, and then she poured as if nothing had been said. The water hit the glass with its polite music. Paul's face went slack, then tightened, then did its usual thing of choosing softness.

"Mum," he said, the warning gentle to the point of mitigation. "That's not fair."

"It's not fair," Dorothy agreed, eyes on Emily. "It's not fair to be forced to eat from a hand you don't trust."

Emily set the jug down carefully, fingers dry on the handle, no betraying slick of sweat. Her voice, when it came, was even as a chalk line.

"I can bring you bread from the tin and butter it in front of you," she said. "Or fruit. Or a packaged yogurt with the lid you can peel yourself. You don't have to take anything I've touched."

The options should have sounded barbed. They landed like mercy. For a heartbeat Dorothy looked caught between humiliation and relief. Then pride found its footing. "I'll have yogurt," she said. "Closed."

"Of course," Emily said, rising at once, her chair making the small, non-abrasive noise she'd taught it to make. She moved through to the kitchen with that signature economy leaving Paul at the table with his mouth open on a sentence that wouldn't decide whether to defend or scold.

"Mum," he tried again, quieter. "You can't say things like that."

Dorothy turned her face towards him and in it, Paul saw, for half a second, the woman from the photographs on the stairs, the girl who had worn pearls like a joke and laughed with her mouth open. The illusion vanished.

"You don't see her like I do," she said, each word precisely placed. "You never see what's in front of your nose, you stupid man. You're weak. Your father always said so."

The last line landed with the weight of an heirloom. Paul

flinched as if she'd thrown something. There were many things he could have absorbed. The first insult, even the second. Not that one. His cheeks coloured in two separate patches as the child in him sat up and reached for an old shield that wasn't there.

"Dorothy," Emily said from the doorway, not Mum, not Mrs Mercer, just the name, a thread offered. She carried the tea on a small tray as if it might change its mind. "Here you are." She set the yogurt pot down in front of Dorothy and had the grace, or the cunning, to place her body briefly between mother and son, to make her frame a screen.

"Paul," she said without turning. "Would you mind checking the back door? It slammed earlier. I think the bolt's loose."

It was not. He went anyway, because the alternative was to sit in the heat of his own woundedness and say something that would ferment. In the utility room, he stood with his hands on the cool enamel of the sink and breathed until the ache behind his breastbone turned from sharp to dull. He heard voices, Emily's low and Dorothy's clipped, and he could not tell, through the walls, whether they were arguing or arriving at a truce.

At the table, Emily poured with a hand that did not shake. "Water?"

Dorothy hesitated, then nodded, the nod a concession disguised as disdain. Emily pushed the glass closer. Dorothy took it.

"I don't poison people," Emily said softly, and the sentence should have sounded ridiculous. It didn't. "And I won't make you eat when you don't want to. I will, however, insist that you have something. For your own sake."

Dorothy blew at the surface and took the tiniest sip, as if hoping to condemn it and being thwarted by it being perfect.

"You twist things," she said, but it lacked teeth. "You stand there making me feel impossible."

"You don't need my help with that," Emily said, and the ghost of a smile crossed her face so quickly it could have been a trick of the lamplight.

Paul came back in, the bolt pronounced sound. He sat and tried to be a man again.

"I'm sorry," Dorothy said suddenly, and both of them looked at her as if a new person had entered the room. She let them look for a second and then clarified.

"I'm sorry this is the part of our life you'll remember," she said to her son. "The bit with the teaspoons and the pills. Not the cricket on the lawn."

Paul's mouth opened and closed.

"I remember the cricket," he said, and the words came out as if they were being dusted off.

"Do you?" Dorothy said, and the faintest grief in her tone was more dangerous than any cruelty. "Then remember I taught you to hold the bat high."

"You did," he said. "You did."

They ate a little more. Or rather, Paul did, contriving forks of pie and salad that he barely tasted, chewing because chewing could be mistaken for a truce. Dorothy sipped tea and frowned at a crumb that had attached itself to the table with the determination of a barnacle. Emily stood to fetch a cloth, smoothed it away, and the entire universe of the room seemed to calm by a degree. She had learned that the sight of a stain being erased soothed Dorothy more than most apologies.

When it was done, Emily cleared plates and Paul reached to help, and she shook her head with a small, neat gesture that saved him from having to perform competence in front of his mother.

"I'll do it," she said. "You sit. Talk to each other."

"About what," Dorothy said, not a question.

"Tell him the story about the time you made Harold take the boat out in a storm and he pretended he wasn't frightened," Emily said. "I like that one." She vanished into the kitchen and left them with an anecdote shaped like a bridge.

Dorothy looked at the water as if it might supply the first line, and then she began. The telling steadied her. Even bitterness can be charmed by a narrative that remembers how to land. Paul listened and laughed, and the laugh was cracked but serviceable. In the kitchen, Emily stood at the sink with her hands in warm water until the sting behind her eyes obeyed.

Later, when Dorothy had gone to her room, Paul found Emily in the pantry folding the good cloth napkins in thirds and then in thirds again. He touched her shoulder. She looked up and, in her face, he found exactly what he needed. There was no reproach, only the quietness of a woman who had already absorbed the day's damage and filed it in a drawer marked Deal With Gently.

"She said..." he began.

"I heard," Emily said. "She's frightened. She hurts. It makes her mean."

He nodded, grateful for the script. "I should have defended you."

"You did," she said, and the lie was kind enough to be true for ten seconds. "You told her it wasn't fair."

He laughed once, a sound like a chip in a plate. "That's not much, is it."

"It's something," she said. "And I would rather you be soft with her than hard. Your softness is why I married you."

He wanted to argue with that. He wanted to present his case, with footnotes and annexes, but the warmth of it did what warmth does. He bent his head, and she let him rest it against her shoulder, the way one does with someone who has not learned how to be held without apologising for the weight.

In her room, Dorothy sat on the edge of the bed and looked at the slice of corridor visible through the half-open door. She had said something unforgivable. She had meant it, at the time. She did not know if that helped. She told herself, stubbornly, that suspicion was a form of vigilance. It made her feel safer than gratitude did. She lay down and pulled the covers up, as if defending her body from an unseen draft, and closed her eyes.

# 20

The police arrived mid-afternoon. In the hour when the house usually slept, when the rain had taken a breath and the river lay flat as tin. Emily had set the morning room as if for a well-behaved tea, with coasters, tissues, and the blue pot poised on its tray like an obedient dog. But when Detective Inspector Rawlings and DC Patel stepped through the doorway, the china felt suddenly like stage props.

Rawlings removed his hat, rain pinpricks stippling the crown. He had the same deliberate calm as before, a manner that said we are all reasonable people here as though it was a test. Patel, neat as ever, balanced her laptop on her knee once they were seated, the machine's small glow washing her hands.

"Thank you for seeing us again, Mr and Mrs Mercer. Mrs Mercer." Rawlings gave each of them that even look, the one that took a quiet measure. "We won't take long."

"What is there left to ask?" Dorothy said, chin high, cardigan buttoned. A paler version of herself sat in the chair by the window, but her voice had kept its edge. "My husband fell. His heart failed. The end."

Rawlings nodded once, as if acknowledging a line he had

read in a file. "We've had further footage from your neighbour," he said, turning a page in his notebook. "Mr and Mrs Latimer have a camera angled towards the lane and the side gate. In addition to the person loitering, which we discussed, there is a sequence, two nights later, in which a hooded figure appears to enter the property via the side gate." His eyes lifted. "And, from what we can tell, they enter the house."

Silence arranged itself around the sentence. The blue pot, absurdly, seemed to listen harder.

"A break-in?" Paul said at last, the words catching. "There was no break-in. Nothing was..." He searched the room for evidence of undisturbed continuity in the clock, the rug, the piano. "Mum never reported anything."

"That's correct," Patel said, her voice even. "There's no record."

Dorothy gave a wet, contemptuous breath. "Because it didn't happen," she said. "The cameras are wrong. Or your neighbour is bored and has decided to make himself interesting."

Rawlings's pen paused. "Mrs Mercer," he said, gentler than the title sounded, "I'm not suggesting anyone's lying. Only that we have images we need to understand. The gate appears to open, and someone enters, and then the recording cuts, which is fine, because it's motion-activated, and then resumes with the gate closing outward. We cannot see the interior of the house. That's why we're here."

Paul looked at Emily. He couldn't help it. His eyes went to her the way water finds the lowest point. Her expression was composed, brows drawn slightly as if working to align facts in a way that wouldn't frighten anyone.

"The week before Dad's fall, we were in Italy," Paul said. "We landed the day he fell." He stalled on the pit of the word happened. "We weren't here."

"And we didn't come here between," Emily added softly. "We

went straight from Heathrow to London. Then the hospital, after Robert's call." She folded her hands together in her lap. "If someone went in, only Harold or Dorothy could have known."

"Quite," Rawlings said. He let the agreement lie a moment and then, carefully, turned to Dorothy.

"Mrs Mercer. Were you aware of anyone entering the house that week? Does anyone else have keys?"

Dorothy's mouth tightened. "I was aware," she said. "Of running my home as I have always done. Which is to say, properly. No one entered without my knowledge. This is Bray, Inspector, not the docks. People knock here."

Patel's fingertips made a quiet, practical rattle on her keys.

"We've cross-checked deliveries," she said. "No one else in the road had contractors or other visitors."

"The side gate sticks," Paul said, strangled. "you've got to know the knack to the latch. Perhaps Dad called someone to fix it."

Rawlings inclined his head. "We saw that. It seemed to open easily in the footage."

Dorothy leaned forward, a small flare of triumph at last. "So there you are. Some child pushing it, a fox, perhaps."

"A figure," Patel said, not unkindly. "Not a fox."

Dorothy's eyes found Emily, and for a second the old suspicion gathered itself, the way a cat coils before deciding whether to spring.

"I tell you there was no break-in," she said. "I think I should know."

Paul sat forward, alarmed by the tone, and touched the arm of his mother's chair.

"Mum," he murmured. The endearment was both warning and plea for her to be careful, to let him help keep her story straight. He had learned to hear the slips, the little gaps in her testimony that could be chalked up to tiredness or to pride, and he loved her fiercely for both. "We don't need to argue with them."

Rawlings eased them out of it as if removing a branch from a stream. "The footage is only part of it," he said, turning a page. "There are other questions." He glanced at Patel, who picked up the thread.

"On the day of Mr Mercer's fall," she said. "We have ambulance timings, phone records, statements. We're confirming who was present in the house before the paramedics arrived."

"Dorothy," Emily said at once, and her voice wore tenderness like a shawl. "And Robert, the neighbour. He crossed from next door when Dorothy found Harold. He called Paul from the garden. We came straight from London."

Rawlings nodded. "Mr Yates's account matches. Mr Mercer senior was alone in the garden when he fell?"

"Yes," Dorothy said. "We do not stand in the garden by committee."

"Had he been unwell that morning?" Patel asked. "Dizzy? Any medication changes in the days before?"

"No." Dorothy's gaze dared the question to persist. "He rose early, as always, to see about his tree. He had his tea." Her mouth pinched at the word. "He did not like to be interfered with."

"Was there a reason he was alone?" Rawlings said, the question as soft as fleece, the words arranged so they would not cut until you pressed them. "No expectation that someone would go with him? Given his heart condition."

Emily kept her eyes on the carpet's border. "He didn't want hand-holding," she said. "He was a dignified man. Besides, he was only looking at a tree in the garden."

Paul felt sweat make a small, disloyal map at the back of his neck. "We should have been there," he said, the defence childish, exhausted. "We were..."

"In London," Patel supplied gently.

"In London," he echoed, and hated the way the repetition sounded like guilt admitting itself into evidence. "I had to pop into work the moment we got off the train. Emily unpacked. When I came back to the flat, we had champagne. And then Robert called and we came straight away."

"The neighbour's footage has no recordings for that day. Which suggests there was no movement near the gate," Patel said. She looked up with those clean, steady eyes of hers. "We don't think anyone else was with him. But we wondered if the stress of an earlier break-in may have been affecting him."

Dorothy's patience, already threadbare, tore.

"He had a weak heart," she said, each word clipped. "It's as simple as that. Leave us alone."

The sentence dropped in the centre of the room like a stone. Rawlings let the ripples settle. He was good at waiting. He could have been a fisherman.

"We're not accusing anyone of anything," he said at last. "But a reported entry into the house raises questions. We've had other incidents in the area. Sneak-ins, people testing doors and gates. Elderly residents are often targeted. It's an ugly pattern. If Mr Mercer had been unsettled, or if someone had been exploring the property earlier in the week, it could help us understand, if not the cause, perhaps, then the context."

Dorothy, perversely, seemed to take this as a personal insult.

"The only people who unsettle this house," she said. "Are the ones who arrive with questions and not answers."

"Dorothy," Emily said, a murmur that was polite, chiding, and loving, all at once. "They're trying to help."

Rawlings's mouth did the subtle twitch it did when something both thanked and rebuked him.

"We appreciate your time," he said, rising. "We'll circulate the footage to patrols. If you think of anything, any small change in routine, any oddity, please call us. And consider reviewing your locks." He glanced at Paul. "The side gate can be latched from within with a second bolt. A handyman can manage it in an hour."

Paul nodded as if given homework. "I'll do it today."

Patel closed the laptop with that gentle finality some people have when ending a conversation you will think of all evening. At the door she turned to Emily as if remembering an afterthought and made it into a kindness.

"And Mrs Mercer? We appreciate your understanding. We know this is a difficult time for all of you."

Emily's smile was shaped like gratitude and also like a veil.

"Thank you," she said.

Rawlings shook hands with each of them, unobtrusively clocking the temperature of palm and eye. With Dorothy he bent an inch lower than necessary, as if tipping a hat no one wore anymore. In the hall he said to Paul, under his breath.

"We'll be in touch," and then the rain received them and the door closed and the house sprang back into the air they had disturbed.

For three beats, nobody moved. Then Dorothy stood, a little too fast, and swayed, and the flare of relief that she didn't fall made Paul angrier than pity would have.

"That's enough of them," she said, as if she'd ordered the visit from a catalogue and found it unsatisfactory on delivery. "Coming into my house with their notepads and their ideas. I won't have it."

"They're doing their jobs," Paul said, a fraction too loud. The strain made his vowels sharp. "There's footage of someone entering the house. We have to..."

"We have to do nothing," Dorothy snapped. "Except resist being dragged through the mud. They're pointing fingers. Accusing me of incompetence. Or worse." Her voice dropped, venom gathering in it like stormwater. She turned on Emily with a speed that belied the day. "And you're enjoying every minute."

It was the *you* that did it, the way it landed, as if the word were a spear carefully weighted. The accusation made the room feel suddenly smaller. Even the curtains seemed to lean in to hear the reply.

Emily's face altered by a degree. She took a single breath, as if steadying a glass on a tray, and put her hand on the back of a chair, not because she needed support but because it read as restraint.

"Dorothy," she said, and the name arrived like a hand held out across water. "That isn't fair."

"Fair?" Dorothy laughed without humour. "You behave as if goodness had chosen your face out of a line-up."

Paul flinched. "Mum..."

"Be quiet, Paul," Dorothy said, not looking at him. "You never see what's in front of your nose, you stupid man. You're weak. Your father always said so. She enjoys this. She enjoys being the one who knows how to answer the door and the questions."

The slap of your father always said so hit harder the second time in two weeks. Something old and hurt in Paul reared up, awkward and armed with the wrong weapons.

"Don't," he said, his voice cracking at the edge. "Don't bring him into this. Emily isn't, she hasn't..." He swung his face towards his wife for a proof she didn't owe him and then back. "She's keeping us from falling apart."

Dorothy's lips folded into a narrow line. "We've already fallen apart. But she is rearranging the pieces."

Emily stepped between them, not physically, quite, but with her presence, the way a person steps between a dog and a mirror.

"Let's not," she said softly. "We're all tired. It's been a lot."

"A lot of questions about why I allowed my husband to die alone on a stone path," Dorothy hissed, the one line she hadn't meant to say. It hung in the air, revealed, naked.

Paul made a sound Emily had never heard from him.

"No one said that," he managed, though the blood had gone from his face. "No one."

Dorothy's breath caught on a cough. It began as the dry bark she tried to ignore and then thickened, knitting itself into a fit that doubled her forward. The room rearranged itself around the sound. There is a particular panic reserved for the ill when they begin to cough and for the healthy who listen. Emily moved first, quick and contained, reaching for a glass of water, her hand on Dorothy's back with a light pat, a napkin passed into the shaking hand. Paul, useless with fear, hovered with palms out, as if ready to catch what couldn't be caught.

"Slow," Emily murmured. "Breathe through your nose. Easy." She counted, quietly, to four, the way the GP had shown her, and offered the water again when the fit loosened its grip. Dorothy took the glass with a furious dignity and sipped as if offended by the swallowing.

The storm passed. Dorothy sat very still, upright again, the colour in her face a false bloom. "I am going to my room," she said, careful with each word, as if stepping on stones in a stream. "If you need me, find a way to cope without me."

She took her cane and left them, the click of its rubber tip along the corridor a metronome for the argument that had not finished. They listened to her progress along corridor, one step, pause, one step, pause, all the way to the door, closing with a gentleness that hid temper.

Paul sagged into the nearest chair and covered his face with his hands. He stayed like that, shoulders stuttering, until the quiet made a shape around him. When Emily sat on the arm and eased his hands away, he let her. He looked younger and older at once.

"She thinks I like this," he said, half laughing on the inhale, the sound scraped raw. "She thinks you like this. She thinks the police are trying to blame her for..." He stopped, because finishing would mean saying aloud a thing that, once said, would not fit back into his chest.

Emily slid onto her knees on the rug in front of him, the way you do when you want a person to see your whole face. She set her palms light on either side of his head and smoothed his hair back from his forehead, a domestic gesture that carried a weird authority of nurse, mother, lover, wife.

"Hey," she said, and the word was a lullaby's first syllable. "Look at me."

He did. In her eyes he found the steadiness he had come to expect and need, no fear, only his wife holding the line while he looked away.

"It's all right," she told him, as if all right were not an ambition but a plan. "We'll get through this."

He swallowed. "I don't know how."

"We do the next thing that needs doing," she said. "We change the gate bolt. We keep the door locked. We make sure she takes the medicine. We call the GP if she coughs like that again. We answer the questions if any more come. We keep calm and carry on." She smiled, tiny and precise. "And we forgive her while we can."

He shut his eyes and let her words settle over him like a blanket ironed smooth. He could pretend, for a breath, that she made a weather he could live in.

"I shouted," he said, shame bubbling, late. "I shouted at my mother."

"She shouted first," Emily said, without heat. "And she was

hurtful. We're allowed to be human in this house. She is. You are."

He nodded, then shook his head, then nodded again, like a man rehearsing an argument with himself and choosing both sides.

"I can't lose you in this," he said, and the confession surprised them both.

"You won't," Emily said, with a certainty that had the density of a vow. She didn't add that people lose each other quietly all the time, one polite silence at a time, and that she had no intention of letting quiet win.

Along the hall, in the library, Dorothy sat on the edge of the bed and pressed the tissue to her lips. A little spot of pink bloomed there, then faded in her stare until it became only paper again. She set it aside. The ache in her ribs pulsed in time with her fury. She pictured the detectives' faces, alert, patient, and hungry, and Emily's modest mouth tidying statements into palatable pieces. Enjoying every minute, she had said, because it felt safer to accuse than to admit fear.

She lay back and stared at the ceiling rose. The plasterwork made a star she had dusted with a feather for forty years. The star looked down at her with its impassive beauty. In the next room, her daughter-in-law made the small, consoling noises her son needed to hear, and didn't hear the accusation levelled at her. Dorothy thought, not for the first time, that if she dropped a plate from the top stair and they found it intact at the bottom, Emily would say she had caught it on the way.

# 21

Frost had crept in overnight, laying its silver fingers across the lawn, tracing delicate veins over the apple tree's bare branches. Inside, the house seemed to breathe the cold into its bones. Windows clouded at the edges, draughts whispered along the skirting boards, and every room felt larger, emptier, as if warmth had been driven into exile.

Emily crouched at the hearth, coaxing flame from logs stacked with precision. She moved slowly, tucking a curl of hair behind her ear, her face calm though her fingers stung from the chill. When the fire caught, she leaned back on her heels, watching the flames lick upward, a fragile victory over the season.

Behind her, Dorothy sat hunched in the wingback chair, swaddled in shawls that made her appear smaller and, somehow, sharper. The wool trailed from her shoulders like battle flags. Her face was pale, her lips pressed thin, her eyes glittering with suspicion.

"Why is it so cold in this house?" she demanded, voice sharp enough to scratch glass. "Are you trying to freeze me to death?"

Emily rose smoothly, brushing ash from her hands. "The fire

will take the chill off in a moment. Would you like another blanket, Dorothy?"

"No," Dorothy snapped, drawing her shawls tighter. "Another blanket will not change the fact that this house is an icebox. It never used to be. Not when Harold was here. Are you economising on me? Waiting for me to perish while you save on the bills?"

Paul stood by the doorway, fiddling with his tie in front of the hall mirror. His brow furrowed as though the knot might hold the answer to his mother's complaint.

"Energy prices are through the roof," he murmured, offering the fact like an apology. "Everyone's feeling it. We've been careful, that's all."

Dorothy's eyes flicked to him, unappeased. "Careful," she echoed bitterly. "That's what you call it. I call it cruelty."

Paul flushed, his gaze dropping. He smoothed the front of his shirt, reached for his jacket. "I've got to head in. Meeting at nine."

Emily stepped forward, her voice a balm, her smile warm and composed.

"Go, Paul. Don't worry. We'll be fine here. I'll turn the heating up a notch." She placed a gentle hand on his arm, urging him toward the door. "You've enough on your mind without fretting about us."

He searched her face, grateful and guilty all at once, and kissed her cheek. "You're remarkable," he whispered.

Emily's eyes softened. "Do your best today."

He left with the sound of gravel crunching beneath tyres, the front door closing behind him like a sigh.

In the silence that followed, Dorothy's cane tapped against the floor.

"Remarkable," she repeated under her breath, sourness curling in the word. "Remarkably good at pretending."

Emily straightened the shawl that had slipped from Dorothy's shoulder, then turned away, her expression cold. The fire popped and spat, casting its fragile heat into a room where warmth refused to stay.

The day wore on in much the same way, heavy and dim, with clouds pressing low over Bray. Emily moved through her routines with measured grace, folding laundry, checking medicines, tending the fire when it threatened to burn low.

From the library came the sharp ring of Dorothy's bell. It cut through the air like a command. Emily wiped her hands on a cloth, set aside the folded linen, and carried the tea tray down the hall. The china clinked softly, the steam rising fragrant with bergamot.

She entered the room with her usual serenity. Dorothy sat stiffly in her chair, shawls gathered about her like armour. Her eyes narrowed.

"Took you long enough," she said. "I could have died of thirst while you were dawdling."

Emily placed the tray on the side table, careful not to rattle a single cup.

"Apologies," she said evenly. "I was finishing with the washing. It's fresh for you now."

Dorothy sniffed, unimpressed. "Excuses. Always excuses. You enjoy making me wait. Don't think I don't see it."

Emily poured the tea in silence, added a splash of milk, and set the cup within reach. She offered no protest, and no defence. Her face was smooth, her movements precise, every gesture one of quiet service.

Dorothy's eyes followed her.

"That's right," she muttered as Emily turned toward the door. "Slope off and leave me here to die. Well, I've got news for you." Her voice sharpened, though it was pitched more to the empty room than to her daughter-in-law's retreating back. "I'm going nowhere. Do you hear me? Nowhere."

Emily paused briefly in the doorway, her head tilting just so, as though she had caught the words but chosen not to answer. Then she withdrew, closing the door with a soft click.

Alone, Dorothy stared at the steaming cup. The firelight flickered across her shawls, shadows dancing over her drawn face. Her hand trembled as she lifted the cup, though she steadied it quickly, her lips tightening with resolve.

"I know what you're doing," she whispered into the empty room. "And I won't make it easy for you."

The house offered no reply. Dorothy sipped her tea, eyes fixed on the door where Emily had gone, as frost gathered once more at the edges of the windows.

# 22

By late morning the frost had given up its shine and retreated to the garden's shady corners, but the house still held a faint chill, the kind that settled in doorways as if waiting to be invited further in. Emily was in the hall with a vase in one hand and a damp tea towel in the other, half-listening for Dorothy's bell, when the knocker sounded with two brisk taps, neighbourly, already apologising for their own insistence.

She opened the door to find Julia Latimer on the step, cheeks pink from the cold, breath making small clouds, a paper-wrapped bouquet pressed to her chest of yellow tulips, too early, really, for this weather. Kindness often arrived ahead of season.

"Emily," Julia said, her smile bright, her eyes quick, "I was just passing. Well I say passing, I was thinking of you, and I thought I'd pop these in. We had them left over from the church arrangements." She lowered her voice, conspiratorial. "They needed a home, and I thought of you."

Emily's face lit with uncomplicated gratitude; she stepped back to let the woman in. "They're beautiful. Dorothy will love the colour. And I've just finished drying the vase after throwing the last bunch away."

She took the flowers with both hands, as if weight mattered to courtesy.

"Come inside, Julia, you'll freeze out there."

The morning room made even nosy neighbours look softened. Julia's gaze went everywhere and nowhere at the same time. The row of photographs on the mantel, the folded shawl on the arm of the wingback chair. People read houses the way they read faces. Emily arranged the tulips in the vase she'd been carrying, moving with that steady economy of hers, each stem trimmed with a quick, neat snip, turned a fraction so the heads faced one another like gossiping friends.

"How is Dorothy?" Julia asked, words cushioned with a concern that was mostly true. "We've been thinking of her. Of all of you."

"She's up and down," Emily said, the truthful version of the polite lie. "The cold tires her. Dr Ahmed's adjusted her medicines." She tucked a leaf back under the rim of the vase. "She's determined, which helps."

Julia nodded, filing the physician's name, the word determined, the fact of the adjusted medication. She made a sympathetic sound, then bit her lip, then plunged into what she was really here for.

"I won't pry," which meant she would do exactly that. "But we had the police back last week, and they said they'd been through our footage again." She leaned forward across the tulips, voice dropping. "That figure at the side gate. Well, it's horrid, really. And them going in. Tom thinks...well." She stopped herself, and then didn't. "You must be frightened. I can't help wondering who it was. It's been on my mind, especially, since, you know, it was Tom who spotted it on the camera."

Emily lifted her head. She had developed an expression for this sort of sentence that was soft and steady, with just enough sorrow in the eyes to make people speak more gently without realising they'd been steered.

"It was kind of Tom to raise the alarm," she said. "We'll always be grateful." She let the detail rest where it caused least trouble. Tom had alerted Robert and Robert had rung Paul. In grief, credit braided itself anyway. "As for the footage, Rawlings says they're looking into it properly. Locks, bolts, the usual sense. We're being careful."

Julia's gaze wandered again, collecting small proofs. She took in the neat row of medicine times on the fridge, glimpsed through the open doorway, the way the fire looked full and welcoming, and the cushion placed on the back of the chair at just the right angle to ease a sore back. She shook her head, admiration overtaking nosiness.

"Dorothy's lucky to have you," she said simply. "I don't know how you do it, and all with a smile."

Emily flushed, the modest pink that photographs well.

"We do what we can," she said. "It's her house. We try to keep it feeling like hers."

The sound of a cane and slow tread came from the hall, preluding Dorothy. She stood in the doorway wrapped in her winter shawl like a general reluctant to acknowledge a truce. Colour had fled her face this morning and what remained was intent. Her eyes went at once to the tulips, then to Julia, then to Emily placing the vase so that the flowers caught what little light there was.

"Mrs Latimer," Dorothy said, the formality meant to suggest limits. "We are not a curiosity."

Julia, who was all good intentions and thin discretion, flustered. "Oh, Dorothy, no, heavens, I brought flowers. And I wanted to see how you..."

"How we are with being interrogated?" Dorothy's mouth tightened. She shifted her weight on the cane. "Don't stand there simpering about luck. I am not lucky. My husband is dead and I have policemen sniffing at my hedges. As for her," A sharp tilt of the head, and the shawl rustled. "She's no angel. More like the devil in disguise. And you are a nosy old bat, so bugger off."

The sentence hit the air like a pane shattering. Emily felt the house stiffen. Even the fire paused its small applause. Julia's face went white and then red in one brittle sweep.

"Oh, well... goodness, Dorothy," she stammered, glancing at the tulips as if to justify her presence. "I didn't... I'll just..."

Emily moved, deft, a dancer smoothing a stumble into choreography.

"Julia, forgive her. It's a bad morning." She let out a small laugh that turned the moment into a weather report. "Come, I'll walk you out. Thank you for the flowers. They're perfect."

She touched Dorothy's arm briefly in passing, light and firm, a signal as much as a comfort, and steered the neighbour gently towards the hall. At the door, with the winter air already reaching for them, Julia recovered enough to be mortified.

"I didn't mean to pry, at all. We were worried. But she's obviously not herself," she said, and then because she could not resist one last peep through the keyhole of disaster.

"You will tell me if you see anyone hanging about, won't you? Tom says these people come back. Once to look. Once to... well. I didn't sleep after Rawlings told us."

"We'll be careful," Emily said. "We've added a second bolt to the side gate." They had not; Paul had promised it would be done by evening. "The police are keeping an eye."

"And you," Julia said, recovering her social footing enough to be kind. "You must be exhausted. Calling at all hours. And her moods." She nodded toward the interior of the house, where Dorothy's realm lay. "Truly, Emily. Dorothy's lucky to have you."

Emily let modesty colour her cheeks again, in a blush they

knew by heart. "We're lucky to have each other," she said, and the sentence made Julia's eyes shine, the way good sentences do.

When the door was shut and the tulips were sitting quietly in their vase and the hall had swallowed the draft, Emily stood for a breath with her hands on the wood and exhaled. Then she turned back to find Dorothy stationed in the threshold of the morning room, chin up, daring her to speak.

"You enjoyed that," Dorothy said. "You like making me the story."

Emily's smile returned, small, tidy. "Only the part where you tell the ending," she said gently. "It's much quicker for everyone."

Dorothy's eyes flashed, but the fight had cost her. She shifted her grip on the cane and retreated down the corridor, the shawl trailing. Emily watched her go, then collected the spent flakes of temper without comment, the way she collected ash from the hearth. On the mantel, Harold's silver-framed summer fixed its squint on the tulips and said nothing at all.

He came home earlier than he'd promised, which still meant after dark. Cold clung to him in the doorway and he shook it from his shoulders as he took off his coat. The smell of supper met him halfway down the hall. He found Emily in the kitchen spooning sauce into a dish with that careful economy that turned dinner into a reassurance. Dorothy's tray had already been taken in, returned and rinsed.

"Julia Latimer brought tulips," Emily said, by way of an opening that wasn't a complaint. "They're on the mantel."

Paul grimaced, reading between lines he would rather were blank. "Did she? That's nice of her. Did mother..."

"She was herself," Emily said, and the neatness of the sentence allowed him not to picture the rest.

He crossed to her, placed his hands lightly on her arms.

"I don't know how you're putting up with her," he said, and for a second it wasn't entirely clear whether her meant Dorothy or Julia or the whole of Bray. "My mother. The things she says." He dropped his forehead to Emily's shoulder, let it rest there like a child's. "I'm sorry."

Emily set the spoon down, turned in his arms, and smoothed a thumb over the crease between his brows, as if folding it away would keep the day from creasing him further.

"Don't be," she said. "It's winter. Everything feels sharper in winter."

He kissed her forehead, a benediction he used when language felt clumsy.

"When this eases," he said, meaning the cough, the police, the frost, the grief. "We'll go away for a weekend. Anywhere. I'll book The Pig, or—no, somewhere you choose. Just us."

Emily's mouth turned at the corners. "We'll see," she said. "She needs us."

"Us," he repeated, the word warming him. He took her hands in both of his and squeezed, a man grateful for something that looked like a plan. "I am so lucky," he said. "You know that, don't you? To have you."

She tilted her head, radiating the modesty everyone had agreed belonged to her. "Pour me a wine," she said softly, releasing one hand to gesture toward the pot. "That's luck enough for this evening."

He laughed, did as he was told. He didn't notice how precisely she had set the glasses to make that true for him. He didn't see how much of his ease had been arranged. He only felt it. And in the feeling, his certainty grew, not merely that he had married the right woman, but that goodness had a shape and it was hers.

# 23

The morning came thin and grey again. Dorothy sat in the library-turned-bedroom with her shawl around her shoulders and the bell within reach, the river a dark seam beyond the glass. The tulips on the mantel had passed their prime and their yellow mouths gaped, petals cupping the last of their colour like a secret they were tired of keeping. She had asked for company, proper company, not neighbours with tulips and questions, and today the village obliged.

Mavis Ellwood arrived at eleven with a handbag that had been old for twenty years and a hat that considered itself an heirloom. She looked like every Tuesday at the church coffee morning had ever looked. She was brisk, perfumed, and her face was powdered to a memory of roses. Emily greeted her at the door with that soft competence she showed everyone, and her coat was taken, her hat lifted onto a hook with the quick warmth in her eyes that made people feel as if they had already been listened to.

"She's in the library," Emily said, and her voice put ribbons on the directions. "Take your time."

Mavis went in with the cautious cheer of someone who told herself this was a social call and not a visit to a sickroom.

"Dorothy," she sang, as if the name were a hymn, "Don't you look smart?"

Dorothy reached for the compliment and set it down where she could see it, as proof that she remained a woman who could receive such things.

"It's the shawl," she said, touching the wool. "It does most of the work." Her breath hitched, but she pretended it was because she'd laughed. "Sit, Mavis. Tell me about anybody but me."

Mavis sat, ankles neatly crossed, hands folded on the leather of her handbag as if keeping it from leaning into mischief. She took in the room with the quiet greed of the well-meaning.

"You've kept it lovely," she said, because the sentence was true and safe. "I always liked this room. Warm even when it's gloomy."

"It's not warm," Dorothy said, sharp. "But at least it's obedient." She let the word settle and then reached for Mavis with a look that made the other woman lean in despite herself.

"Close the door," she whispered, suddenly conspiratorial. "I don't want her hovering."

Mavis hesitated, then did as she was asked. The latch clicked with the softness of gossip.

Dorothy waited a theatrical half-breath, then bent her head, the shawl sliding a fraction, and the voice that came out of her sounded younger, slyer, the one she used to deploy with Harold when they'd shared a secret in company.

"She wants me gone," she said. "I can tell. Everything she does, tidy, tidy, tidy, making my house behave as if it belongs to her. She smiles as if her smile are medicine, but they feel like poison, and I'm meant to be grateful while she rearranges my life."

Mavis's mouth opened and then closed. A lifetime of village courtesy told her to say now, now, and stroke the air.

"She's been very good to come and tend to you," she ventured. "From what people say. She's ireless. You're fortunate, Dorothy. It isn't everyone who gets..."

Dorothy's hand came up, palm out as the old schoolmistress in her briefly resurfaced.

"Not good," she said, almost amused. "She has been practised." She leaned closer. "I wouldn't trust her as far as I could throw her. And I never could throw far."

Mavis breathed through her nose, the way you do when a draught opens under a door. "What makes you say that?"

"She's after my money," Dorothy said simply. "She's after the house. And Paul, bless him, he's too stupid to see what he married. He told me goodness has a shape and it's hers." She turned her face a fraction, the movement made the light slide along her cheekbones, making her look suddenly feral. "It is not goodness to make a person disappear in their own home."

Mavis shifted, and took a moment to decide which drawer to put this in. Was it resentment or grief?

"Change is always difficult," she offered. "For all of us. We say thank you the wrong way sometimes. It's an age thing, you know that. I told the vicar as much, my patience fits me less well than it used to."

Dorothy ignored the homily. The urgency in her had the crackle of frost.

"Do you know what tea tastes like to me now?" she demanded, the question grabbing Mavis by the sleeve. "Not every time. But often enough. Bitter. A tang under the milk as if the pot remembered something it shouldn't. And the food? Some mouthfuls are just wrong. I know my own house. I know when a taste doesn't belong." She gave a small, brittle laugh.

"You'll say it's the medicines. They all say that. They pat me in their minds and move on."

Mavis stared at her friend.

"Steroids and such," she said, feeling the room tilt. "They do put a taste on the tongue. My Frank said everything was tin for a while." She took a breath, found her own centre, rebuckled it. "You're tired, that's all. Tired and frightened. The world looks different when you're made to rest in it."

"Frightened," Dorothy repeated, tasting the word like a new jam. "Yes. Of being erased. Of everyone thinking the version of me she presents is the only one that counts." She set her fingers on the arm of the chair and tapped once, a metronome for her fury. "She'll smile me into a corner, that one."

Mavis found her smile, the one pasted on for difficult parishioners and funerals with more wreaths than mourners.

"Oh, Dorothy," she said softly, and it meant how would you like me to help you back into the world we both recognise. "You've always had the upper hand. Everyone knows that. Emily's young. She's doing her best. Poor love. It isn't easy. You aren't easy."

Dorothy sat back. In the small collapse of posture, something old and stubborn seemed to loosen.

"Poor love," she echoed, and there was venom in it. "She knows exactly what she's doing. If I were to die tonight..." She let the sentence hang and Mavis felt it brush her cheek like moth wings and shuddered. "There'd be a rota of casseroles at the door by lunchtime tomorrow and everyone would say how wonderful she has been. And they would not be wrong, only incomplete. That is her gift, Mavis. To make incompletion look like truth."

The old woman looked to the photograph of Harold for permission to disagree and found none. She leaned forward and set her hand briefly over Dorothy's, a rare trespass.

"Listen to me," she said, and the old authority returned to her voice. "You're ill. You're angry. You feel outflanked. All sensible. But the part where you whispered about... poisoning." She made herself finish the ugly word. "That's not fair. On her. Or on you. You'll hear it back in your own head tonight and it will frighten you. Don't plant that thought and water it. Please don't."

Dorothy's chin tipped. She almost laughed. "She doesn't need to poison me," she said, suddenly airy, as if she'd decided to treat the thing as a joke before it bit. "Life's doing it fine. But I'm not as mad as they make me sound." The last sentence arrived wearing more fragile armour. "I notice things. That is all."

Mavis seized the change of temperature as if it were a rope thrown to her. "How is Paul?" she asked too brightly. "Working hard? He always did like a shirt that meant business." She launched into local bulletins. There were new pew cushions at St. Michael's that were too plump, the WI cake sale scandal when Hilda's Victoria sponge came second, the frost on the allotments tearing through the leeks. Conversation did what conversation does when fear has to be gentled, it placed warm, ordinary things on top of the colder ones until the chill receded enough to survive.

After a time, Emily tapped lightly on the door and brought in a plate of shortbread and a fresh pot of tea. She poured, smiling. "I won't intrude," she said, setting cups down just right. "Ring if you need anything."

"Thank you, dear," Mavis said, melting back into politeness. "You're a wonder."

Emily's eyes made the smallest bow at the praise.

"Enjoy your chat." She left with her usual economy, the door closing with a soft kiss that sounded like privacy.

Mavis sampled the shortbread, found it impeccable, and

complimented it as if compliments might lay blessing on the room. Dorothy ate half a biscuit without noticing, then put the remainder down with an expression that suggested it had confessed something awkward on her tongue. When, at last, coats were required again and goodbyes rehearsed, Mavis kissed Dorothy's cheek and promised a lift to church when Dorothy felt up to it. In the hall, she pressed Emily's hands in both of hers and said, with feeling, "You are a saint," and left relieved to be back in the familiar tranquillity of the lane.

Dorothy watched her go from the chair by the window, the shawl loosened, the tulips looking on in their blown-out splendour. The words she had whispered lay where she'd put them, uncollected. In the quiet, they sounded less like truth.

Emily had not lingered at the door, not exactly. She had moved away as any considerate daughter-in-law would, to the edge of the hall where a draft fussed at the runner and the blue pot's steam thinned into the air. But the house's acoustics had their own ideas. It carried phrases like cups on a tray. She's after my money... I wouldn't trust her... poisoning... The words had drifted through the gap with the precision of things not meant to be heard by someone else. Emily had stood very still, the tray's weight pleasant in her hands, her gaze on the small fracture in the skirting board that she had been meaning to fix with wood filler when time allowed.

When the front door closed behind Mavis and the silence folded back into itself, Emily waited a moment, and then she went in, the modest smile already in place, as if she had spent the intervening seconds tidying.

"Can I get you anything?" she asked, and the question had both politeness and inevitability in it.

Dorothy turned her face away, the gesture girlish in its refusal. Her lips pressed into a line that might once have been capable of mischief but now held only sting. "I'd rather sip arsenic," she muttered. "Than have another cup of your insipid brew."

For a fraction of a beat, the light in the room seemed to dim. Emily did not blink. The expression she wore was the one the village had come to recognise as her tranquil, attentive signature.

"I'll bring you some hot lemon, then," she said. "It's kinder to the throat. I'll bring it now."

She withdrew without waiting for consent, the soft click of the door a courtesy to a listener who did not know whether she wished to be alone or to be witnessed. Dorothy stared at her reflection in the darkened window. Mavis's kind eyes had slid away from the word poison, as all kind eyes do. Dorothy felt shame and satisfaction do a strange minuet in her chest.

"I notice," she said aloud to herself, a test to see whether saying it again made it more true.

When Emily returned with the cup, the lemon scent preceded her, bright and false as winter sun. She placed the saucer within reach and did not step back at once.

"It's very cold this afternoon," she said mildly. "Shall I put another log on?"

Dorothy eyed the cup, then the woman holding the room together with string.

"Leave it," she said.

"As you wish." Emily turned, paused, and looked over her shoulder with that small, unassuming smile that asked nothing more than the right to be there. "Ring if you need me." She left again. The door closed. The house resumed its listening.

Dorothy lifted the cup and brought it slowly to her mouth, as if expectation itself might be a poison. She held the liquid on her tongue and waited for the tang that would prove her right. Lemon and tea and heat. Nothing else. She swallowed, annoyed at the disappointment of surviving another sip.

# 24

By evening the cold had settled into the house as if it had paid rent. Frost made a halo on the windowpane of the library-bedroom. Dorothy sat propped against pillows that remembered the shape of her back, with her shawl gathered like a small mountain at her waist. Every few breaths a cough unspooled, dry at first, then snagging, then loosening again, as if her lungs were trying to knit and unknit at the same time.

Emily's knock was the sound a polite thought would make if it had knuckles. She came in with the tray balanced on one hand with a glass tumbler, pills in their little cut-glass dish, a carafe of water that glinted in the lamp's light.

"Your bedtime things," Emily said, and the sentence arranged the room.

Dorothy eyed the tray the way one eyes a stranger who insists they have been here before. "I don't like the water so cold," she muttered, the words snagging on a cough.

"I'll let it rest to room temperature next time," Emily said, and somehow managed to make next time sound like a promise rather than a sentence. She set the glass within reach, then the water, then slid the dish of pills into position. "Whenever you're ready."

Dorothy took the glass and sipped, eyes on Emily's face as if daring it to flinch. Emily bent to tuck the blanket in beside her knee. Dorothy wanted to tell her not to tuck. She wanted to tell her that being tucked stole a layer of self she couldn't spare. But the blanket lay warm and heavy across her legs now, and the fire in the grate was low but obedient, and breath was briefly easier to borrow, so she let herself be contained. "Give me more water," she said, which was as close to a polite request Emily would get.

Emily refilled the glass and nudged the pills closer to Dorothy.

"Evening dose," she said. "Two of the small white, one of the pale blue, and the steroid."

Dorothy looked down at the neatness of the arranged pills and hated the way her fingers trembled when she reached for them. She swallowed them one by one, the water cool against the heat in her chest. The steroid sat metallic on her tongue for a second before going, leaving nothing but the idea of itself behind.

"Horrid," she said.

"But necessary," Emily said.

Paul stuck his head around the door, the workday still clinging to him like a scent.

"Only me," he said. "Just popping in to see you before bed." He said it as if she might fine him for staying longer. He crossed the room and bent to kiss Dorothy's cheek, and his lips met the lavender of her skin and the dry whisper of powder.

"You get some rest," he told her.

"I rest all day," Dorothy said, which was half a rebuke and half a plea she didn't intend him to hear. He squeezed her hand anyway in a boy's gesture that had survived its boy.

He looked past her to Emily, who stood with her hands lightly laced as if catching sunlight.

"Thank you," he said, under his breath. "For everything."

"Go and change out of those work clothes," Emily murmured, the domestic absolution that was also instruction. "I'll be in soon."

He went, and his departure left the room rearranged around its women again. Emily tucked the lower corner of the blanket with a competence that said I have made a thousand edges behave.

"Ring if you need me," she said, the bell already placed within precise reach. "I'll leave the door on the latch."

Dorothy watched her go and felt the old stubbornness stir, the one that said she would not be turned into someone who simply rang a bell when thirsty.

"Close it properly," she said, quickly, surprising herself. "It's draughty."

Emily paused.

"All right," she said at last. She eased the door to, and the soft snick of the latch felt like a decision being made three rooms away.

When she was alone, Dorothy took another sip of water and tried to name the taste that climbed the back of her throat and sat there like a small idea that refuses to leave. Metal. The steroid's ghost. Not poison. Not anything she could point at and say, there. Just the infuriating and intangible knowledge that even water now tasted off.

She set the glass down and let her head sink back against the pillows. The lamp made a small circle on the ceiling that looked like a hole in the night. Sleep came quickly.

She woke in the dark with a start. Her breath had gone somewhere and forgotten to tell her where it was. She chased it with her mouth open, gulping at the cold air, trying to catch the rhythm that would allow the next minute to exist. Her chest felt tight and hollow at once, like a room with all the furniture pushed against the walls.

"Paul," she tried, but the name arrived as vapour.

Her son did not answer. Outside the door the grandfather clock took its time, the tick loud as footfalls in an empty church. She counted three, then four, then lost count because panic was taking over. She pressed the heel of her hand to her sternum and felt nothing useful but the thud of a heart insulted by its effort.

"Emily," she tried, lower, because anger fed breath better than fear. The room offered her the thin echo of her own voice and the soft, infuriating steadiness of the lamp's circle on the ceiling.

She reached for the bell and knocked it with clumsy fingers. It made a genteel, ridiculous sound that would never wake anyone who didn't want to be woken. She considered the water and rejected it. Water only reminded the body of drowning when it was already frightened. Instead, she closed her eyes and pictured the old apple tree, the way the blossom had once come in a rush, the way Harold had stood beneath it and declared himself a fine gardener. Memory is a better inhaler than any prescribed one if you catch it just right. Her breath began to come a little easier.

Dorothy let her head sag sideways on the pillow and fixed her eyes on the bottom edge of the door, where a sliver of hallway always lived even when the door had been shut "properly". Tonight, the sliver was a bright line, the colour of butter. She heard nothing outside, and yet the light altered, in that minuscule way light does when it passes around a shape.

A shadow crossed the gap, as though something standing very still on the other side of the door was deciding what to do.

Dorothy's skin tightened along her arms as if frost had laid its hand there. She tried to say Who's there and found that the words were the size of a breath she did not have. The shadow thickened, then thinned, as if the figure had swayed, as if a listening head had tilted. The light wavered and the shadow slid away without a sound, the way steam disappears if you decide not to look at it properly. The line under the door narrowed back to a sliver.

Dorothy stared at the door until her eyes watered and the bright line blurred into two and then into one again. She wanted to call out a third name, one the house had not heard for months.

"Harold," she whispered, and the syllables fell like small stones into a deep place.

She felt the panic loosen its grip by degrees, mean as a miser, granting her breath in reluctant coins. Each inhale scratched, each exhale made a small complaint, but the rhythm of her breathing returned like a sulky servant summoned back to duty. She let herself sink, because she didn't have the strength to fight it.

As her eyes gave up their watch, Dorothy held the certainty in her chest like a hot coin. Someone had been at that door, listening. And she was sure they were waiting to hear her take her last breath.

# 25

Dawn arrived like a whisper. The curtains in the library-bedroom took the first suggestion of light and made it a gentle, faint glow on the stitched leaves of the fabric.

Emily came as she always did, with the breakfast tray balanced on one hand and her other hand steadying the door so it would open with its careful, considerate click. Good morning was already arranged on her mouth.

"Dorothy?" she said softly. "Morning, love."

She set the tray down on the table. The china sounded smaller than usual, as if the air had thickened and turned the note inward. Dorothy lay higher on the pillows than she had when Emily had tucked her the night before. The shawl was folded at the foot of the bed in a square of obedience, as if its wearer had not wanted to make trouble. Her face was pale in a way that had nothing to do with winter, her mouth hung a little slack, as though it had forgotten its tightness, and her hands, always so purposeful, even when doing nothing, now rested without pose on the coverlet, half-curled, as if they had been surprised by sleep while holding a thought.

"Dorothy?" Emily stepped closer and listened. She reached out and touched the back of Dorothy's hand with two fingers. The skin was cool, but then she had been cool yesterday. She lifted her hand to Dorothy's throat, to the little soft place where the pulse announces itself when it wants to be found. She waited, her face composed into readiness. She bowed her head very slightly and then she stood straight and said, not loudly, but with a clarity that carried down the corridor, "Paul?"

A beat, and then louder, the shape of desperation in it because the shape mattered, because the house needed to know this was not just a request.

"Paul!"

His feet were already on the stairs when she called. He appeared in the doorway without the shuffling that usually announced him. His eyes went first to Emily, then to the stillness on the bed, then to the tray, a fast, baffling triangulation, and then back to the bed as if the third point had betrayed him.

"Mum?" His voice misfired on the second letter. He crossed the room at a speed that didn't belong to a man raised in quiet houses and put both hands on Dorothy's shoulders as if sensible pressure could call a person back.

"Mum. Mum." He shook her, not roughly, but with a boy's panic and a man's wish to be told what to do. Her head lolled once and settled in a way that made something behind Emily's ribs pull tight.

"Paul." Emily's hand found his forearm, warm over the tendon, and held. "She's gone."

He froze in the angle between belief and refusal, and for a moment he was a silhouette cut from paper, his arms, shoulders, and head bent over the past. The next sound he made was raw and private. He let go of his mother and stood back as if instructed by an invigilator.

"I should..." His gaze flicked to the window and then to the door, looking for a switch marked reverse. He stepped to the curtains and parted them a fraction, letting more of the thin morning in, then closed them again immediately as if the light were impertinent. He smoothed the edge of the blanket where his hands had creased it. He found the bell and laid it square on the table, though there was no longer anyone to ring it. He did all of it with the jerky concentration of a man trying to put back the last minute with his fingers.

Emily stayed where she was, steadying the room by remaining still in it. She watched him without commentary, because she knew the moment people begin to narrate a shock it hardens around the wrong words. She touched Dorothy's hair once in an old-fashioned gesture of mothering that belonged to nobody now, and then she drew the sheet up an inch, just enough to deny the air its voyeurism.

"We'll call Dr Ahmed," she said, when the sound of her own voice could be added without breaking anything. "He'll come. He'll know what to do next."

Paul nodded, and reached for his phone and then put it back in his pocket, as if he had been about to call the wrong number. He looked at his mother's face as if it were a puzzle he had been set at school and had forgotten how to start. He pressed his lips together until they whitened.

"She was breathing roughly," he said to Emily, rather than to the air. "Last night, in the night. I heard her. I came down for water. I was in the hall, and I thought I heard the bell, but it didn't ring." He swallowed. "I listened outside the door, and she seemed to settle. I should have come in."

"You were here," Emily said, choosing the true thing that would not undo him. "She knew that."

He nodded again, slower. He reached automatically for the

glass of water on the tray, then seemed to remember and moved his hand two inches to the carafe instead, as if the decision had been made for him by a small, officious angel at his shoulder. The movement left a faint crescent of moisture on the tray's polished wood. He wiped it away with his cuff, quick, embarrassed, and then looked ashamed at having done something so ordinary when ordinary had been cancelled.

He sat on the chair by the window and put his hands over his face. Emily took her phone from her cardigan pocket and called the number she had stored under GP. When she said her name, her voice was the one she used for heavy things carried carefully.

"Yes," she said. "We think... yes. This morning. She was comfortable." She listened. "Thank you. We'll expect you."

When she ended the call she placed her hand on Paul's shoulder and left it there. They stayed like that for a while.

Dr Ahmed arrived with his coat still damp from the short walk from the car, rain stippling the shoulders. He had brought the small bag that contains reassurance and a stethoscope and the forms that make official what everybody already knows. The face he wore into the library was neither cheer nor sorrow but that professional, ordinary kindness that keeps people from falling apart on the good rugs.

"I'm very sorry," he said, to both of them and to the room. He sat at the bedside with the care of a guest and asked permission with his eyes before he did anything with his hands. He felt at the throat where Emily had felt, he watched the chest without drama. He listened, briefly, to the silence through his stethoscope, because ritual matters even when it proves only ritual. Then he straightened and looked at Emily first and then at Paul.

"She's passed peacefully," he said. "Likely in the early hours."

Paul nodded and then shook his head and then nodded, a man rehearsing whether consent is the right response to death. "Was it..." He made a vague circle in the air with his finger, the shape of a word he couldn't bring himself to say.

"The cancer," Dr Ahmed supplied, gentle. "Her lungs were very compromised. The breathlessness, the fatigue, you've seen how much harder her body has been working. This is what I'll record." He added, as if anticipating a question no one was ready to ask, "We need to let the medical examiner know but I'll make it clear this was natural causes. No ambulance. No police. I'll complete the certificate, make the call and notify the registrar."

Emily let out a breath she didn't remember beginning. "Thank you."

The doctor set the sheet aside so that Dorothy was no longer half and half but whole, a woman who had once made rules and now didn't need them. He adjusted the blanket with a small, respectful squaring, a professional's version of a curtsy.

"Have you someone to help you with arrangements?" he asked. "A funeral director you prefer?"

Paul lifted his head. His cheeks were wet in two unembarrassed tracks.

"Bridges will handle the cremation," he said too quickly, as if the words had been waiting in his mouth. "They helped with my father. She should be with my father. She wanted that." He stood suddenly and then sat again, as if his legs hadn't yet received the message from his intentions.

Dr Ahmed glanced at Emily, not for permission but to locate the steadier ground in the room.

"Once I've lodged the certificate and the necessary forms are in place, the director can advise you. Given her history, there's no reason for delay." He got up with a small sound from his shoes; the floor had dried his soles. "I'll go and write what I need to, now. Take your time." He nodded to Dorothy, to the mourning couple, and then he left them to their private grief.

In the kitchen, Paul sat at the table with his elbows planted and his hands flat, the way a man sits in interview rooms in television dramas. He stared at the wood grain as if it might unfurl a way of being that didn't ache.

Emily set a cup before him and touched his fingers as if guiding a child's hand to a pen.

"Drink," she said. Her voice wrapped itself around the imperative and made it a kindness. "Just a sip."

He obeyed, then put the cup down too close to the edge and reached automatically to pull it back, as if he had caught it in the act of leaving.

"I should ring someone," he said. "The undertaker." He pulled his phone from his pocket, and the screen lit his face a strange, healthy blue. A name sat near the top of his recent calls, G. Bridges & Sons, and his thumb hovered a moment too long before he scrolled past it, as if remembering that grief ought to be seen to arrive before it could be seen to organise. He scrolled again, more slowly.

"Robert," he said. "Next door. Then... then the rest."

Emily heard none of the wrongness in that brief hitch. She heard only a man trying to lay a path across a sudden marsh. "I'll tell the Latimers," she said quietly. "And Isla. I'll be here when they come. You just do Robert."

He nodded and made the call. When he said the words, she's died, his mouth shaped them with the carefulness he had learned for saying I do and I'm sorry and yes, that's fine, all the ceremonial sentences that change your life. He listened and said thank you twice and yes, please, and then hung up and took another sip of tea, because Emily's hand was still near his and it made sense to do as it suggested.

Dr Ahmed returned later with paperwork, the official script catching up with the day. He sat again, this time at the kitchen table, and explained the steps.

"I've completed the medical certificate," he said, tapping the form with a finger that had signed too many to require ceremony. "I've noted malignant disease of the lung as the cause. The registrar will be in touch, but you can ring them as well. It tends to be quicker. The funeral director will guide you on the cremation forms and I'll complete my section. You won't need to attend hospital. Given her age and diagnosis, there's no requirement for post-mortem. We spare people where we can."

Paul nodded too vigorously, then checked himself.

"Thank you. That's... that sounds right." He looked like a man who had just been given permission to stop holding a heavy thing, but then remembered he would need to pick up another.

"If you think of questions later," Dr Ahmed added. "Just ring me. Any time."

He rose, offering his hand because rituals have their use. Paul shook it hard, as if the grip itself could anchor him. Emily took it lightly, and smiled to show her gratitude.

When the doctor had gone, the telephone began its small work of voices coming and going, condolences phrased with the tidiness people put on grief when they haven't yet seen it. The vicar's voice, baffled and kind. Julia Latimer's, too loud, then too soft. Arrangements layered themselves like paper as names and times were confirmed, and the promise of the arrival of men in dark suits who know how to fold a look into sympathy.

Paul wept. Not the dignified tears that belong to men in films, but the real, inconvenient kind that left his shoulders shaking, breath hitching. He pressed the heel of his hand against his eyes as if he could keep the grief from making a spectacle of him, and then gave up and let it be ordinary. Emily moved closer, sat beside him, and guided his hand back to the cup again.

"She's with Dad now," he said eventually, hoarse, the thought he had chosen to survive on. "She'll like that. She hated the cold."

"She will," Emily said. "And we'll get through this." The words, which on other days could sound like a plan, today were only a thread, and a thread was enough.

He swallowed. "I'd like it done quickly," he said, then flushed, as if speed made him cruel. "Not to be rid. But, so she isn't... waiting." His hand strayed to his phone again, not quite touching it, as if you could warm yourself by association.

Emily touched his wrist and left her fingers there for a count of four, her private way of saying I see you choosing what helps.

"We'll do it properly," she said. "Swiftly but properly." To her, efficiency was mercy.

In the library-bedroom, Emily went in alone and pulled the sheet higher to cover Dorothy completely. She stood for a moment with her hand on the linen, a small valediction that nobody would notice, and then she lifted the shawl from the foot of the bed and folded it in half and then in half again, her thumbs smoothing the corners as if finishing a task she had promised, at some point, to complete.

By noon the first of the calls had turned into visits, and the house did what good houses do when death comes calling. It made space. Paul moved between rooms, slower now, as if grief had filled his bones with sand. He paused in the doorway of the library one last time before the funeral director arrived, and his eyes went to small things as if the large could be managed through them. He reached out, his hand hovering over the water glass as if to clear it away and spare it from becoming something that had belonged to a dead woman. Then he thought better of it and stepped back, the restraint looking, to anyone watching, like reverence.

"Come on," Emily said gently from the hall. "They're here." He turned. He let her lead him.

## 26

Two days after the dawn that unstitched their house, the dining room had the air of a set laid for a play that no one wished to perform. Morning light stranded itself along the polished table. In its centre, a small arrangement of bright tulips had begun to slump in their glass. Paul sat at the head of the table as if trying the chair on for size, hollow-eyed, a man who had not yet discovered where to put his hands when there were no instructions.

Across from him, the undertaker occupied the upright chair with the practised compactness of someone used to making himself smaller than grief. He had a discreet folder, a pen that didn't click, and a voice pitched at the precise frequency that suggests both authority and softness. On the folder's tab, in tidy block letters was the name Mercer, Dorothy.

Emily had laid out a plate of plain biscuits, though no one was eating. She stood beside the undertaker, not looming, simply within reach of every necessary sentence. Her tone was calm, the edges of her words smoothed the way you run your fingers over silk to find the nap.

"We'd prefer cremation," she said, not filling the statement with excuses. "As soon as the forms allow. Dorothy wanted the same as her husband."

The undertaker inclined his head.

"Of course, Mrs Mercer." He glanced at Paul to confirm and found only a nod that tried to be decisive.

"We have availability at The Oaks this Friday, early afternoon. There would be time to gather a few close friends, or we can arrange a very quiet service. No orders, a single piece of music if you like." His pen hovered. "Alternatively, Thursday morning might just work."

Emily's eyes flicked to Paul, offered him the chance to speak, then spared him the labour. "Thursday morning," she said gently. "Quiet. We'll keep it simple. Just a few friends from the village. Dorothy hated fuss." She added, because she knew men like options to exist even when they decline them, "If Paul thinks of a hymn later, we'll ring."

Paul watched her mouth shape the details and felt relief arrive like heat after a long walk in cold air. He swallowed.

"What would I do without you?" he whispered, meant only for her.

"You don't have to think about that," she returned, pressing his hand under the table, the squeeze perfectly measured to feel present, not performative.

The undertaker made notes that would later turn into phone calls and schedules. "Dr Ahmed's certificate is lodged," he said, leafing to a blue form with a reassuring stamp. "I'll submit the cremation papers this afternoon. If you have a photograph you'd like on a small table by the curtains..."

Emily had already set one aside in her mind, of Dorothy and Harold on a summer lawn, a glass of something pale between them, both smiling at the person behind the lens as if they'd been interrupted mid-discussion and were forgiving it for the camera's sake.

"We do," she said. "I'll have it ready."

"Flowers?" he asked, glancing at the tulips as if they might volunteer.

"Just something white," Emily said. "Not Irises. Nothing showy. She disliked fuss."

Paul let out a sound that might have been a laugh if anyone had been brave enough to call it one. The undertaker nodded, pencilling white, simple. He slid a consent page across the table to Paul with the gentle gravity of a man placing a child into someone's arms.

"If you'll sign here. This authorises us to proceed once the registrar confirms."

Paul took the pen and positioned it as if aiming. His hand shook, then steadied under Emily's resting fingers. He signed Paul Mercer in letters that looked briefly unfamiliar, each line landing a fraction too hard, the ink dark against the cream. He stared at his name for a heartbeat, as if he'd surprised himself in a mirror.

"Thank you," the undertaker said. He gathered the forms with a tidiness that showed he had practiced this movement hundreds of times and yet never allowed himself to make it thoughtless. "I'll take care of everything from here. A car will come for you at eleven."

Emily walked him to the door. He paused in the hall, hat in hand, and looked at her with an awkward sincerity that improved him.

"She was fortunate to have you at the end."

Emily's modest smile did its work. "We were fortunate to have her," she said, and the sentence lay in the air between them, useful and true enough to stand on.

When she returned to the dining room, Paul had shifted in his chair and was rubbing at the place on the table where the pen's point had impressed the paper. He looked up, guilt flaring as if he'd been caught smudging something sacred.

"Do you think Thursday is too soon?" he asked, as though confessing a selfishness.

"No. I think you chose well," she answered. "It's kinder not to ask yourself to wait."

He nodded, relief and dependency knitting a tighter weave. "I don't know how you keep it all straight."

"I write it down," she said, which was the nearest she ever came to admitting the scale of what she managed to keep straight. She set the biscuits nearer to him as if appetite could be persuaded by proximity, then left him alone to his thoughts.

Detective Inspector Rawlings and DC Patel came in the afternoon. They stood on the step with their hats in their hands, coats beaded with recent rain, the posture of people hoping they might be mistaken for condolence rather than interruption. Emily led them into the morning room where the fire performed its polite arithmetic and the tulips, stubborn to the last, held what remained of their yellow.

"Mrs Mercer," Rawlings said, voice lowered by half a step. "Mr Mercer. We're sorry to intrude. We heard about your mother. We just wanted to share our condolences."

"Thank you," Emily said. She did not offer refreshments. This was a conversation that wanted to be brief.

Rawlings cleared his throat, the paperwork version of a cough. "We only wanted to update you. There are still lines to close regarding the footage from the neighbour. It seems that the figure was spotted leaving the train station, though they were already wearing their hood, so we haven't got any further with facial recognition. Since your father's fall came some time after both visits, we don't imagine the intruder was complicit in his injury. But, as I say, we're continuing to review. We'll only be in touch if absolutely necessary."

Paul, who had been standing by the mantel with his arms folded as if trying to keep himself together, bristled. The movement of shoulders squaring, and chin lifting was small, but it changed the temperature of the air.

"So, you've wasted our time and upset my dying mother over nothing?" His voice was tight, the sentence honed by nights of practising arguments he would never have to deliver.

Patel's face softened.

"We didn't intend distress," she said gently. "We have procedures we need to follow when footage suggests a forced entry. We're mindful of the circumstances. We're not pursuing anything further at this time."

Emily stepped closer to Paul and laid a hand on his forearm, the exact weight that says not here, not now.

"They're only doing their jobs," she said, and heard, beneath her own words, the echo of the undertaker's, the doctor's. The house had become a stage for professionals, and she had learned everyone's lines like the perfect understudy.

Paul unclenched his jaw by force. He looked at Patel and something in him wanted to apologise to someone who wouldn't ask him to. Instead, he nodded once and turned away to the window, where the garden lowered itself into early dark.

Rawlings, reading rooms as if it were part of his training, replaced his hat respectfully beneath his arm. "We'll leave you to your arrangements," he said. "If anything changes, on either side, you'll hear from us. Again, our sympathies."

Emily saw them out. At the door Rawlings turned back to her.

"You take care now," he said. "And call me if you see anything suspicious at all." Then he touched the brim of his hat in an old-fashioned movement that suited him, and stepped into the damp air.

When the door closed, Paul sank into the nearest chair like a man no longer maintaining an appearance. His shoulders sagged and his hands dangled between his knees, open and useless.

Emily did not ask what he was thinking. She knew he would not be able to tell her in any case.

"At least it's over now," she said softly. The sentence was ambiguous enough to accommodate every burden from the police, to Dorothy's illness, to the waiting.

Paul stood suddenly, pulled Emily into a hug that was all need and no elegance, and pressed his face to her hair.

"Thank God I have you," he said into the quiet, and the words hung heavily between them, as binding as a vow.

She held him tight for as long as he needed it.

# 27

Winter light fell through the crematorium's small stained-glass windows and came out the other side thinner, as if filtered of anything too warm. The chapel was all pale oak and polished brass, and the air hummed with that particular hush people bring with coats buttoned and gloves held rather than worn. The coffin rested beneath a spray of white flowers that were simple, nothing showy, because fuss had been Dorothy's nemesis.

Paul rose when the celebrant nodded, a folded sheet of paper held like a passport that might be rejected at the desk. He swallowed, checked the page as though it might have changed its mind since the pew, and walked to the lectern with the gait of a man approaching a door he half-expected to be locked. When he began, his voice carried a wobble that felt borrowed from a younger self.

"My mother," he said, and stopped there as if the two words were a hill. "Dorothy was..." He adjusted the pages, the paper shivering lightly in his hands. "Indomitable. If you knew her, you know that." A breath. "She liked standards. She liked rules. She liked... us to be better than we were yesterday. She..."

He glanced up, eyes catching on Emily, who sat in the front row with her ankles crossed and a handkerchief at the ready. He seemed steadied by the sight of her.

"She kept a tight ship," he tried to joke, and the mourners made the small cooperative sound that tells the speaker he isn't drowning alone.

He went on, hitting the anecdotes as if they were buoys he'd planned ahead. He talked of the apple tree, the cricket bat held high, the way she could tell if a bed had been made with care or haste. When he finished he looked up abruptly, paper held neatly, and placed it face-down on the lectern as if hiding evidence.

He looked, for a strange heartbeat, over the heads of the mourners to the chapel door, as though orienting himself by exits, then forced his gaze back to the coffin and the white flowers he had chosen and might not have picked if left to himself. He returned to the pew, sitting with the care of a man who had rehearsed sitting and now doubted everything about it.

Emily dabbed delicately at the corner of her eye with the quiet mechanics of grief as it is supposed to look among people who will remember how you behaved. A hand reached from behind and rested briefly on her shoulder. Mavis Ellwood's powdery gesture noted in Julia Latimer's whispers which hovered like static a few rows back. The celebrant invited a moment of silence, and in that minute, with the air hushed and the faint sound of the curtain's runner somewhere behind the flowers, suspicion slipped in and sat down quietly in the back pew.

Afterwards, outside under a sky the colour of pewter, the murmurs began.

"So beautifully done," someone said, and meant the service but glanced at Emily.

"Such devotion," another offered, pressing her fingers.

"Like a daughter to her," the phrase repeated itself from mouth to mouth, the community's way of writing a footnote to the chapter they'd chosen to keep. No one remembered Dorothy calling anyone a devil. Memory is tidy when it needs to be.

Emily received the compliments with a small incline of the head and her modest smile engaged.

"Dorothy looked after us," she said, as if returning dishes washed. "We only did the same for her."

She made space for Julia's awkwardness, for Mavis's tremulous blessing, for Robert's damp handshakes. She nodded thanks to the celebrant, who had said all the right words and left the wrong ones to evaporate.

Paul's face had the rawness new grief gives even to men practised at withholding. He stood a fraction too far from the gathering, then stepped in too close, then retreated again as if triangulating where the proper amount of bereaved should be. His phone vibrated in his pocket and he jolted, fumbled, thumbed the screen to darkness without looking.

When Rawlings and Patel appeared at the far edge of the mourners, hats in hand, not intruding upon condolences but not absent either, Paul's jaw set in that small, mechanical way that looks like dentistry. He turned his back before he realised, then pivoted again and shook Rawlings's hand too firmly, as if proving he had nothing to hide by the strength of his grip. Patel's condolence was brief and human, and he responded by nodding as if she had asked him to sign something.

The curtain didn't move until after the chapel emptied, since the staff believed in sparing families the sight of the chamber emptied. Still, when the undertaker touched Paul's elbow and told him gently that the car was ready, he jumped as if caught.

~

Back at the house, the quiet tried to behave the way it had after Harold's funeral, but absence has different weights depending on who has left. The photograph they had propped on the mantel for the service of Dorothy and Harold in summer, had come home with them and smiled insistently on the table in the morning room.

Emily moved between guests, resuming that gentle circulation the village had christened angelic. She poured drinks, gathered coats, took delivery of a casserole from a neighbour who swore she didn't remember baking it but thought someone else might have and meant well. She offered the right sentences to the right people and sent them away feeling they had done something without requiring them to name it. When at last the door closed behind the final mourner and the house inhaled its emptiness, she found Paul in the study that had been Harold's and lately felt too large for any one person.

He sat at the desk, the eulogy pages unfolded beside an envelope he had opened with more force than he meant to. His thumb rubbed at a smear of ink on the corner, as if willing it to come off the paper and onto him instead. When she came in, he flinched and put the papers into a drawer, shutting it with a smile that was almost sheepish.

"You were good," she said softly, crossing to him. "She'd have liked that."

"She'd have corrected my grammar," he said, the joke spoiling in his mouth even as he made it. He leaned back, then forward, then set his elbows on his knees and pressed his knuckles into his eyes in the way of a boy who has been told to be brave and is trying to remember the instructions.

She sat beside him on the arm of the chair, not quite in his lap, and traced one finger along the line where his sleeve met his cuff.

"It's done," she murmured. "You did the hard part."

He nodded, then shook his head, then nodded again, as if grief had thrown the switch on his instincts and now everything repeated.

"I kept... thinking," he said. "All through it. About the time... the timings. Should I have gone in?" He spoke the words as if they belonged in a filing cabinet marked Things Men Control. "Ridiculous. I'm..." He cut himself short. "I'm tired."

"Then be tired," she said, making room for his failure to say what he meant. "You've earned the right to stop tying everything together."

He made a small sound that wanted to be grateful.

"What do people do," he asked, looking up at her with the helplessness he hated in himself. "In the weeks after? When the forms are done and the food runs out and the house... goes quiet?"

"They plan a time to breathe," she said, and he looked startled by the practicality of it, as if she had named a tool he had forgotten existed. "We should think about getting away, even for a few days. Somewhere with a horizon. You need to give yourself space to grieve properly after losing both parents so close together."

He frowned, because the word horizon came with the price of admitting there would be a future on the other side of today. Then, slowly, he nodded, as if the idea had been there already and only needed permission.

"I don't know if I can... not yet. There's so much to do."

"Not tomorrow," she agreed. "But soon. After we've seen the solicitor and everything is clear."

It was gently said, but still, the sentence made a faint, cold sound as it settled, like the subtle click of a drawer being opened in the mind.

"We'll go somewhere quiet. Just you and me."

His gaze slid to the window and then to the doorway, as if he expected someone to arrive and catch him wanting to be happy again.

"Money feels… obscene to think about right now," he said, voice roughening. "Even though it's the thing that changes what we can do. Probate, accounts, the house. I keep thinking I should have asked her things. About passwords. About preferences." He gave a small, mirthless laugh. "As if Dorothy had any preferences beyond the word no."

"She had very clear preferences," Emily said, and made the word kind. "And only some of them were unreasonable. We'll honour the ones that mattered and release the ones that hurt." She threaded her fingers through his and held. "And we'll make careful plans. Not giddy ones. We've had enough of chaos."

He exhaled, relief moving through his face.

"We," he repeated, leaning on the pronoun as if it were a banister. "I don't deserve you."

She let her smile be small and almost embarrassed.

"Then it's a good thing marriage isn't merit-based," she said, and the line made him laugh, and the laugh made him look briefly like the man he had been on their honeymoon, head tipped on her shoulder, phone facedown for once.

"When do we see the solicitor?" he asked.

"Tomorrow afternoon," she said without turning. "He'll explain probate. There's the Bray house, the investments Harold set up, what remains of the pension. We'll take it slowly." She rested her hands lightly on his chest as if anchoring him to something warmer than accounts. "We'll make the most of what they built, Paul. That's what good children do."

He swallowed, blinked, looked aside. "It sounds a bit opportunistic, when you say it like that."

"It sounds dutiful," she corrected. "You're allowed not to feel guilty for being the son they loved."

He nodded, and in the nod was a flinch, as if the word son had grazed scar tissue. She pretended not to notice.

Later, when the house settled into that furtive quiet it wore now, he went upstairs to the old study and stood by the locked drawer as if he'd come in for something and couldn't remember what. He checked his phone to find a notification for an email that he dismissed too quickly and then pocketed it and returned to the landing, listening for a sound in the rooms below. The floorboard by the third stair gave its usual complaint, and he stepped over it without looking, the way people do who have learned a house too well.

In the kitchen, Emily rinsed two plates, dried them, and placed them in the cupboard in a neat stack that seemed like the most natural movement in the world. She did not look up when Paul entered but only glanced at his reflection in the glass of the window.

"Come on. Let's try to sleep."

He nodded. On the way out he touched the edge of the photograph on the mantel with the backs of his fingers before he turned off the lights.

# 28

Paul lay awake beside Emily, eyes open to a ceiling that offered nothing back, sheets cold where his legs had kicked them loose. Every creak in the house was a footstep from a memory he hadn't invited, like a voice that stopped speaking when he tried to hear it.

He turned his head to the clock: 2:41, then 3:07, then 3:19. He relived days in untidy loops, snagging always on the same barbs. Dorothy at the kitchen table, pinning him with the old verdict, 'you're weak' as if she were handing him back a prize he'd never wanted. Dorothy coughing behind the library door, the bell's genteel chime that had started to feel like an accusation. Dorothy bending over his father on the stone path in the garden, though he hadn't been there to see it, the imagination refusing to respect fact.

He tried to picture the good things, but the mind makes its own choices in the dark, and his kept turning to little failures he couldn't edit. He remembered the slit of light under his mother's door two nights ago, the way he had stood in the corridor with his hand on the latch and found his feet locked to the runner.

He told himself she was sleeping. He told himself breath is private. He told himself there would be another minute.

"I feel guilty," he said into the ceiling. The words were small and ugly and came out in a rush, as if he had surprised them into leaving. He swallowed. "I feel guilty," he said again, softer, as if practicing a language.

Beside him, the bed shifted. Emily turned toward him in the dark, the warm hush of the duvet lifting and settling. Her hand found his chest, the heel of it resting over his heart.

"You did your best," she whispered, the sentence shaped to fit around whatever remained unsaid. Her breath touched his jaw. "She knew you loved her."

He wanted to ask how she could know what his mother knew, and he wanted to believe she could. He wanted to say that love might not be the right tool for the job he had been set as her son, that love had not unlocked her door when he'd stood there with his hand against the varnished wood and decided not to knock. He said nothing. The quiet around them accepted the omission the way a lake accepts a stone, with a small inward movement and no echo.

Paul covered her hand with his and pressed it harder against his chest, as if the extra weight might keep his heart from arguing. Emily's thumb moved once, slow and sure, the way she soothed the rim of a cup as she set it down.

"Try to sleep," she murmured, and the word made a shape for him to lie down in. He tried it. He tried stillness, then turning. The ceiling did not change. The numbers on the clock did. Paul lay with his eyes open until the window found its way to grey. Inside his chest the guilt sat, heavy as a paperweight, not eased by morning's light.

~

The study still smelled faintly of Harold's aftershave and the beeswax polish Dorothy liked on the desk. Light came thin through the window, laying itself on the leather blotter where Harold had written cheques with slow, exacting care. Paul sat in his father's chair as if expecting it to reject him and kept both feet flat on the carpet like a boy in assembly.

Papers had been gathered into dutiful piles. Insurance, Utilities, Bank. There were envelopes that seemed to multiply when he looked away. A grey one from the registrar lay on top, a cream one from the undertakers beneath, the solicitor's letterhead, Firth & Rowe, square and important on the next. He had opened some things with unnecessary neatness and others with the ragged impatience of a man trying to catch up with his life.

He picked up a bank statement and stared at it with the intensity of someone hoping numbers might explain character. He ran a thumb along the edge until a corner softened. From beneath the blotter he drew a smaller envelope addressed to him in Dorothy's tight hand and stared at his name. He didn't open it. He slipped it back under the leather as if postponement were a form of denial or respect.

Footsteps paused at the doorway. He shut the top drawer quickly, the movement too smooth to be innocent. When he looked up, Emily was already crossing the threshold, the morning on her skin, a mug of coffee in one hand, her face knotted with kindness.

"There is so much to sort out," he said, as if getting ahead of accusation. He gestured at the small, ordered chaos. "The solicitor, all the bank accounts, the reading of the will." The last word came out flatter than he meant, as if it had landed on something hard.

Emily set the coffee down and came around the desk. She

knelt beside his chair with the unconcern of someone who remembers when kneeling was agency rather than supplication. She rested her head lightly against his shoulder, the weight of it a precise comfort, her hand finding his sleeve and smoothing a crease he hadn't noticed. "I know it seems like a lot to take in and your mother has left a huge hole in your life," she said, voice low. "But you still have me."

He nodded, the movement catching, his gaze skittering over her hair to the drawer he'd shut and away again. "I know."

"And you mustn't worry about the will." She angled herself so that he could not avoid her eyes. Her tone sat on that line she had perfected between practical and tender. "You're their only child. It should all be very simple."

He nodded again, slower.

"Yes," he said, as if agreeing to the terms of a contract that might yet surprise him. He reached for the solicitor's letter and let his fingers rest on the letterhead without lifting it. "Simple."

"Everything can be done step by step," she said. "We'll see the solicitor at three. We'll list the accounts and give them to him. The house will be valued. We'll make a plan." She lifted her head, looked at him, and added, like an afterthought offered as a gift, "You don't have to be ashamed of practicality. It doesn't make you unkind to arrange what must be arranged."

He exhaled his relief, or the thought of it. "I keep thinking about the logistics," he admitted, and the word sounded too technical for grief. "When to call, who to call." He stopped. "It's stupid."

"It's not," she said. "It's how you stay upright."

He glanced at his phone, face-down on the desk. A faint smear of fingerprint on the glass gave him away. He flipped it over, checked the blank screen as if confirming innocence, then set it back down carefully. "Robert's expecting a call about the garden," he said, though he hadn't mentioned it before. "He wants to tidy it for us." He swallowed. "She hated leaves on the path."

Emily's hand tightened on his sleeve and released. "Then let him. We'll call him after the solicitor." She tilted toward the piles with a half-smile. "Do you want me to sort these? Or would you rather throw everything out of the window and start a new life as a shepherd."

He tried on a smile; it didn't fit.

"Sort," he said. "Please. I'm..." He rubbed a palm over his sternum as if smoothing out a thought. "I feel like I'm going to miss something and that missing it will be the thing that matters."

"You won't," she said, and made it sound like a fact rather than comfort. "And if you do, I'll catch it." She gathered the Bank pile and pressed the edges until they behaved. "Tell me about your father," she said, a sideways step onto firmer ground. "What would he have said if he'd walked in and found you doing this."

Paul's mouth tugged.

"That the pens are in the wrong pot," he said. "That the window should be open a crack. That there's no point thinking about a thing until you can see it on paper." He reached to tug the sash window two fingers higher, as if summoned. Cold came in and made the paper edges lift. "He'd have taken the top sheet off each pile and written a number in the corner."

Emily smiled. "Then write a number in the corner," she said, handing him a pen as if she had found it rather than anticipated it. He did, and the act steadied him in that visible way small tasks do.

She moved around the desk and lifted the blotter to find a paperclip. The motion exposed the corner of the envelope Dorothy had addressed to him. Emily didn't look at it directly. She was the kind of woman who understood the courtesy of pretending not to see the thing you had seen. She replaced the leather carefully.

"If you like," she said lightly, still moving papers into lines, "I'll call the utilities so you don't have to say it out loud ten times. And I'll make sure the gate lock has been fixed." She gave him half a look. "Properly."

He flushed and nodded and didn't say that he had already checked it at dawn, standing on the step with his coat over pyjamas.

"Good," she said, reading the nod as consent to all sorts of mercies. "We'll take this to three, then I'll make you eat, and then we'll go for a walk, and if you're really unlucky I'll make you look at the sea on a property website."

He almost laughed. "You hate the seaside," he said.

"I hate what people do to it," she replied, which sounded enough like a principle to end the subject. She rose, pressed a kiss to his temple and lifted the Insurance pile. "More coffee?"

He reached for her wrist as she turned, a boy's impulse again, the hand closing and opening before it quite landed.

"Don't leave," he blurted, then recovered himself. "Just stay with me, for a minute."

"I'm not going anywhere," she said, and she sat for a while, leafing quietly through paperwork.

When she did go, and the door closed behind her, Paul exhaled and lifted the blotter. He took out Dorothy's envelope, broke the seal, and slid out a single folded page. He held it without unfolding, listening to Emily busy herself in the kitchen. He refolded the paper he hadn't read and put it in the top drawer. He wiped his thumb and forefinger along the desk's edge as if polishing could erase the act of not knowing. By the time Emily returned, he was sitting upright again, a pen in his hand, a number written neatly in the corner of the next sheet of bank paperwork.

She set his coffee down, saw the numbers where there hadn't been numbers, and smiled. "There," she said. "Already better."

He nodded, the movement small and obedient.

"Already better," he echoed, and stared at the shut drawer as if it might hum.

# 29

The bell over the village shop door had a particular winter jangle that was brisk, apologetic, and determined to sound cheerful despite the cold. Paul ducked in with his collar turned up, the air warm with coffee, bread, the faint chemical sweetness of floor cleaner. He meant to buy milk and a newspaper.

"Paul." Mrs Winship, who had sold newspapers to him since school, came out from behind the till with the gravity she reserved for births, deaths and the winning raffle ticket. "How are you bearing up, love?" Her hand closed over his forearm before he could answer. "We were all saying how your Emily has been a rock. Held everything together."

A man in a high-vis jacket nodded from the queue.

"Wouldn't wish it on anyone. Your mum was a strong character. Old school." The phrase had a way of scrubbing history until it gleamed.

"Strong," echoed Julia Latimer by the biscuit display, already rehearsing the line's next use. "And Emily? Well she's like a daughter."

Paul felt himself lengthen under the praise, as if standing straighter could make what they said more true.

"She... she has been extraordinary," he said, and the relief of a sentence that asked for no defence made his throat feel looser. "I couldn't have done any of it without her."

"Exactly." Mrs Winship patted his arm once, decisively. "You tell her we said so. And you tell her dinner's on us if she ever wants a night off the cooker. Chicken pie. Proper pastry." She added, half-whisper, "Detectives been and gone, haven't they? Nasty business. People snooping around. Still, nothing's come of it." Her face composed itself into respectability. "And I suppose they're paid to poke. Everyone can see what's what."

"Everyone," Paul repeated. He smiled until his teeth felt like props, paid for and reusable. He bought milk, two apples, and a newspaper he probably would not open. On his way out, a chorus of "give our love to Emily" followed him through the door. He let the bell swing shut on gratitude and gossip and carried both home like things that might spill.

In the kitchen Emily was rinsing a jug, the sleeves of her cardigan pushed to her elbows, wrists neat as if sketched. He set the items on the counter and, unprompted, gave his report.

"I stopped at the shop," he said, arranging the milk so the label faced forward, because order felt like virtue. "They all asked after us. Said you were a rock. That you held everything together." He smiled at the memory as if retelling it would keep it true. "Julia again. And Mrs Winship. She's offered to make us a chicken pie with proper pastry."

Emily laughed softly, the sound tidy and warm. "You see? The village has finally accepted me." She turned the tap off with two fingers. "I just did what anyone would."

"Not anyone," he said quickly, with more fervour than the room required. "You." He stepped in and kissed her cheek, grateful to have something to do with his mouth that wasn't explaining.

She wiped a comet of water from the counter with the edge of a tea towel. "I'll take 'rock' if it means you eat the pie," she said. "Put the milk away before it sours."

He did. Later, when he repeated the praise once more over coffee, then again at the top of the stairs, he heard himself and did not stop. It was a story that fitted him, and a man in need of shape will wear anything that drapes well.

Isla came with a bottle of red and a professional smile that had been softened at the edges by rain. Emily ushered her in from the porch with a quick tug of warmth, shaking her umbrella free over the step so the tiles wouldn't puddle. The house smelled faintly of woodsmoke.

"I wasn't sure about red," Isla said, holding up the bottle. "It felt respectful. White felt... flippant?" She grimaced at herself. "I'm overthinking."

"Red's perfect," Emily said. "We've had enough cold."

They settled in the morning room. The curtains were open just enough to show the river thinking in the last hour of light. Emily poured the wine with her careful hand. Paul came in a moment later, hair damp as if he'd stepped into rain without noticing. He sat on the edge of the armchair and then deeper into it, as if obeying instruction. He said Isla's name with relief.

"How are you?" Isla asked him, the kind of question that suggests a thousand exits if you want to take them.

"Up and down," he said. "And sideways." He tried to smile and didn't quite manage. "We keep moving forward. Registrar, undertaker, solicitor. The house doesn't like pauses."

"Grief loves admin," Isla said, and that won her a small,

grateful look from Emily as well as Paul. She took a sip. The wine was decent.

Paul began to talk. At first it came in pieces, like how mornings were heavier than nights, how there was still so much to arrange. Then, as if a track had clicked into place, the story of Dorothy's final weeks unfurled with a surprising neatness. He spoke of Dr Ahmed's last visit, and of steroids and the new infusion the GP had suggested but not had time to arrange, of Dorothy's breath "catching, then easing," the phrase too polished to be accidental. He described the bell. He talked about pausing at her door on the night she died. About not checking. Emily listened without correcting, and Isla listened without comment.

He kept his gaze on the middle distance, as if remembering a place just beyond the room. He did not stumble. He did not reach for dates and find them missing. When Isla asked a question about the time he'd been outside her door, he answered with the kind of detail that belongs to people who have told their version often enough to have filed off the burrs.

"Just before two," he said. "I looked at my phone at 1:43. I remember thinking it was a bad time to be awake, neither night nor morning. But I wanted a drink, and I heard something fro her room, so I lingered, but it didn't come again, so I assumed she was asleep."

Emily's expression did not betray the faint recalibration Isla felt in her own head. He said, twice, "She died peacefully," and placed the words on the table between them as if they might tip if set down carelessly. When Isla asked nothing, he hurried to fill the quiet. "The doctor was kind," he said. "He said there was no need... for anything further." He made the last phrase sound like mercy.

Isla watched the story for a seam and couldn't find one. People who are raw forget whether they told you a thing already.

They reach for a name and come up with a description, or they halt, backtrack, cross themselves with detail. Paul did none of that. His account ran smooth as a set piece, the lines clearly marked. It shouldn't have made her feel colder. It did.

She took another sip and said, lightly, "Do you remember anything... odd? The night before?" She made it sound like superstition, a grandmother's question.

He shook his head at once, too quickly.

"No," he said, and then, as if to soften the speed of it, added, "Only the usual. The light under the door. I thought about knocking. I didn't."

He swallowed, adjusted his glass two inches away from the edge of the table, then two inches nearer, as if trying to remember where he usually put it.

"I feel guilty about that," he said, and Isla saw Emily's hand find his sleeve, thumb settling in the groove his jacket had made.

"You did your best," Emily told him, her voice a steadying beam. "You loved her the way she could bear."

He nodded, obedient and exhausted, and Isla smiled, because that was what she had come to help them do. The room warmed a degree at the look she gave Emily. Of all the things she could have said, Isla said none. She held her tongue where she could have placed a question.

Paul poured himself more wine and then seemed to remember something, set the bottle down untouched and reached for water instead. "I need to keep my head," he said, tapping his temple with a crooked smile. "Too many forms to fill in."

The smile didn't reach his eyes. They were busy with the desk beyond the door, the envelope keeping a secret or a warning, or both.

"I brought a second bottle," Isla said to the room at large. "But it can sit. I'm not here to seduce anyone into bad decisions."

"Shame," Emily said, the smallest flash of mischief passing over her face before duty resumed its place. "We could use one or two."

Paul laughed, and his recounting resumed before anyone asked, the same notes in the same order. Isla let it wash over her a second time and found no snag, no desperate flourish. There was nothing to catch at because nothing had been allowed to fray.

When she rose to leave, Emily hugged her with both arms and the right amount of pressure.

"Come again soon," she said. "Not to talk about any of this. Just to sit."

Isla promised she would. At the door, Paul took her coat and held it for a moment, fingers at the collar as if the fabric might tell him a secret.

"Thank you," he said, the words hoarse in a way that made them heavier. "For listening."

"Always," Isla said. She met his eyes and found them clear, open, frank. The look of a man with nothing to hide or one who had picked a story and crawled inside it until it fit. She smiled, because that was required, and stepped out into the lane.

# 30

By the time spring came round, the house had learned a new silence without edges. The bell on the bedside table was gone, the blue pot boxed and carried, shawls folded into the airing cupboard and then, later, removed altogether. The mantel was clear of old photographs, replaced by a bright collection of snaps from their honeymoon. On the kitchen table, a fan of interior magazines lay open like travel brochures to a country called Afterwards. There are paint swatches pegged with paperclips, a tape measure coiled like a domesticated snake, pages turned down at velvet sofas and modern lights that promised to make the ceilings taller.

They ate at the little table by the window because it felt kinder to conversation. Emily had laid a cloth and set two shallow bowls of something simple and warm. A candle burned in a plain glass, throwing a steady coin of light on the wood.

Paul looked around with a kind of wary wonder, as if the room might vanish if he looked too full at it.

"I can't believe the paperwork is all done. It's finally ours," he said. The sentence released something in him. His shoulders dropped, his mouth softened. He was careful, even now, not to speak too loudly in case he woke a grievance in the walls.

Across the candlelight Emily smiled, the flame catching in her eyes and turning their brown to something a degree warmer.

"It's yours," she said, and if there was an echo of a vow in it, it was one that left a space for him to step into. She reached across the table and he took her hand, his thumb finding the smooth groove of her knuckles as if it had been made for that exact fit.

They ate and talked of small decisions with the attention people usually reserve for large ones. Which bedroom should become a study. Whether the piano should stay, though neither of them played. The magazines made promises as only magazines can, of chalky greens, a velvet the shade of night sea, a lamp shaped like a question mark.

"We'll do it slowly," she said. "One room at a time. There's no rush." The words were modest, though the stack on the table contradicted her.

Between courses she got up to fetch the next dish and left him alone with the candle and the quiet. His eyes softened as they ran along the skirting where he'd once watched a line of dust and resentment collect. He traced the place under the sill where the draught had troubled Dorothy and found it gone. When Emily came back, the flame steadied itself as if reassured by her return.

She poured them wine and leaned back in her chair, candlelight polishing the planes of her face.

"I keep thinking about the maps," she said, less to change the subject than to open a door at the end of it. "The charts of the Med." She smiled, slow and private. "How much I'm looking forward to the adventure you've planned. I can't believe that in a few weeks we'll be sailing across the med. It will do us the world of good to get away, and be alone together. Just the two of us. Not another soul around for miles and miles."

The phrasing drifted between them and settled on the table with the careful weight of something expensive. Paul watched the words take their place among the paint chips and the neat cutlery.

"We'll switch our phones off," he said, surprising himself with the ease of saying it. "No emails. No calls."

His free hand hovered over the magazines as if deciding which colour matched the idea of silence. She nodded her encouragement at the plan for isolation.

"We'll follow the wind and stop where the water is just the right kind of blue." She reached for her glass, then put it down without drinking. "It will be so good for you," she added, softer. "You need a horizon that isn't the end of this garden."

"Us," he said, correcting her without resistance. "Good for us." He squeezed her fingers and felt, with a gratitude that embarrassed him, how surely she answered pressure with pressure, as if her palm had learned the language of his bones.

They talked routes and ports, and he mentioned a cove he had seen once, in a magazine years ago before any of this, she mentioned a harbour she'd found on a blog at two in the morning, all white houses and a bakery that looked like a postcard. Neither of them said aloud that a boat is a small world where everything that matters is within reach, where decisions can be made without witnesses, where water receives what it is given and keeps its counsel.

When the plates were cleared and the candle had burned halfway down its glass, Emily gathered the magazines into a single stack with the edge of her hand and squared them without looking.

"Tomorrow," she said, almost to herself, as if the word were a good piece of furniture that would find its corner. "We can choose tiles." She blew the candle out and the smoke rose and thinned, polite as always.

"Tiles," Paul echoed, enjoying the feel of the ordinary on his tongue. He brushed his hand along the back of her neck as they passed in the narrow place between table and chair, and she turned her face into his palm like a woman who had learned the exact amount of tenderness a room could bear.

These days, Paul slept quickly, as if rest had finally found him and was impatient to be used. The day dropped from his shoulders in one piece. His mouth slackened into an expression he would not have chosen in waking, something softer than he allowed himself in mirrors. The rhythm of his breathing evened and deepened, a small engine willing to do its work without being supervised.

Beside him, Emily lay awake with her eyes open, returning the room's stare. The darkness was not empty, it held the usual inventory of her mind at work. Her hand rested lightly on his chest, a small weight that could be, if asked, mistaken for affection in the night. Her palm sat over the place where his guilt had lodged for weeks, where the breath, when it came, rose and fell away again. She felt the steady lift, the measured drop, as if counting were a way to keep time from dispersing.

He turned toward her in sleep, the way people do when they learn, even unconscious, where solace is likely to be found. She stayed very still, measuring. Emily shifted a fraction, as if testing the weight of her own hand. The night breathed once, twice.

# EPILOGUE

Dawn. I sit at the dressing table and fasten my robe tight around my waist. The house is quiet now. Paul's reluctantly gone to work, leaving me to enjoy the peace. No pills. No bells. No witnesses.

I watch my reflection settle into something warm enough to trust. Soft eyes, careful hands, steady competence disguised as love. That's what people remember, and that's what made them warm to me. All these gestures that look gentle.

When the call came that Harold had fallen, that his heart had gone, I held Paul in our flat, and let the shock drain him. I'd timed everything perfectly, in the end. Our return from honeymoon, the neighbours' cameras catching a hooded figure I'd arranged to drop by days before on a secret little errand no-one need know about. I'd had them slip in through the side gate, in through the door that was always open, and make one small switch that no one would suspect. I never went near the garden. I didn't have to, and besides, I was out of the country. Harold simply needed the wrong pills. Or none at all. A heart that fragile becomes a clock you control. It just stops. Neatly.

Dorothy lasted longer than I'd expected. Her lung cancer

gave me a window I needed, but she saw something in me that no one else ever has. She wheezed, begged for air, then sleep. I gave her both in the end, until I took one away. A hand on the face in the dead of night. A bell stifled. Quiet pressure, with no theatrics. It's remarkable how easily a body accepts an ending if the room feels calm.

I crawled back into bed, and Paul knew no different. I felt him wake not long after, and find me fast asleep. I heard him crawl out of bed and head downstairs, pausing at her door. I waited for his worried cry, but it didn't come.

In the morning, I found her as I'd left her. And I told Paul she slipped away peacefully. There had been no peace in the end, but he didn't need to hear that. He collapsed, and I held him. He didn't see anything except the story I gave him. The doctor signed what he needed to and the village murmured its sympathy while I made tea.

Now the house is settling around us. His parents gone, his grief is soft and grateful. The paperwork is all complete. Properties, portfolios, pensions are all his. All tidy. He calls it ours, and looks at me with thinly veiled questions, and I say it's all yours, which seems to relax him. And that's the trick. If you let people feel safe, they don't notice you rearranging the edges.

But he's drifting. And so I guide him. He thinks he's planning our little escape to the Mediterranean. He thinks it's all his idea, this sailing trip, alone on the yacht he's always wanted. Just the two of us with time to "heal." He says it's the least he can do to thank me for everything. I encouraged it all, of course. Quietly, because that's how my plans unfold best. I've already told Isla he's not coping. That the losses have hollowed him out. Poor Paul, I said over wine. The sea air will do him good.

At breakfast he smiles when I touch his shoulder. He doesn't notice how easily he follows directions, my hand to his cup, his mouth to the rim. Habit, love... the difference is mostly paperwork. I set warm toast in front of him and he asks what he'd do without me and I smile because there's no need to answer.

On the counter we've laid out maps of blue water, the promise of islands and open horizons. To him, they're hope of a future. To me, they're places where accidents look like fate, and when a small misstep can make a person vanish in spray and sun. Where the only witness is the sea.

He folds the newspaper. I rest my hand on his shoulder again. He looks up at me with such uncomplicated trust. Soon, we'll be at sea. No neighbours, no cameras, no gates. Just water wide enough to swallow anything or anyone.

And when he's gone, everything will be mine. All mine.

# AFTERWORD

Age, Death, and (Un)Detectable Crime

A grim truth sits behind this novel: when the victim is elderly, a suspicious death is easier to miss.

In England and Wales, only a minority of deaths are ever escalated to a coroner. The Ministry of Justice reports that in 2024, 31% of all registered deaths were reported to coroners; of those reported cases, 46% involved a post-mortem, and 21% led to an inquest. Notably, 42% of deaths reported to coroners required neither post-mortem nor inquest because a natural cause was later accepted. In plain terms, most deaths—especially among older people with multiple illnesses—are certified without invasive investigation; by simple arithmetic, fewer than one in six registered deaths undergo a coronial post-mortem. From September 2024, England and Wales introduced a statutory Medical Examiner system so that every death is scrutinised either by a medical examiner or a coroner, a reform intended to close some of the gaps that let suspicious deaths pass as "natural." (GOV.UK)

That oversight gap is what made Harold Shipman possible.

The public inquiry concluded he unlawfully killed at least 215 patients—most of them older women—and expressed concern about dozens more. The case exposed how easily a trusted practitioner could weaponise death certification and the appearance of frailty. (PMC) The inquiry went on to call for "sweeping changes" to death and cremation certification—loopholes that allowed Shipman to kill undetected for years. Many of those recommendations underpinned later reforms to certification and oversight. (PMC)

Why are older victims particularly vulnerable to misclassification? Research on elder homicide notes that comorbidity, social isolation, and caregiver control over access to clinicians can make a killing look like deterioration. The literature also shows that domestic homicides of older people are frequently committed by intimates—partners or adult children—and they are often framed by narratives of "natural decline." (Centre for the Study of Emotion and Law) In the UK, analysis of domestic homicides among older victims (2010–15) found that nearly half were perpetrated by an intimate partner, and almost as many by an adult child (parricide), underscoring that family members are frequently the offenders—precisely where suspicion is least welcome. (N8 Policing Research Partnership)

Cremation adds another layer. Once remains are cremated, the possibility of later toxicology or re-examination is effectively gone—something Shipman exploited by steering families toward cremation. Cremation is now the norm in the UK (roughly 80% of deaths in recent years), which makes timely scrutiny crucial. (The Cremation Society of Great Britain)

Real cases of relatives killing older family members are mercifully rare—but they do happen, and they show how plausible "natural causes" can look until someone asks the wrong (or right) question. In 2018, Barbara Coombes confessed to killing her 87-year-old father years earlier and burying him in the garden; the case revealed how an elderly man could simply vanish into paperwork and assumption. (The Guardian) In a different pattern of offending, Benjamin Field murdered the 69-year-old writer Peter Farquhar, staging his death to resemble alcohol-related decline while grooming him to change his will—a case that initially looked like a sad, ordinary passing. (The Guardian) And inheritance-linked poisonings continue to surface: in 2024, Dr Thomas Kwan received a 31-year sentence for a poison attack on his mother's elderly partner—an attempted murder triggered by grievance over an estate. (AP News)

None of this is offered as a handbook—quite the opposite. The point is that systems built for compassion at the end of life can be manipulated. Older victims present with plausible medical explanations; families and professionals are primed for kindness; and high cremation rates foreclose second looks. The Shipman Inquiry remains the starkest warning: systems that rely on trust, cursory checks, and minimal challenge to a doctor's narrative can be deadly. That is precisely why the UK's newer medical-examiner oversight and strengthened coroner pathways matter: they add friction, require corroboration, and create a record that can be tested if concerns arise. (GOV.UK)

Even with reforms, uncomfortable probabilities remain. When only a portion of deaths are ever escalated, and only a portion of those receive full post-mortems, some murders of older people will still be missed—misread as stroke, heart failure, or "decline." The best protection is vigilance around the death, not heroic investigation after it: robust safeguarding for at-risk elders; willingness by clinicians to challenge convenient diagnoses; and systems that treat "natural causes" as a conclusion to be justified, not a default to be assumed.

Fiction, here, is not a mirror so much as a warning light. The

Mercers are invented; the vulnerabilities their story exploits are not.

Made in United States
North Haven, CT
15 January 2026

86823226R00142